PART FOR THE HOLE

Peter Gould

©Whetstone Books

Brattleboro Vermont, 2026

PART FOR THE HOLE by Peter Gould

COVER ILLUSTRATION: Gabriela Morac, Espacio Panoplia, Calle Mariano Matamoros 308-A, Oaxaca de Juárez, Oaxaca, Mexico

COVER DESIGN: Timothy Thrasher Graphics, Brattleboro, Vermont

BOOK DESIGN: Chloë Marr-Fuller, alooDesign, Arlington, Massachusetts

First Edition copyright April 2026 by Whetstone Books, Brattleboro Vermont

ISBN # 978-0-915731-13-8

All rights reserved. Except for applications in criticism and marketing, all reproduction of this text and illustrations is subject to the written approval of the author, graphic artist, and the publisher. PART FOR THE HOLE is a work of fiction.

Printed in the United States of America

Other books by Peter Gould

Burnt Toast *(Alfred A. Knopf)*

A Peasant of El Salvador *(Whetstone Books)*

Macbush *(Whetstone Books)*

Write Naked *(Farrar, Straus, & Giroux)*

Marly *(Green Writers Press)*

Horse-Drawn Yogurt *(Green Writers Press)*

Red Nose Girl *(Whetstone Books)*

To my friends and family in Mexico

*"The book never stops insisting that
its pinhole aperture is a wide-screen lens."*
—Jessica Winter

"…to be an artist was to see what others could not."
—Patti Smith

PART FOR THE HOLE

Chapter One

Call me Bob. Bob B.

I rescued the National Endowment for the Arts at gunpoint.

Not a brag. And if you don't want to believe me, don't.

I'll push on anyway. When you have an urge to tell the truth, ignoring it can be harmful to the health.

Teaching high school English is my day job. Herman Melville had his. Mark Twain, too. They had day jobs. Women writers? They all have day jobs; you want to talk about that?

Weekends or after dinner, that's when I write. And in the mental spaces I don't let that job into, that's *where* I write.

A friend of mine in my Tuesday night writers group is Assistant Chief of Staff for a U.S. Senator. That's his job, at least for now, but his work is writing novels, under an alias. Some of the group know his real name, but we're not telling. When he appears in this story, I'll give him a fake name. An alias for his alias.

I still get a daily paper. I sometimes bring in a news story that catches my eye, to share with a class. We read it out loud; we talk about it. If something strikes me, there's a chance it'll resonate with a few of my students. Even shake them up. Soon most of us are talking, and around it goes. We look at how it ties in to what we've been studying. If there's time, we write about it, too, and that's the class. Block scheduling, but eighty minutes go by quickly.

A few months ago I saw this one late at night. Next day I brought it into afternoon AP English:

Seized Artist Says He Had to Paint a Nude

MEXICO CITY(AP)–*A Mexican artist seized at gunpoint off the street says his kidnappers forced him to paint a nude portrait of a wealthy woman.*

Witnesses saw armed men seize Julio Parra off a street in the southern city of San Cristobal on April 11. He wasn't heard from for four days. Relatives and friends feared Parra, who was imprisoned in the 1970's for links to militant leftist groups, had been kidnapped for political reasons. His case won attention in national newspapers.

But in an interview published Tuesday in the newspaper La Reforma, Parra said his captors were interested in his art, not his politics. He said he was picked up off the street, covered in a cloth and driven to a "run of the mill" room, where the kidnappers told him why they wanted him.

"This is a whim," Parra quoted the kidnappers as telling him.

"There is a very rich lady who likes your painting a lot... and she wants you to paint her." Parra said he was given paintbrushes and forced to look through a hole in the wall at the model, who would pose nude for about an hour at a time.

That's the article. I haven't changed a word.

I reached down to my front right pants pocket—my favorite pair of Spanish Civil War chinos. Heavy green cotton, button-up fly. Antifascist trousers. I had on a blue denim work shirt, sleeves rolled up, three-tiered pink coral bracelet on my right wrist. If you looked closely, you'd see spatulate fingers, visible veins on the back of both hands, a burn scar on the middle finger knuckle—a relic of an old encounter with a woodstove during a brief back-to-the-land stage in my life.

I was leaning on the front of my desk, about twenty students looking up at me. There was a lot of wood and old brick in the room, pictures of dead writers looking down from the walls. I pulled out the article, excited to share it, as I recalled how the story had made me smile the night before.

I unfolded the newsprint and I was about to share it out loud, and then: I just didn't. At the time I didn't know why.

Afternoon class, definite lull in the day?

A deep drowsiness did threaten, which my students—even my best students—were fighting to resist. Well, one or two of them had let it carry them away. Before I reached for the news piece, I'd been saying something, mouth moving, brain on automatic. The fluorescents were on; a powerful spring sun bore in. The room was hot, bright. Nothing clicked. Time was playing with me. Moments stretched like a cat.

Kyla and Jermayne, the senior couple in the back, had moved their chairs closer to each other. They always did. Their legs pointed toward me and their backs lay almost horizontal, chins toward the ceiling, as if last night, instead of doing their homework together, they'd watched the video, "How to Make Two School Desks into a Bed." Every inch of Jermayne's right side touched the corresponding inch on Kyla's left. Where flesh could contact, it did—at the feet, sandals kicked off; the thighs, two matching rips; bare midriffs; arms intertwined like the snakes on a doctor's note pad; cheeks— his: chocolate brown, covered by a soft, sparse, never-shaven fluff, hers: pearl white with a loose blonde wave before her ear.

Those two clasped hands at the end of their serpentined arms lay covering Kyla's lower belly, but respectfully off-center and up a little, as if to say "we've been there, but we're not going there right now. Not in English class. Not in public."

Every once in a while, one of them would surface with a simple hand gesture—his left or her right—which I interpreted to mean "Yo, we're listening, Mr. B. Don't stop."

Were they disruptive?

That's a judgment call. I excused them.

We had an understanding: they wouldn't be inappropriate. They'd sit up when they had something useful to say, or it was time to connect with the other students, or to write. And they both wrote beautifully, as if inspiring each other. They inspired me. I loved their love, discreetly and not as a voyeur, honestly (I'll try to prove that later)—and they knew it.

LOVE like that in all caps, it carries me right to the stacks in my brain where big loves from literature get shelved, like Romeo and Juliet, Lancelot and Guinevere—I go there often. There's so much murder around, blood, torture and mayhem, so much cynicism, rage, nihilism, deception, that I don't mind seeing real love, and teaching it. Jermayne and Kyla were my Paolo and Francesca: students, memorable ones, who, as Dante wrote, "*reading* about fond kisses, put down the book and read no more that day."

Love that's so beautiful it can make you forget you're in Hell. That's what I teach. I'll teach it till they drag me out of here.

I looked away from those two and scanned the rest of the students. All colors of the rainbow. My eyes paused on a few of them—Bolo, Becca, Cheeto, Ravinia, Tyrell—then landed in the first row on the big upright white student in tropical camo and mirror sunglasses.

Garth. He was hard to miss. He waved to me—a quick inside-to-out whip, four fingers through a ten degree arc. We'd agreed he would do that from time to time to signal attention, since he never moved, and I couldn't see his eyes.

I make as many separate agreements with as many students as I can. Hold them to it. What looks like anarchy has a deeper order that an outsider could miss.

Too quiet, after too long, I remembered the scrap of newsprint. It was still pinched between my thumb and finger. I thought about the name again, Julio Parra. That's when I realized: this moment I'd got stuck in had stretched itself out on purpose, waiting for me to catch up, long enough for a recognition to happen. For his name to hit me.

I know that man, I thought.

I know Julio Parra. Or, I *used* to.

With no plan or reflection, talking again, I pointed away with my left hand, refolded the newsprint with only my right, and stuck it back in my pants. Rabbit in a hat trick. A magician's misdirection:

all eyes to the empty active pointing hand, none to the limp holding hand quickly moving toward the pocket.

Why did I do that? Some idea that had no words told me: keep this one close, don't share it yet. Take it back home. Move on to something else. Anything. I did. I can't remember what. Then time hurried again, and soon the class was over, and the day.

Later that night, I sat at my kitchen table, unfolded the article, and read it over.

> *...Relatives and friends feared Parra, who was imprisoned in the 1970's for links to militant leftist groups, had been kidnapped for political reasons. His case won attention in national newspapers.*

I'd been to San Cristobal in the 1970's. At the local university, students were still sifting the fall-out from 1968. What a year. There are student and worker revolutions all over the world against the established orders. In the U.S., they kill Martin Luther King Jr. A hundred U.S. cities go up in flames, LBJ resigns over the Vietnam War, Bobby Kennedy is murdered, then in the late summer there's the Chicago police riot outside the Democrat convention. Tear gas clouds in every country meet up with each other as they spread all over the world.

But Mexico, Mexico City, that's the worst of all. They're just about to host the Summer Olympics. Student demonstrators show no sign of leaving Tlatelolco Plaza. They're an embarrassment to the State and to the ruling political party, and they're threatening to shut down Latin America's first-ever Olympic Games.

The tanks roll in. All sides of the square. When the demonstrators try to leave, they can't. No one really knows how many people are murdered. Hundreds. Maybe more. You can look it up. Afterward, they hose the blood away, down the gutters to the sinking sands—like when the Spaniards mowed the Aztecs down, in the same place—

Mothers and fathers pour into the Plaza, searching for anything,

an ID, a sneaker, a piece of a familiar shirt—weeping street clean-
ers on their knees, scrubbing: what Tlatelolco is, it's a rehearsal
for the Dirty Wars about to happen in Panama, Perú, Grenada,
Nicaragua, El Salvador. Especially Chile. Especially Argentina.

The Mexican President holds a press conference. Killings?
What killings?

Add this one to your list of massacres that never happened. The
Mexican army says "we never fired a shot." A few survivors get out
of the city and hole up in far-off states like Chihuahua, Guerrero,
Yucatán. Sympathizers take them in, and student activism, crushed
and bleeding in the capitol, comes alive in the provinces.

I met Julio at the Hotel Chayo in 1970. Anyone tripping through
San Cristo stayed at the Chayo. It was squalid, but cheap and pass-
ably clean. You'd never get me to stay there now. But I loved the
clotheslines criss-crossing the three-story inner courtyard, full of
peasant shirts, weavings, misappropriated tribal dresses—I loved
the sounds: songbirds, music, typewriters, the many languages of
tourists...

Some travelers arrived from the undeveloped Pacific coast; I
was one of them. A few came from the sacred mushroom country
to the north. They arrived at all hours of the night, and shared
the contents of their dirty plastic bags up on the hotel roof. You
washed the cow dung off the white caps with bad tap water. You
held your nose, you chewed and swallowed. Diarrhea and nirvana
hit you at the same time.

Julio was a Tlatelolco refugee. He hadn't come for shelter, or
for the beach or the psychedelics. He was there to organize. He'd
come back to where his people were from. I learned all this about
him over breakfast: eggs a la mexicana, tortillas, café con leche—

I went to hear him speak. It was a late afternoon, beneath a
stupefying sun. He stood on the front steps of one of the big old
churches—sanctuary promised just a few steps away A small crowd
gathered in the shade of a big old Indian laurel tree.

Julio was in his twenties—a well-read, passionate speaker with a clear light in his eye. He spoke about the massacre he'd lived through, and others to come. He spoke of corruption, racism, inequality, the imperial evil of the neighboring country—my country—to the north, and the local elite class who cooperated—

I was standing in a doorway when the blue car sped up, braked, four men jumped out and dragged Julio away. A cop who had been standing at the crowd's fringe hollered then, waving his club, telling everyone to go home.

That was the last time I saw him or heard of him. I didn't know whether he was alive or dead.

Till now. He was alive, and the same thing had happened to him again. Alone in my house, but celebrating a reunion with the younger versions of us both, I poured myself a Corona from the sixpack I'd bought on the way home. I keep glasses frosting in the freezer. I even have one of those round Corona trays with the buxom black-haired Mexican glowing against blue sky.

I know. I'm sorry. It's a nice tray.

Toasting a man whose youthful face I could almost remember, I pretended he was there grasping my elbow, smiling at my Spanish. What does he look like now? I let my mind take this reunion wherever it wanted to go. I had a big fresh pad of lined paper by me, and a couple of pens. Didn't want to lose any ideas.

First, I considered the coincidence.

I suppose it was possible that other people around the country were sitting in their kitchens reading about Julio, maybe reminiscing along lines similar to mine. But no, I was certain that I was the only one within a thousand miles. The story had chosen *me*, had come to me especially, compliments of a night-shift news editor I'd never met.

It was toward this moment only that Julio Parra's name, which I had nearly forgotten, had stayed in storage all those years in my mind! For an instant I cupped my hand over the bit of newsprint, turned slowly to look out the window, like the good guy in a Bogart film, as darkness fell over—well, I'm not going to tell you the city; I just can't.

But in an interview published Tuesday in the newspaper La Reforma, Parra said his captors were interested in his art, not his politics.

His art, not his politics? He is a painter now. Is he no longer an activist? Not an organizer? Did he disappear twice, like some of those wounded students did after 1968? They spent lost years in the awful, infamous Black Palace Prison in Mexico City. When they were released, they disappeared themselves into business, banking, English teaching, painting, suicide.

Some of our own antiwar activists got co-opted and comfortable, turned into traders of stocks or stories. Everyone has a price.

When I saw them drag Julio away, what happened? Did they beat it out of him all at once, break his legs, electro-shock him? Or did they offer him a deal? Something in trade for his politics? Or did he just gradually let it go dormant? He's an artist now: does he have a family, a Zapotec Indian wife with thick glasses, an artist intellectual from an ancient indigenous family for whom art, craft, spirit, have always been just a breath away?

She wants him to live. To survive with her. When he gets too agitated, turns too active, she counsels him, "*tranquilo, tranquilo, hombre.*"

He puts away his books. He picks up paintbrushes. He follows her example—she who comes from a people who make art every day: wood carvings, weavings, lacquer ware, tin angels, painted wooden animals, black pottery, wax flowers—Art takes him over and mostly pushes politics aside—so that, decades later when he's kidnapped again, it's for his painting now.

It's a whim.

That seemed plausible.

I opened another Corona. Leaned forward on the kitchen table. I read the story again. I wished it were longer than it was.

There were so few details given, so many to fill in:

Julio Parra leaves his house in the morning. It's an ordinary day in his city, San Cristobal. He's going to his studio. He's left his phone at home, doesn't want it interrupting his work. He's wearing jeans, leather sandals from the marketplace, a colorful sweater. Later he will remember that he did not satisfactorily embrace his wife. He will regret this lack of a mindful connection, and will feel more separated from her for those four days because of his lapse of concentration when they kissed.

He vows to do better if given the chance.

If given the chance.

He is going down to the Zócalo, San Cristobal's central plaza, before getting to work. He will meet three artist friends for morning coffee or cocoa. They'll talk about their current work, they'll feed on the busy human pulse around them, and mark time before returning to their solitude.

Maybe they're all experiencing a lull in their creativity. They may talk about that. They've been friends for a long time, from the early days in the left-wing graphics collective when he'd first moved here.

Julio's two children walk with him, occupying both his hands, till he drops them off at the school nearby. He watches them run up the school steps. He loves the high voices of the children running in the school's interior patio. He admires, as he always does, the orange trim of the entranceway against the ochre of the wall. He watches other parents hug their kids and send them in with a wave, an embrace.

Then he starts the long descent down a street of antique paving stones that have just been swept, in the morning light whose clarity he'll remember as soon as it is denied him. The daily industrial and automotive haze hasn't built yet and the view to the mountains is clear. South toward the coastal range. North to the Sierra de Juárez. Streets have been swept; piles of yesterday's dust and trash wait at each corner for the noisy old truck, the men with big shovels, to come through and pick them up.

He has to angle a few streets to the right to pick up the main route to the plaza. This brings him across a mixed-use neighborhood—patches of adobe wall not yet plastered and painted, worm-eaten doors leading through passages one-person wide, into deep apartment blocks around courtyards, many families opening up to each other from balconies; these people, he understands, have to be involved in each other's lives. They have no choice.

He passes gypsy auto enterprises: homemade tire re-wraps, chop shops, hand-hammered exhaust-pipe makers, windshield repairers. The low corners where the buildings meet the sidewalk just a step from the street are full of years' accumulation of iron filings, rust flakes, paper, cement dust, bits of sulfide slag and diesel soot and bouganvillea blossoms, cemented there by urine where street drunks stopped and leaned and sighed, one hand against the wall, during the night.

Julio Parra is concentrating on all this beauty in passing, sidewalks not yet full of people—though two women with split-reed shopping baskets are standing and talking by a doorway several strides away—so that he fails to notice the Jeep Cherokee coasting beside him, keeping his pace.

He pauses to look through the ironwork of an open window and the Jeep stops, too. His attention has been caught by a colonial painting inside; the room is the front parlor of a time-machine house: an impossibly elaborate glass chandelier hanging over a never-used polished mahogany table, a maroon sofa covered with thick clear plastic, a blue tile floor—he is looking in this window when a hand lightly touches his shoulder. He turns around and a burly man in a polo shirt, mirror glasses, baseball hat, a thin-lipped smile, says, obsequiously,

"Pardón? Would you help us, Señor? My friend here says the Municipio is that way, and I say it is over there, and we are having a hard time with the street map, please—"

He indicates the two doors swung open effectively blocking the whole sidewalk, a man in the driver's seat with an old tourist street map open on his lap smiles up at him; Julio turns and bends in, crouches off-balance near the front passenger seat to take a closer look and that is when the man who first touched him, using all his weight, leans hard against him and propels him right into the car. The driver whips the gun from under the map, plants it under Julio's left armpit and whispers harshly not to make a sound if he wants to ever see his kids again.

Man on the street pushes Julio all the way in, yanks the front door closed, jumps into the back, pulls that door after him, throws a blanket over Julio's head and upper body from behind the bucket seat, pushes another gun into his neck and with a screech that Julio thinks must wake up, startle, deafen, the whole observing neighborhood, the Cherokee's two rear tires find the rough stone surface through the dust, and the car jumps forward, pushing him back against the headrest, backseat man uses the gravity to pull the blanket tighter around him and the seat—

No one notices.

Or they do, and they don't.

Like that painting by Breughel, and the poem about it by W. H. Auden, Icarus of the melting wings, falling from the sky—such a huge event; the story will be told and retold for thousands of years—but no one on the ground at that moment pays attention. It's just us, watching from our place of privilege—I mean, at a distance from the plane of the painting—and everyone on the ground just goes about their business.

The day beginning. The sweeping. The clank of iron from the

heavy metal recycler up the street, the call of the man from the truck that drives by slowly, selling full gas canisters, guard dogs on rooftops looking down at the sidewalk, barking, spinning, snarling at their own tails—did they see what happened? Do they understand? Would they like to intervene?

No one notices. Three children walking together have already passed the car, intent upon each other and their own mission: make it to school!

The women with market baskets turn quickly and move up the street.

A driver at the next intersection drags on his cigarette, waiting for the light to change; he does notice, but glances away, not wanting to invade the privacy of this sequester, this sudden, intense physical intimacy he's not supposed to share. What if the two men are cops, what if the guy is a wanted criminal—no one wants to be a material witness—

Across the street a young man presses his girlfriend against a dark red wall. Her arms are at her side. He is pressing her so hard she has to almost fight for breath. They are kissing, kissing, never having made love, only this, never ever been alone together in a house, a room, a bed, but just when the man almost comes in his own pants she sees Julio launched into the car seat, sees the auto speed away; she gasps, widens her mouth—the man's tongue pushes in further, he thinks she is having her first-ever orgasm with him and he is so glad, but it's not the inbreath of ecstasy; it's the kidnap she is seeing, the mental note she makes—

Julio knows the neighborhood well. In four car-lengths they make a hard right turn and head uphill. Since his first helpful lean down toward the open door, perhaps eight seconds have gone by.

The car bounces up the rough street; he feels them head away from the city center towards the better neighborhoods in the hills. It all comes back to him: how it happened the first time, what, twenty-five years before? Why is it happening again?

Adrenalin's running him now and he thinks five thoughts at once: why him? Why move on him now? What has he recently done? Are they going to finish the job this time and kill him? What does he have in his pockets? Thank God he doesn't have his phone, with all his contacts, with him. If he clamps down hard on his lips, his groin, will he master the urge he has to cry out, to sob, to piss?

While he's thinking all this he's also straining to visualize where they're taking him. And while sending his senses out to locate himself, he is puzzled by the almost good-humored lack of tension in the car; the muzzle of the driver's gun eases up and leaves him; the man behind him chats quietly to the other, loosens the blanket a little, and then says, to Julio:

"Sit tight, Maestro; you're gonna be all right."

The driver still hasn't spoken. He hits a button on the dash and "Radio Capital" fills the car with bad music. They drive in a deliberately disorienting maneuver, left and right turns, back down, back up, five minutes, no more: hill stop, engine still running. He hears the scrape of iron on stone, familiar sound of a driveway gate being swung open. The Jeep jerks uphill briefly—man loves to burn rubber, Julio thinks; must not be his own car—turns into the heavy gate, which swings shut behind them as the engine quits.

Silence around him, still under the blanket. Someone from outside the car opens the passenger door and pulls him gently up, out of the seat, walks him across what Julio takes to be a small courtyard, into a door, up a steep tilted flight of stone stairs his feet tell him must be centuries old. No level lines, rough stone edges—

Now he feels himself on a landing, down a hall, now inside a room. Hears a door close behind them. Someone pulls the blanket off him. He looks around. The windows are covered with sheets; light comes through but no view possible, and little air. Thick colonial earthquake-proof walls. He thinks it may be an old convent, a nunnery; there were dozens of them in the city, a place to park nubile colonial women while the fathers and brothers went out conquering.

A truly sleazy specimen of macho Mexican humanity is leaning against a wall in front of him, picking his teeth, then doing a poor yawning imitation of a junkyard dog. Got the yellow eyes right, but that's about all. Julio takes it all in. The only man who has spoken so far touches him again on the shoulder. Julio swings around to face him. Still the baseball cap and shades.

"*Tranquilo, Señor*," he says. He makes the universal two-hand calming gesture.

"Sí."

"This is a whim," the man says, apology creeping into his tough voice. "There is a very rich lady who likes your painting a lot... and she wants you to paint her."

To paint her! Julio fights the urge to laugh, but notices serious business in the air. Then he relaxes just a little, sensing he may have a chance to see his home again. He notices the table, the paints, the brushes, the oil paint sticks, sketchbooks, canvasses. A brand new easel against an interior wall.

No model.

"Don't make any trouble, Maestro, and you'll get out of here," the same man says. "You have my word. My word is good. I'm going to be sitting right outside here; you need something; you tell the big guy and he'll tell me. Some food, a soda, the baño—You try to get away and we are all going to be very sorry." Then he is out the door and Julio hears him moving a wooden chair on the stone floor.

He turns to the guard-dog man, who hasn't moved yet except to pivot his big head around the toothpick fulcrum in his left hand. The other hand is on a gold-plated gun half in his grip, half in a holster, strap hanging open. Slowly the man flicks the toothpick away; Julio even hears the tiny crisp sound of it hitting the floor. The man straightens up and, with the slightest head-lean to the left, indicates a crack in the plaster wall, and an eye-level conical scar in the plaster where a chisel has recently worked.

"*Por allí,*" the man says; "through there."

A hole? Through a hole in the wall?

Julio breathes in and out, exaggerated puff of cheeks, the first full breath he's taken since being pushed into the car; takes four steps to the hole and looks through.

Is this unusual in Mexico, in the rest of the world? Is it a well-kept secret?—kidnapping artists, sculptors, potters, etchers, photographers, songwriters? Maybe that's how we'll get past the old system of arts patronage. That only ever made a few people happy anyway.

Now it's people crazed with the power their money brings, saying, fuck commission work, fuck the arts council, fuck the grant, fuck the agent, fuck the gallery district, fuck even the money! We'll just kidnap the artists and make them do what we want! Hold a pistol to their head. You wanted to be a painter, huh? Do it now or you're a dead man. You'll be a photo next year on someone's *Día de los Muertos* altar. Day of the Dead.

Writers, too, will need to double lock their doors, put up cameras, or write in safe houses but it's no use; the goons will crash in, screaming, hey, man, look at me! My boss loves your novels, man; you put her in your next one, or that's all you wrote.

Did the wealthy model dream this up on her own? Why? Why did she do it?

He said he was picked up off the street, covered in a cloth and driven to a "run of the mill" room, where the kidnappers told him why they wanted him.

The rich industrialist, oilman, drug lord, is going away on a business trip. His wife parts the blinds and watches the driver hold the car door open. Shiny black Mercedes SUV. As soon as it's gone, she picks up the phone. Action! Two guys in the Jeep and the hired guard.

She's amazed at how easily the caper comes off, how well her plan works, how powerful she is! In no time at all, really, she has the artist where she wants him. An empty property her husband owns. A short walk from her own house. She's already arranged the rooms. She's been waiting.

She watches through the hole as Andrés pulls the cloth off the artist's head and shoulders. Watches Julio stagger a little and as he leans in her direction, she is already undressing, tossing her expensive clothes right on the floor beside her as if this were a reckless assignation and she was proving her willingness to him, her disdain for clothing, her eagerness for anything.

Naked, she leans both her arms above the opening and watches, feeling the slight breeze—her windows are uncovered—livening her skin, exciting her breasts. Then, day-dreaming now of Gauguin or Goya—no, Modigliani: she's studied his paintings, for the wanton look in the eye, the curl of lip—she leaves the wall and lies back on her day-bed and feels the hot glance of the artist, *her* artist, feels his initial shock, then feels his glance made hotter as it is squeezed under pressure through the hole in the wall.

She takes her time arranging herself. She knows in theory what a model needs to do—be still—but first she settles slowly, moving her legs and back into the position she has planned for the paint-ing, enjoying the texture of the cloth on her skin, the intentional relaxing of muscles she rarely gives a thought to, into a pose she can hold. A pose she has practiced, in her own room, times when she was alone—There!

She has fantasized about this day, planned it for a year since she saw his paintings at Bellas Artes and saw him, too.

She was amazed at the idea that struck her then, and doubly amazed that she would even consider the idea and take it seriously. She was at the opening reception of his last exhibition, had seen him animatedly talking in a group of friends. Had held a champagne in her hand, standing near the chamber music players, watching him... Maybe their eyes had met once briefly as he worked the crowd. But she had looked away quickly, thinking he might read her expression, see her plan, recognize the relationship that, as far as she was concerned, had already begun.

Her husband is older, protective, instantaneous in their bed. He married her young. He likes his *aguardiente* more than he likes her. But she's a trophy and he guards her heavily like a dragon sprawled asleep on treasure. He never satisfies her; he doesn't care.

No other man has ever seen her body. None. She cannot see the artist now, but she is certain of her beauty, certain even of his unprofessional unartistic arousal on the other side of the wall. She has skin the color of cinnamon; long, gleaming black hair to go with the dark eyes; optimistic breasts, full hips, a wedge of pubic hair dense and black, matte finish. A silver and turquoise ankle bracelet on her right leg.

How do I know all this?

She is lying on a tapestry, one knee slightly raised and tilted to the outside, the kind of pose the artist could call passive, but she is thinking, no, get this straight, Julio, I am the active one, I planned this, I gave the signal to drag you off the street, I am the one keeping you on that side of the wall. The one who could get up and get dressed and leave, tell my temp workers, kill him.

I'm the one who'll tell you when the time is over and you can go. Paint that if you can.

Untouchable, at ease, she touches herself for a moment. A peep show. He moves his eye away from the hole, puts his lips there, like Pyramus to Thisbe, whispers through the hole, it is okay to move, Señora, just please get back to your original pose. He looks again. The arms, por favor. Sí. She breathes a little heavier. Does he?

Parra said he was given paintbrushes and forced to look through a hole in the wall at the model, who would pose nude for about an hour at a time.

The big yellow-eyed man paces—strange mutation of a museum

guard. He's thinking: weirdest temp job I ever had. Private security's my specialty. Rent-a-cop. Definitely a growing profession. Looking ahead to his next interview, he pictures his beefy body, cap on his lap, squeezed into a plastic chair across a desk in Human Resources:

"Señor, tell us about your last position."

He laughs to himself.

His name is Horacio Robles Sánchez; he's a big mestizo Mexican, not a Zapotec; he has an overhanging belly and a tiny behind, a huge silver belt buckle pressing like a chastity belt on the place where his rampant imagination strains him. There's his pistol holstered to the right of the buckle. He had it out for a while for a show of force; then, tired of holding it, he put it away once Señor Parra stopped noticing.

Horacio wears cowboy boots with upswept pointy toes and elevator heels, a white shirt his wife ironed this morning, oiled black hair combed back, a gold star filling on his right front tooth: an ornament. He is sweating little drops above his moustache and big staining pools under his armpits, looking at the bare walls of the hot "run-of-the-mill" room, thinking, "this place could use a little decoration, nothing to look at—that's a joke, man; there's plenty to look at it, but it's only that one little place, you got to squint through the little hole one eye at a time. One man at a time. *Lo que quiero decir es,* what I mean is, *chinga,* I want to look through that hole in the wall... the rich woman, my employer, to see her naked; her *cosita,* a man like me, he needs to see these things..."

Julio quickly gets down to doing preliminary studies—appreciates the fine quality of the materials they bought him, English brushes, R & F paint sticks; he recognizes the tag from the art supply store where he shops. As he finishes the studies, he hangs them on pushpins; one of the stucco-adobe walls is so old it gives way to the pin, dust snowing to the floor. Old colonial convent:

the nuns, did they have holes like this to spy on each other, or tell each other their secrets? Eye, ear, mouth. Take turns. Breathe heavy, like phone sex?

The guard, Horacio, sees the multiplying images of the woman he's never seen, never met. He watches the artist change medium, put a canvas on the easel.

"*...About an hour at a time...*"

Julio stretches, readies himself. He needs to rest his eyes before beginning on the canvas. He lets the guard look through the hole—how can he not? He's the prisoner; the big guard has the gun. The woman is immediately aware that another male gaze is focussed on her. The guard snorts, sees her eyes flash, her thighs cross, hands cover her nipples, but he stays peering through the hole, only moves when Julio, back and neck stretched out now, touches him, "excuse me," on the shoulder—

Did I get it right, Julio? Is this how it happened?

Chapter Two

The scrap of paper had nothing more to tell me.

Could this story possibly be true? Or did the artist make it up? To fan interest in his work? Planned it with his wife, the intellectual Zapotec writer. Was there really a kidnapping—okay there was, but was it staged, a publicity stunt? Maybe they hired the crew, and the model, too—all from some hungry hipster theatre troupe who needed the work. Friends of Julio. Came up with the idea over mezcal and guacamole and tostaditos one Friday night at Julio's and—Marta's—dinner table. To make the paintings of this nude even more fascinating to the public. Value-added art. I could picture the scene at the table, as the beer and mezcal flowed, friends jostling to play the kidnappers, or be the naked model!

Weren't Andrew Wyeth's "Helga" paintings worth more because of the strange sneaky way they'd been created and stockpiled? Shown to the world at just the right time—

No, that was fun, but I dismissed that; there had to be a rich woman, and the plan had to come from her; something in the story convinced me of that. Well, or maybe from her husband, a present for her, using his own hired guns, his most trusted guards—knowing she wanted a nude portrait of herself, the only way he was ever going to permit it. Giving him a strange perverted rush of power, thinking about what was happening back on the ground, as he flew away in his private jet to close a deal. And what happened with the painting, the sketches, when they were finished? Did Julio roll up some of the studies, trot home, kiss his wife, for real this time, then paint some more from memory?

Can anyone believe Julio Parra unless he has a show? No!

Yes—and an opening. Will the people attending turn around and take a second look at a young woman in the big hat and sunglasses who teases the edge of the crowd, cranes her neck—that neck!—at the canvasses, and then leaves quickly? Wait! Could she be—?

I wanted to see the paintings if I could, to see whether they were great. Since—I felt this suddenly—whenever great art takes place, not commercial production art, but intensely felt, intensely displayed emotional art—this kind of art is *always* a result of kidnapping, I mean when an artist's life gets taken over by the necessity to create, even to focus sharply through a hole at the object of their observation. Otherwise there's no intensity in the work.

Why not look at all art, film, writing, that way? Did a kidnapping take place? Pablo Neruda wrote something about that, didn't he: something about poetry arriving of a sudden to take hold of him, pull him right off the street—

Say you're an artist waiting for inspiration, sharpening pencils, meditating, cleaning your studio, doing watercolor sketches, quick self-portraits of "the artist without an idea"—then suddenly, when you have made yourself available but least expecting the visit, you're hijacked by the problem, by the project. You're roughed up and thrown into the vehicle curbside. With a gun at your head, a guard at your door, you're compelled to see the work through to its completion—an experience full of stiffness, pain, shoulder twisted to focus through a difficult vantage, solitude no one else could fathom, the model moving, her surface shifting, won't sit still, hard to see, demanding—finally at great expense you finish the work, and always it leaves you feeling, it could be better; shit, I could have done better!

You wake up on the street with your neck stiff, your head hurting, forgetting how you got there; the dream is over—the guard has already clocked out, going to pick up his pay. You will get paid too, sometime, but it's never enough, or it is nearly irrelevant, skew to the process. Someone else—a dealer, a first buyer, an auctioneer—will profit more. Much more.

Your guard almost disappears around the street corner, but you want to follow him and tackle him; you call out to him, wait, bring your gun again, hold it to my temple, lock the door again, don't leave me, this time don't feed or water me; pistol-whip me a couple of times, scream at me my work's not good enough; don't leave me.

I put myself into Julio's head, the experience over, back on the street:

Amigo, no te vayas—"

"Don't go away; make me keep painting—bring her back, the woman with the cinnamon skin, the pale thighs; I didn't get it right, how her hair shines, how the light comes in on the left like Vermeer! How will I live in my house again, my studio? How will I ever get back to work?"

Thus in thought, I went to bed. Well, not a bed. It's a mattress and box-spring on the floor. A thrift store floor lamp looks over it. Hardwood floor coated with generations of varnish. Old posters on the wall, in solidarity with my student days, with the people I met on my travels. A real black, white, and red Navajo rug. Oak bureau, neat.

My "run-of-the-mill" room.

Chapter Three

I own a two-family house—wooden with clapboards, real modest, needs work. I live on the top two floors alone, and rent the bottom-floor apartment usually to medical students, a visiting nurse, or sometimes a young family who stay a couple years and then move up in the world. It's a quiet, multi-ethnic middle class neighborhood that's kept most of its trees. In springtime, we all step outside and remember in a rush how many of those trees are the blossoming kind.

I ride my bike to school most of the year. The sounds of the city and the expressways are distant enough. My daughter finished college and my wife left to join a woman's collective somewhere out west. We keep in touch. I like to teach. I like to write. I stuff envelopes and sometimes knock on doors for Progressive causes. I'm not about to tell you what I look like. I keep in shape.

I come downstairs, combing my hair back with my fingers. I honor the tradition of breakfast. Do it right there at home on a rag-rug place mat handwoven by some Salvadoran *madre*, a mother-of-the-disappeared. Grapefruit, good brown toast, butter, fair-trade coffee, Mexican eggs, and the morning paper.

I get up extra early so I don't have to rush. It's a comfortable routine I keep.

"Seized Artist Says He Had to Paint a Nude" is still where I left it on the table. I know I'm not ready to share this one with the class, but I don't know why. I can live with that.

I'll look for something else. I go down and get the paper. Used to be, it was on the top step to the porch. Boy stopped his bike and put it there. Now I have to check the bottom steps, the path, the small front lawn, see where the moonlighting driver flung it as she sped by, trying to get home before her kids woke up. I find the paper under a parked car and head back to the house. Yesterday's mail is in the box by the door; I forgot to take it in yesterday. Among the fourth-class—all I mostly get anymore—is a letter.

I usually sleep alone, but not always. There is a woman, Sarah, who takes the train down from Vermont, has been coming to see me for about four years now. Veteran of so many movements, nearly went to jail on some trumped-up bombing charges. Went missing instead.

We love each other like dear old friends, but even when she is poised above me, smiling, dangling her hair over my face and taking in a deep breath, we both know—you could say it's an agreement—that we're keeping each other warm for old time's sake, and keeping in practice, should real love come colliding with either of us one more time. There's no one to tell us we can't express our affection in a way that brings us both pleasure. That's how I see it. A letter from her usually means she's coming soon.

Back in my kitchen, the content of her letter confirmed, I check the paper again. I cut out an article and chew it over with my toast, one about a politician going beet-red in the Senate Chamber while speaking about the National Endowment for the Arts.

Maybe you're one in a hundred out there, maybe you can see where my mind is heading. I gave you hints, after all. Maybe I haven't thought it through yet—I know I haven't—but the identical impulse which drove me to put Julio Parra and the rich-naked-woman-funded-art-project article aside, leads me now to spend more time with the account of Senator Stern's humble wish: that not a penny of Joe Taxpayer's money ever again go to some filthy left-wing AIDS-infected, tattooed, immigrant, welfare-chiseling, nipple-pierced, anti-Christ flaming faggot-fist-buggering poet, painter, pissaint pronoun-popping woke performance artist, singer, sculptor, writer, commie, Jew, or mime.

This one will do, I think; the class'll like this.

Senator Stern is from the state next door. We'll get a good discussion going about this one. I fold it and put it in my pocket. Same pocket, different pants. Enjoying a burst of mindfulness, avoiding the certain "where-did-I-put-that?" moment sometime in the future, I slip the Julio Parra article into my engagement book, halfway in so that the headline shows. I put it with the rest of what I'll take to school.

Do I realize that I am now engaged, and where the combination of the two articles will take me? No, I really do not, but I have some hints, and I'll figure it out. That's what they give us planning time for.

The day is warming already: in a nice white cotton Yucatecan shirt, I ride to school. Winter's potholes are not fixed yet; I slalom among them, and behind me in the stolen milk-crate bungeed to my rat-trap, my faded leather backpack bounces about.

I love the school I teach in. A while ago some of the land in this county found a little fame. It offered places where people came to re-activate themselves. They dropped out of graduate school. They fought against war and environmental destruction, objecting conscientiously to what was most repugnant in their republic. Then, after years of working at carpentry, odd jobs or crafts, doing gardens and wood-butcher carpentry and newsletters and after-school programs for needy kids, some of them became school teachers.

My school has a better history department than most small colleges do. You want to find a long-bearded fly-fishing Trotskyite teaching about the New Deal? A rabble-rousing, football-coaching JFK-assassination-conspiracy buff? A steel-trap-minded woman teaching ancient Greek history to twenty breathless, excited juniors? You can find them right down the hall from me. Seriously.

While I'm still on my bike, let me ask you a question. Let's go back a little: I went a little overboard about Senator Stern just then, didn't I? By now you know I can get excited about 1968, and other big years, too. I have strong opinions about teaching. I love to correct student papers. That makes me one of the few. I have theories about individual rights, and about responsibilities in school and in our democracy. I can go on and on about love. But almost nothing gets me up in the morning, more than the radical right's position on government support for the arts. So when I see some actual news on the subject, I gravitate to it.

You'll say, come on, Mr. B.; it's such a little issue, a tiny amount of money. You leftists have such tunnel vision, you bend yourselves out of shape about spotted owls, endangered newts. Why don't you focus on something big, like redwood trees, opioid addiction, terrorism, white supremacist fascism, women's health, climate change, or that big chunk of space rock out there, hurtling toward the Earth?

And I do, I do concentrate on all that.

It all wakes me up at night.

For me, art is more important than anything. Anything. And if there's a way besides marketing to help artists put food on their table while they're telling their stories—I'm all for that.

There's this great book of criticism called *Shards of Love*. A woman writing about civilization's artifacts. She was moved by Eric Clapton's "Layla." The song made her feel like an archaeologist cradling a scrap of Etruscan pottery in her lap. María Mendoçal, that's the author's name. She used to live near here. Before she's finished with it, her chapter on "Layla" has taken on all of twentieth century cultural history, and Spanish mysticism, Dante, and what music does for civilization, for any civilization, about its origins and more—

But all the arts, not just music. They tell us all you need to know. If you're actually digging in history's layers, unearthing old societies, all you have to ask is "Who's in that mosaic? What did they draw on their dinner plates? What did they write about? What show did they put on?"

Art is love or grief or wonder or anger, transformed. And you can learn so much about a whole people from just a tiny piece of that art, a shard you discover, a shred of cloth, a line from a song. That's a figure of speech: what we call "synecdoche," a part for the whole. "We" being English teachers. I'll have a lot more to say on this particular subject before long.

Every time I hear a senator or president or talk show host or blogger rail about government support for the arts, I want to throttle them—no, okay, *carjack* them and take them to Europe or Japan or Mexico and show them how national support for the arts works. What is so bad about it?

They say, "Artists shouldn't get a free ride. Let the market place determine what gets done, and leave it. The government has no business paying for any of it."

Then they'll turn around and vote fifty billion dollars for an over-priced bomber fleet to fly over the world incinerating the cultural treasures of our enemies. And did the market place determine the dominance of Lockheed Marietta? Or Haliburton? Or Palantir? No: the politicians bought by the Defense industries did. And then, the government's contracts did, too, with the money they take out of my pay.

I'll admit I never did like my tax dollars funding a crucifix bathing in a pitcher of piss. Does anybody? I'm not into shock art.

Extreme ideologues in art or politics are no friends of mine. But they're the exception. They're so unrepresentative and so rare, that they're probably not the shard that some future archaeologist is going to pick up. That's all I'm saying.

Well, one more thing. Here's my opinion, and you can have a different one. Most artists the world over are pretty normal, hard-working people. They deserve support because they are in a profession that is not easily monetized. The support they get helps them with paying their bills, and being charitable themselves. They ought to get paid for their day's work. And their small amount of income expands in place right where it is, giving benefits to the communities where those people work. Especially to the children.

Is that worth an exclamation point? The children!

The creative economy, they call it. I do have more to say, but it can wait. It's the end of my commute.

I parked and locked the bike outside of school. My Fuji ten-speed was state-of-the-two-wheeled-art when I bought it. I never thought it would look old. The frame's the color of key-lime pie. I put on new handlebars, the kind with the ends pointing up so I don't have to lean over so far. It's easier on my back and I get a better view of parked-car doors swinging open up ahead. The milk crate bungeed to the back rat trap says "WEST LYNN CREAMERY: Penalty for Misuse." Come and get me.

I entered the school. A solid old building made to last, about seventy years so far. Long ago some clairvoyant architect designed wide halls and high ceilings. They must have known that two short generations later, North Americans would eat supersized meals, stand a foot higher and fifty pounds heavier, carry a backpack bigger than a Himalayan trekker's, and as one century turned into the next, girls already way taller than their grandmas would wear four-inch designer heels as they passed from "Advisory" to "Accelerated Functions."

The designers also must have known what was coming. They left the pipe chases accessible so decades later the place could easily get rewired for the internet. Over the years a succession of school boards had shown asbestos salesmen, ceiling droppers, and vinyl hucksters the door. Without much work to be done on the building, the board had more to spend on learning and teaching and crowd control, which is arguably what we were all there for?

You name it; we've got it: tai chi, yoga, digital editing, mural painting, modern dance, a TV station, student-run restorative justice circles, healthy food cooked on the premises, a teen mom's and dad's support space.

There's often an artist-in-residence or two disrupting the school's routine, and we've learned to love that. We've got dancers, writers, and visual and video artists coming here to help us tell our story. They don't stay long. They leave a good taste in our mouths after they're gone. Every artist finds out something different about us. We're diverse and proud of it. So many stories waiting to be told.

Much of their funding comes from the NEA. With creativity and artistic expression permitted, actually encouraged, the school becomes a safe place for students to empty baggage, to get over home and family trauma if they need to. A lot of our students, knowing safety when they see it, stay in the building long after the last bell, till it's almost dark and the custodians, sympathetic but firm, tell them they have to leave.

I know, there's always a few misfits, but no more than there are in your local post office. You know about the Iroquois confederacy? Go read sometime about the systems those illiterate pre-Conquest savages put in place for collectively dealing with individual raging males.

I let myself into my room. I probably ought to lock it but I don't. It just doesn't seem appropriate. I want people in here, on their own time, if they need to be.

I don't care what color you are, what your gender, or how bad it is at home, I welcome you to my class, and my class will be hard. I'll sit and talk with you if you want. I'll loan you lunch money. I will be fair, including I won't take out, upon you, any anger I'm carrying around from somewhere else. You will be safe in this room.

I know; no school is safe any more. If I can, as much as I can, I'm ready to throw myself in the line of fire.

As I look around, I think about the talk I've heard, how we're letting the old melting-pot U.S. culture paradigm go. It's gone. No one's going to cook us all up into some vaguely light brown stew—some people get touchy about that. Many of us will stay in our own neighborhoods, with some mixing in and out. Together we'll all be Americans and we'll be connected—like, *very* connected—but we'll still show the discreet ethnic parts like strong stripes in a tapestry, verses in a song, squares in a quilt, no one above the rest, all equal, all fair.

One from many. That's the ideal.

Chapter Four

Another post-lunchtime lull; my third class hadn't started yet. Students straggled in. Kyla and Jermayne had come in first and arranged themselves in back. Surrounded by comfortable high-school hubbub, my mind within was connecting dots. I hadn't moved on from Julio Parra—I had a feeling he'd be with me for a long while.

But this would be Senator Stern's day, and he was also no stranger to me. He was a leader in the attack against the NEA. In his own way, he seemed to take to the issue as passionately as I did. But I had picked apart his passion long ago. His speeches steamed and bellowed in inverse proportion to his commitment. He was looking for money and votes, and white conservative Christian men wrote the biggest checks where he came from. They all had it in for artists. And for free-loving women, disgusting effeminate men, and any kind of trans people. They stank of love, they threatened the social order.

Men like the Senator, they got FURIOUS in all caps whenever they saw artistic types living without the super-ego restraints their pastors drummed into them from the pulpit. Still lashing back at the sixties and seventies, decades later. Damn it to hell, they think, if I can keep a tight rein, why can't you? Scratch a fury like that, and you find the itch called envy right under the surface. Some people just can't stand it when they see others having way more fun.

But like Walt Whitman said, art has to have soul. The NEA is one of, but not the only, guarantors of soul. You hold the marketplace at bay in some places and soul has a better chance. You can have two million fanatic brain-dead Jesus freaks with not a trace of soul. You can have one non-market-based poem with more soul than all of those put together. Sigmund Freud—

"Hey, Mr. B.," a voice said; "can I talk to you?"

I looked up leftward from my desk. Garth was standing a few inches from my head. Caught me dreaming.

When I say I looked up, I mean, not all the way.

You only had to connect with a view of Garth's midsection to know who it was. He wore camouflage every day of the year. Wooly in the winter, cotton on warm days, nylon mesh when it was truly sweaty. He owned what seemed to be an endless collection of multi-colored camo, from vintage to just-minted, from ski-patrol to Desert Storm to Jungle Drug War. And the young man was big—wide and muscled like a bouncer at this week's hottest club. He was broad-shouldered, and still growing.

I knew who it was. Anyway, the reflective sunglasses would be in the way. Why bother looking all the way up?

Garth was powerful and disciplined, having been frequently knocked around and bruised at home till the Old Man started looking really small. His politics ran far off the charts to the right, but he was smart, and well-mannered ("Yes, sir; No, sir.") already practicing for the military he was a year too young to join.

"What is it, Garth?" I asked wearily, always trying, always failing, to disguise the affection in my voice. How could I begin to like someone whose politics were pure Pinochet? Yet I did.

"Here's my paper, Sir. Sorry it's late."

The assignment had been "Write a fictional dialogue demonstrating the debate on affirmative action or Diversity/Equity/Inclusion." Pretty vague assignment. They could pick their speakers. I wanted to see whether they could navigate clearly through two opposing points of view. I thought doing it as fiction might free them from some inhibitions.

I gestured to the pile on my desk: "I haven't started reading them yet; no harm done."

That was that, I thought, but he didn't go away.

"Mr. B?"

"Yes, Garth?"

"Uh, Sir, pardon me—" He looked around, checking for listeners. He bowed toward me and spoke confidentially.

"I saw you hide it."

"Hide what?"

"That piece of paper."

"Paper?"

"Yesterday."

"Yesterday...?"

"Yes, Sir. You know what I'm talking about. I'm trained to see stuff like that. I don't miss much. You gonna tell us about that one today?"

I leaned back a little and waited, till he got my non-verbal cue and took off his shades and let me meet his blue-eyed Eagle Scout gaze. Some people as conservative as he was look smug; the glance is a little twisted, like a hand-caught-in-the-cookie-jar look. Some others look as if someone long ago took a sledge hammer to that part of the brain where tolerance sits.

Garth, though, just looked at you with an actual glow in his eyes; they seemed to say, "I've done the reading; I've read stuff you'd never touch, been to all the websites; I've thought it all out and I'm probably not gonna change, but I'm not a conspiracy nut, and this conversation we're about to have I guarantee it'll be fun for us both."

"Garth," I said, "soldier to soldier, if you drop by after school I'll tell you what I can about it. It's not ready for general consumption. Okay?"

I knew he would be proud enough to keep that secret. He wore camouflage, but he leaned more toward espionage, spy stuff, and less to active duty soldier.

"Yes, Sir," he said, with the emphasis all on the "Sir." He would have saluted if I had deserved it.

As I watched him head back to his seat, I caught myself wondering how much I would tell him, how much I wouldn't. The Julio Parra story was still there, bothering my field of vision, breeding something in me: an idea, a paradox, even a plan?—but it wasn't yet in focus. Blurry and bound to be strange, it was, in Horatio's words, "a mote to trouble the mind's eye."

I didn't mind the irritation: I'm a literature teacher, after all. Reading's like sex. Understanding is like a big climax you're building toward: it's not as much fun if you come too quickly. I like to pace myself and then hang there at the edge for a while. Almost understanding. When I think I have it, and then instead it slips away and it turns out I don't, I laugh. I can wait.

Borges said it best:

Certain twilights and certain places try to tell us something, or have said something we should not have missed, or are about to say something; this imminence of a revelation which does not occur is, perhaps, the aesthetic phenomenon.

We had a good discussion, after all, that day. I found more of the text of Senator Stern's speech on the internet, and read it to the class, restraining my hilarity as best I could.

Gently, I coaxed out a talk about the National Endowment for the Arts. Why did the students think some people got so exercised about it? How did most artists get money to begin to live on? What did they think about government support for the arts? I mean, real art, not propaganda. Had they ever heard of the WPA? No, of course not. That's the Works Projects Administration, FDR's program to save twenty million unemployed North Americans—artists included—from terminal Depression.

Who was FDR? You don't know? Hell. Okay. Back to the basics. Franklin Delano Roosevelt. President number 32.

I read them a quote I had up on the wall, that I'm sure none of them had ever looked at. From an artist who worked for Roosevelt's army of artists when they first hit the ground:

"This is the first time in history that many thousands of artists are working completely without censorship, without even the indirect censorship of the art dealer or collector. I believe this is the most quickening impulse in painting alive in the world today... It will form a record of the deepest value."

What he was saying was, the marketplace could censor you more than the government did. And he named names: the dealer, the collector—

One of my students, Cheeto, was all over the discussion that day.

I spell it like that to make sure you pronounce it right. But when his friends called him that, what they were saying was Chito, a nickname for Monchito, which is itself a nickname for Monseñor. Like our word, Monsignor.

All my students have a story. I said that already, didn't I? Any one of them could reward a deep dive, and a deeper—

Cheeto's actual name is Romero Romero, an odd name his parents chose for him during their escape from the gangs of El Salvador. They hid every night in some bush or ravine or cardboard-and-tin shanty town between El Salvador and Texas, always praying to their hero, Archbishop Oscar Romero, murdered years back in his own church by a killer bankrolled by the U.S.A. Romero had been begging the U.S. to take back all its military aid and go home.

Sleeping shallow and scared, also feeling the first signs of her pregnancy, the woman prayed, "Monchito," (what the Salvadoran people called their archbishop), "you get me to El Norte safely and I will name this child after you. Twice, because my surname, as you know, Monseñor, is already Romero."

Oscar Romero has been sainted now, by the Church in Rome, so maybe he has more power to answer prayers. The family made it across safely, and ended up in my city. To my benefit.

Our Cheeto, Romero Romero, was short and stocky with a winning smile. Just like the archbishop. He carried the kind of weight that most North American Caucasian beef-fed boys store for a couple of years and then they spurt eight inches and get tall and skinny nearly overnight. Cheeto seemed resigned to never having that spurt. He liked to wear long soccer jerseys down to his knees, favoring only the ones from the teams named for indigenous heroes, like "Moctezuma," "Cuahtemoc," "Caupolican..."

I know. We're dropping Indian team names in the U.S., but not in Latin America. Things are different there.

Cheeto was studious and quiet. He had a wide toast-colored

face, with dark brown eyes and thick glasses. He was one of about two thousand Salvadorans who lived in the neighborhoods around my house. They were safer here, in the heart of the beast (Che Guevara's old name for the USA), than they were back in the country that the beast was devouring.

Safe at least till ICE and the Border Patrol come invading their homes.

They were also safe for a reason that many Americans don't get. Their families are strong! They come here, often alone, but they're drawn by their family's gravitational pull, no matter where it is. One of them makes it here safe. And then others. And no one feels okay, really okay, till grandma is here, and till there's a warm kitchen and food that is pure nostalgia, and a family room where they can all hang out.

For some reason, in the discussion that day, Cheeto caught fire. He took aim at the Senator, the undercover racist, who had oil and big pharma money stuffed in his pockets and hate speech with a violent anti-immigrant tone bursting from his mouth.

He had heard it all before, while in his mother's womb, and in the dinner discussions as he grew up in the safety they had fled to. It all came together for Cheeto. Making connections, he kept raising his hand, both adding to the talk and pushing it in a direction I neither expected or quite understood at first. As a teacher, it's just about my favorite thing: to lean back against my desk and watch a discussion I've set in motion running on its own, with little need for further magisterial prompting. Remember that deeper order I talked about, in my classroom? On good days we had more than just order; we had comfort and trust, too; people could talk freely. We found a direction. The whole class could move to a different position without much input from me.

Cheeto had been with me since September. He knew that every book I taught had been written by a person nearly desperate to record a story so "momentary in the mind" (Wallace Stevens said that) that they would willingly go without food, sleep, or sex to get it down just right. That's the kind of stuff I like to teach.

These writers nursed a truth so pure. They mustered all the life force contained inside them and stood it up against the force of an obliterating, hostile history. Cheeto knew that, but in simpler words than I've just used. His own story, some of which he told that day, overflowed with burning villages, death squads, disappearing relatives, drug cartels, gangs... He suddenly pictured himself taking his own story and making it into living art.

Cheeto lived two thousand miles from the place where his family's memories abided. He wanted to collect these memories and grant them permanence, even if he himself never went back to meet the trees, the rocks, the streets, the relatives who remained. He understood that this mission was quixotic. An uphill fight. An artistic fight. It was hard enough to sit in the classroom and hold on to remnants of his culture while the dominant local one bombarded him. Have you been to a Scholastic Book Fair lately?

Cheeto was not the only one in my class who lived with that problem. I was sensitive to that, and I think the students were, too. They understood that their public self was different from their private self, and for some of them, this private one had connections to some distant origin place that both defined them and tantalized them. War's mad destruction had wasted their homes, and also wounded them: even the ones who hadn't yet been born when their parents left it all behind.

Adolescence often brings submerged pains to the surface. Maturing individuals start to explore the inner reaches of their psyche. Some of the material they find can be disturbing. But they have to deal with it. That's one thing Sigmund Freud got right.

Now add to the pain that Cheeto felt, and usually did a good job in hiding, the knowledge that the mythical mothering country he pictured was being rebuilt without him there. Who was footing the bill? The U.S. had previously sunk billions of dollars into guns and bombs for the rulers; now they were no longer interested.

No, now, to rebuild the country, the folks like Cheeto's family paid special taxes on everything they needed to buy: bread, milk, cooking oil. They paid protection money to gangs and cartels. Or they borrowed and saved and hid enough money to pay a *coyote* to transport a loved one north of the Rio Grande.

In a few fenced-in industrial zones, deals were struck for tax incentives to attract foreign corporations. Somewhere under the ruins and the factories lay the stories. Villages half-destroyed by civil war, then abandoned by forced emigration, held synecdochal shards of life. This is what Cheeto was talking about that day: how would any of the old stories survive?

Every part of the past that could not help a corporation make a profit or a gang take power would all be erased: bulldozed, burned, or painted over. Magnificent works of art—songs, stories, novels, dances, paintings—would never be born. The wrong people were winning the main chance to define the country's next generation by controlling what was remembered about the past.

Then of a sudden Cheeto tuned out and started writing excitedly, and was lost to the class for the rest of that hour. I figured we'd see what he had written, some day in some regenerated form. I figured, too, that he wouldn't make history out of his family's story. Anyone could do that. He would make something new, never made before. What artists do.

I let the rest of the class read or write, too.

"Thirty minutes with your self," I call it. No phones. They can catch up with their reading. They can work on their essays. Even write real letters. I keep stationery, stamps, and envelopes, free for the taking, right on my desk. Maybe someone owes a love letter or a thank-you to someone. To me it's all good, as long as they're writing. When's the last time you got a letter?

While the class is quiet I meet them individually, talk about their papers—I love the serious quiet as I try to give them more than just my written reaction: comments about the feeling tone, suggestions of where else they could go with this thought, tricks for letting the self show through. It's better than a letter grade, though I have to do that, too. I have taught myself over the years to see each paper as powerful and true, worthy of my deepest respect, reflection, comment.

I expect their work to be that way, so usually it is.

Chapter Five

At 2:45 I was sitting at my desk again, reading Garth's paper. This was his second go-round with me, first Sophomore English and American Lit, and now Junior A.P. Last year was a continual recognition scene for him. He got through puberty, grew about a foot, shaved his head, took on his mercenary disguise, fell in love with a college girl who had a car with a huge backseat, devoured everything I gave the class to read, and more, and became a writer. He knew I genuinely liked him, in spite of his Cro-Magnon worldview, and since no other teacher even gave him the time of day, he would have followed me to whatever class I was teaching.

Like it says in Julio's article, I was "interested in his art, not his politics."

Garth was a walking military museum. Today he had dressed like one of the marines that LBJ sent down to the Dominican Republic to prevent that lefty nationalist from claiming victory in the 1965 election. Took the DR two generations to get over that little intervention. Garth was one of those invaders, right down to the black steel-tipped landing boots. He put his big body into a front-row school desk and rode that desk with a loud floor-squeak out of line and closer to me.

"So, Garth," I suddenly plunged in, changing the subject before we had one; "what do you think about what we were talking about today? About government support for the Arts. About Senator Stern. Cheeto really got into it, but you were pretty quiet. Haven't quite made your mind up about that one, have you?"

"No, Sir," he said; "you'd think I would have, but I don't know. It's one thing I can't make up my mind about."

"Why not?" I asked.

"It doesn't fit."

"Meaning you've thought about it before?"

"Yeah. I mean, my aunt helped to save an old theatre in Indiana. I love her. She, like, tolerates me. She's always saying it would never have happened without the NEA. It was full of old dudes jerking off under their hats. Now it's kids performing "The Lion, the Witch, and the Wardrobe.""

"You're right it doesn't fit," I said; "Still, you're so sure about everything else you believe in."

I was kidding, letting him know I could see him, see into him.

"It's an act, Mr. B," he said; "I'm not half as sure about anything as I seem. It's fiction like that paper in your hand. You know that."

I acted surprised. But I was pleased that he was letting down his guard. To me that made him look even stronger, bigger in his uniform.

Vulnerability in men, that's good.

"Look, Garth," I said, surprising myself, but holding him in my gaze for a moment; "talkin' about being sure—would you be willing to take a risk, to fight, for something you *were* really sure about?" That sounded really clichéd. But they weren't really my words. Remember that unfocussed idea I told you about? First it was just bothering me; now, emboldened by my giving it a place to lodge, it was starting to speak right through me. If I had thought about it first, maybe it would have come out different. At least not so trite anyway.

You shouldn't really trust voices that come through you. You don't know where they come from, much less where they're going.

"Sure I would. No problem with that. Would you?" he asked, turning it right back to me.

I never had to, I thought. Ever. Or if I had to, I practiced avoidance. Never used my fists. Didn't push back at bullies. Didn't fight to keep my wife. Couldn't think of a reason why my daughter shouldn't move out west to be near her mom. Not a fighter. Never. Life was easier that way.

"I'm not sure I ever have," I told him; "but maybe I would now."

He gave me a smile. We were both silent for a moment, and then that moment stretched out, as if we had just decided to do something together, but we didn't yet know what.

He broke the silence. "There's something else."

"What's that?"

"Back to your question. That Senator Stern guy? I hate his guts. So if he's so dead set against the NEA, that means I'd have to be for it, big time."

"Why do you hate him?" I asked.

"Tons of reasons. He's a windbag. And a liar. And a sleaze. He takes money from anyone who'll give it to him. He's unfaithful to his wife. With prostitutes. He hits on teen-age girls; everybody knows it. He pretends to be religious to get the Christian vote. He only comes around when he's up for election. That's the worst thing: he forgets where he came from."

In Garth's book, loyalty to family, place, country, and truth counted large. I didn't have to ask him how he knew all that about the senator. When he came across someone he ought to like for his politics, but somehow knew he didn't like, he did his own sleuthing about them. Like I said, he was more into espionage.

Maybe he'd outgrow the soldier act someday and use the camo collection for duck-hunting. I pictured me and him in a blind by a salt marsh, cradling our shotguns (he'd loan me one), passing a flask of Bourbon back and forth, talking about the old days. And about literature, of course. Watching that wooden duck bob on the bay.

I liked that picture. Wooden duck.

I took in what he told me. And then, after a deliberate pause, "So are you ready?"

"Ready for what?" he said.

"You ready to see that piece of paper?"

"Yeah," he said; "thanks for reminding me. I mean, that's why I'm here. One of your famous newspaper articles, right?"

I pushed *"Seized Artist Says He Had to Paint a Nude"* across the desktop toward him. I sat there while he read it. Looking out the window at the calm the school buses had just left behind. Jim Marconi—Chemistry—was out there in their wake, scooping up emptied soda cans. Spring sunlight. Pale promising green of trees newly leafing out. Small skinny trees, sparsely spread out in a recent re-planting. Diesel soot dust devils whirled about. Now that the buses were gone, the student cars started out of their lot. Windows open, heads and arms out. Wind whipping baggy pants of kids waiting for rides. Everyone wired for sound.

"Wow," said Garth. He looked up at me and then he dipped down to read it again. I liked that. Watching him read, I felt him descending the levels I had gone down in those five paragraphs— the mystery, the pictures, the danger, the possibilities, the layers of truth.

"Wow," he said again; "why didn't you show this to us? Can't have nudity in the classroom, Mister B? Too R-rated? Think you might lose your job?"

"No," I said; "that wasn't it at all. Not worried about my job.

It happened real quickly; I got it out to show you all and then, I don't know, I stuck it in my pocket before I even thought why."

"Well I guess you've thought about it now, otherwise you wouldn't be showing it to me." He smiled: "Or maybe you think I can help you figure it out."

"I got it covered, thanks. You can maybe add something, but I thought about it most of the night."

He took that in and sat there, waiting for me to explain. He looked relaxed, amused, like he was a moment away from putting his combat boots up on my desk.

It's in the silences, when a student comes to see you, that you really begin to know each other.

"How does it strike you, Garth?" I asked him.

"All right," he began slowly. "You see here where it says 'they forced him to look through a hole at the model?' Shit—excuse me, Sir—they wouldn't have had to force me! I mean, who was forcing him? How'd they force him? And then, did he try to get away? You don't run away from something like that."

"Run from what?" I asked. Thinking about the nude. Maybe Garth had never seen a woman totally undressed. In the back of a car, you don't get to see it all.

"The assignment, Mr. B. The artistic challenge. Whatever."

That told me more than I had ever known about my student. Politics was really like a circle. He was so far right, he was left. We were together, on the same position about art, about being kid-napped, about the impossibility of turning away. He had jumped right over the image, maybe picturing her for a moment—as I had, of course—but then he'd landed where I was now, in the meaning, the metaphor, in all the possibilities.

"So why did you run away, Mr. B?"—his turn to ask me—"why didn't you show it to us? You afraid to take a real good look at it?"

He made a pistol gesture with his right hand. "You need some-one to hold a gun to your head?"

"No, but thanks for the offer," I said.

Then I decided to tell him what I'd come to. I say, "I decided," but I distinctly felt that something not yet named was pulling my strings. Like I said, where was this coming from?

"It's not that. All of a sudden I realized I just didn't want to show you all. I don't want to talk about it. I don't want you guys to write about it."

I let that hang in the air for a minute. Then I added the thought that sprang into shape in my mind that very second, catching me by surprise.

" I don't want anyone else to even know about it. Almost anyone else."

"Why not?" he asked.

"I want to do it."

"Do it."

"Right."

"Like, *do* it."

"Yes."

"Do what?"

"What it says."

"I still don't get it."

"I want to grab somebody off the street, or wherever, push their head against the wall, hold their eye up to some hole as hard as I can and make them watch something really beautiful, I mean extraordinary, surprising, and, and then, make them write about it."

"Write about it?"

"That's what I know about. Writing. I don't know painting."

And then I added, "if I could do that with you all, I would. Believe me."

He listened on without responding.

"You've seen me almost there," I said. "Seen me about to shake somebody's bones to get them to focus on this point I know could save their life. And they don't get it."

"Yeah, I've seen you," he said. He'd been with me almost two years.

"If I could do more, I would, but there's laws against corporal punishment. I'd get in trouble. That's how I'd lose the job."

And then I went on: "There's something about this article that hit me upside the head—"

(Besides the fact I knew the artist; I didn't tell him that. Like any good mission specialist, I'd already begun to compartmentalize what my team would know.)

I finished my thought. "—as if the whole thing could be, I don't know, useful. "

I knew he was right with me, even willing to make leaps, to improvise, till he had more information. Despite our political differences, Garth trusted me. Maybe like he trusted no one else. I was grateful for that, and for a lot more. Whatever it was we decided to do, together, not yet knowing what it was, we had already begun to do it. Now his army clothes looked just right. The classroom vanished and we were two infantrymen planning how to take out the bunker up ahead.

I'm not too spiritual a person. Spending so much time and space in literature, I get my glimpses of spirit from the great global works of the Humanities. For daily living, I go by Buddha's Four Noble Truths—the problem-solving approach to life. You can apply it on a grand scale, like, how can we cure the world's suffering? Or a small scale, like, damn, how can we fix this flat tire if we don't have a jack?

It's pure pleasure for me when I meet other people who share that ancient practicality. I will be talking with someone, beginning to hash out a plan, something that could involve a bit of risk, and nothing negative comes from the other quarter. Not: what kind of idiot are you? Whoa! Do you know you could get in a lot of trouble for this? Get *me* in a lot of trouble, too?

Instead: what are we going to do; can I help you state the

problem more clearly? Do you have a plan? A timeline? You see any possible difficulties? How can we solve them? Why don't we try such and such? What materials do we need? Come on, when do we start?

Give me friends like this all my life.

Garth asked a few pertinent questions and then he just sat there, boots on my desk now, the smile growing over his face, where a blonde beard was just beginning. Having me for English had taken on new value.

Then, he stood up. The implied salute. I saw into his thought process. I saw something like, "the fewer words I say here, the more I come off like an action hero."

Feeling the urge for a cinematic exit, he said, "Let me know what you need me to do. See you tomorrow, Mr. B."

And then walked out not looking back.

Chapter Six

Later the same afternoon I'm in my kitchen again. Reading again.

"This is a whim," Parra quoted the kidnappers as telling him. "There is a very rich lady who likes your painting a lot... and she wants you to paint her."

Dinner's done. Big pot of chili I had left simmering in the crockpot all day. Dishes still on the table, along with the phone, some corn chips and guacamole, a Corona, three or four books in various stages of being read. You do it for a lecture you're preparing, right? You find appropriate passages, mark the pages with a torn piece of paper you scrawl a note on. Why not do the same thing for an action, a covert op? Same writers: Elmore Leonard, Pablo Neruda, Dante—Emily Dickinson: maybe not for strategy, but for wild inspiration.

A few others. Writers, mostly dead ones, who I know will give me words for what I am only just beginning to think.

My mother always used to tell me "if you don't like somebody, Robert, get to know him; then you'll end up liking him."

I'd found that to be usually true. Certainly always true with my students. At my tenth college reunion, and then at my twentieth, I found myself talking to people I had avoided during my four on-campus years. Had written them off, misjudged them, never got to know them. And now talking to them I found them wonderful, accomplished, attractive, hip. But I particularly loved to hear what we had in common. What we had *always* had in common, if I'd ever just dismounted from whatever high horse I was on way back when, and taken the time to find out.

So.

So, what if I picked someone—what if I had a good reason to pick someone—whom I personally could not stand, who might dislike me also, intensely, if he even knew me at all, and we got to know each other under *difficult* circumstances, and I helped him—okay, *forced* him—to see what we had in common? What if I pulled him in off the street? Could I change his thinking? Would he become my ally?

And, thinking on another level now, it would be nothing personal. The kidnappers yanking Julio Parra into the car, the guard at once menacing and bored, had nothing against the man. They were not interested in his politics; he said. They were doing an assignment.

Anyway, you get past that quickly when things take an elemental turn, when your environment—and your point of reference—are radically changed. Then your politics is revealed for what it really is: only another act, just like high-school teaching, like camouflage and black boots, like public penitence, like the fulminations of a Senate orator.

Get over the act, get to basics.

The way I looked at it, this whole story was about art. Julio's art.

Art is one of the basics.

Which brings me back to that figure of speech I was talking about before: the "synecdoche." Dusty attic word. I'll line it out for you if your ancient Greek has dimmed. Sin. Eck. Dough. Key. Say that out loud three times. A part for the whole.

You want a common example? All right.

You ask the farmer how big her dairy herd is. She says, "I've got sixty head." Obviously, she's got more than their heads. You don't even milk the head.

But synecdoche is more than just this word trick. It is the deliberate decision to let a single entity stand in for something a lot larger. How could those Greek philosophers know so much? Indeed, who was the first to give a name to this conception? It's not just the shard of pottery in the archaeologist's hand as she brushes away the dirt and dust and sees in her mind's eye the whole civilization, its lives lived, loves loved, laws passed, leaders elevated and brought down.

Any time any of us is lucky enough to contemplate—a good word, contemplation, since it suggests a protected space within which a real act of awareness takes place—when we discover our self contemplating a single finite work of art that shakes us, pushes us from our position, changes our body chemistry and our comfortable through-line to the future, our safe opinion about something, we're experiencing synecdoche. It may be metaphor's most powerful engine, releasing atomic proportions of heat or thrust as something very big is compressed into or through something very small. That's certainly what was happening to me. All from that little article.

Desperate gold miners in Alaska take a whole subarctic river and step-valve it down through rubber hoses incrementally decreased in size. When the whole river shoots out a four-inch nozzle in the miner's hands, the water flies a hundred horizontal feet with enough compressed force to tear a whole cliffside to bits in seconds, hopefully revealing a sunlit vein of gold. That's how strong synecdoche is. Metaphor gone critical, compressed to its limit.

When I told Garth that I wanted to grab somebody and push their head against a hole in a wall, and look through it, and get that person to see, to feel, to write; one obvious question he could have asked me then was, "Who?"

Chapter Seven

"That's the story, so far," I said.

"So far," Sarah said, looking across the restaurant table at me. Sal's. A steak and burger place with Italian-themed sides. She had come down from Vermont on the train. We'd phoned once in the interim. She does nothing, I mean nothing, online. Email, cell phone: nothing. The surveillance satellites do not see her.

She traveled light, like me, and was in the passenger seat of my sedan before the curb police could lose their patience with my being in the way. She swirled the iced tea in her glass. We were waiting for a steak. One portion, two plates, two forks. It had been six weeks since her last visit. Too much time. We didn't have a schedule, but we were regular, and I liked how my life changed when she was with me. Changed right away.

We saw each other when she needed to, when she needed an infusion of city noise, night life, political talk, nostalgia, love-making, and meat. Legend has it—it even came up in her trial twenty-some years ago—that when the New York City bomb squad burst into her apartment, there was a half-devoured still-warm hamburger on her dinner plate. Obviously an urban legend. Or the wrong apartment. Back then Sarah was a vegetarian.

They missed her by five minutes. And then by seven years. But after she was found and arrested, brought to trial and acquitted, she had become a small-town quasi-hermit who needed to remember, every couple of months, who she'd been and where she'd come from. She came to the city for that.

I helped her remember—all to my benefit. Hers too, I guess. There was always a wary chill about her at first; but after a moment of that, she was warm to the touch.

Looking at Sarah across a restaurant table, or the breakfast table at home, was a complex pleasure. She looked good. Clean Vermont air, daily yoga, and outdoor exercise: long solo walks with no chatting, no earphones. Her blue eyes looked out from under dark chestnut hair. Her skin positively glowed.

Years ago we'd met in the middle of a two-acre vegetable garden. I was married. My wife and I were halfway along an endless row of sweet corn seedlings, maybe ten inches high. We were pulling weeds, protecting the tender plants so they could grow up healthy and tall and feed the raccoons later on in the summer; if we grew enough of it, maybe the animal pests would leave a few ears for our table, our freezer.

Michael, who lived in the room next to us, walked down the corn row with a woman in tow. "This is Sarah," he said. "She's gonna live here. She can stay with me till we help her make a room of her own."

The determination in Michael's voice intrigued me: what he said was not a request for a probationary period. Her coming to live with us was a fact he would defend if anyone challenged him.

Since I did not yet know her history, his attitude puzzled me. I looked at Sarah and the look she gave me back was direct. It said, "find out more about me if you can." I don't mean to imply that the look was unfriendly. It just didn't yield any ground. At the same time, I had no desire to look away. She was strikingly beautiful. She made you search for adjectives, then and much later when we met again. Ironic mouth. The shiney sable hair. Erect posture, broad, wiry shoulders. She soon became the best of all of us at splitting wood for the various stoves. And while she lived at our farm, she minored in truck and tractor mechanics.

Out there in the garden, I looked away before she did.

If you had told me just then that, twenty-five years later, I'd be divorced, teaching English in a city high school a few states away, making occasional love to Sarah and recruiting her for my first-ever guerrilla action, I would have said: that's interesting; I didn't know that; thank you. Good ideas, all of them.

Our group was atypical. The population changed but little. About ten of us crowded into the kitchen at the round dinner table. There was no leader and no agenda. No spiritual practice. No rules. We raised pigs, chickens, a couple of Jersey cows. We sold vegetables, baked goods, and books: some of us were writers, and the world out there was interested just then in what we had to tell of our lives.

My wife and I had both dropped out of graduate school and moved to the farm, to be with friends. When people asked us, we said we simply wanted to be more like whatever peasants our soldiers were killing somewhere in the world. There was both arrogance and innocence in that desire; it was misguided solidarity, but it was sincere.

We weren't in the first rush back to the land, or even in the second. Most of us who stayed for a time found a chance to confront something in our existence, and not via therapy or drugs. We achieved a kind of wholeness which would stand us in good stead in later lives when the day to day life on the farm had faded from memory. That's what happened to me.

My wife and I had come to do something different—even to see whether the monogamy our parents had taught us had its place within the coming collective reality of the future. Neither of us anticipated that it would be the unspoken objective of everyone else on the farm to break up our marriage, to call our vows into question like any other silly patriarchal rule made to be broken.

We held out for two years, stayed for two long winters. Moved away, pregnant, to preserve our family unit. Before we moved, Sarah became friend, confidant, and lover to us both.

She had come to the farm to hide. At Michael's request, we helped to hide her. We pieced together, from what she told each of us in complementary versions, the whole story of her life till our farm harbored her. We became two participants in the network of friends who shared her secret.

Sarah believed the country had been hijacked, and she believed, like I do, in the power of education: that if enough people learned the truth, we could alter the disastrous path our country had set out on. She joined a study group in the city. They met once a week, had speakers, read Howard Zinn and Chomsky; de Toqueville, Marx, Emma Goldman, James Baldwin, Malcolm X, and Chairman Mao.

You know about him? His Little Red Book?

Goddamn rapist.

None of the people in her study group knew that one third of them were undercover agents, working for, among others, the FBI, the CIA, or the local police department. None of the agents was aware of the others' existence. One of them knew how to make a bomb, another said he could get the materials, another one never shut up; he raved like a hellfire preacher about the need for less study and more action, and there was one who smoldered that non-violence had had its chance and was never gonna work. All of them were *agents provocateurs.* It all came out in Sarah's trial.

This is in no way to excuse what happened, to deny how the innocent folks in the study group allowed it to change. And not to cover up Sarah's participation. I don't even know how she took part. Let the men use her apartment for a bombshop? Make the pre-dawn phone call that cleared the few occupants of the building? Did she drive a car? I never asked.

When the jury learned what I've just told you, there was no way they would ever have found her guilty. They let her walk. They held a press conference outside, excoriating the undercover agents who'd changed a naive optimistic study group into a terror cell. It was a sting. The jury didn't like stings.

It was a sunny day. She walked out of the Federal Building, and caught the caravan back to Vermont.

After seven years underground, Sarah was schooled in secrecy. There was nothing I couldn't tell her. Not a word would ever leave her confidence. I'm different; I'm a school teacher; sometimes my excitement as I think out loud, my desire that a student understand—this point! now! get it for a lifetime!—makes me raise my voice, talk too much, even makes me wonder later whether I can get back what I've spilled.

But that night in the restaurant with her I told her everything quietly and easily, eagerly and carefully. I waited for more than her two-word reply. I guessed that the time she spent in framing her response was mostly taken up with speculating how and where she would fit in to the part of the story yet to happen.

"All right. Let me get this straight. You see this article, you think you know this guy, this artist, Julio Parra. The story gets under your skin."

"Yeah."

"So now you want us to do some copycat crime here."

"Um, yeah, I guess you could call it that."

"Okay. We go get some guy. You'll tell us who. We put him in a room. I could seduce the fucker and blackmail him, make some kind of deal with him, but I gather that's not what you have in mind."

"No."

"I get to keep my clothes on. I'm not the nude on the sofa."

"No."

"That's a shame. Sounded kinda fun."

"Yeah, no, not you ," I said; "you just help me teach him a lesson."

"An English lesson."

"So to speak," I said, grinning.

"So to speak," she agreed.

"Not that I've figured out yet how you can help," I added, after we tried to picture it for a moment.

"You never had a teacher's aide?" she asked with a smile.

"Not this kind," I said.

"I'm not familiar with this Senator," she said, "the guy you want to get to. What's he like?"

"He's a lying blowhard ultra-conservative, lecherous misogynist pig, Jesus freak, violently homophobic, anti-semitic, anti-communist, sexist, racist, transphobic, hates Muslims, women, abortions, contraceptives, the IRS, day care—"

"Is that all?" she asked; "why don't you just invite him out to dinner with us. There's nothing here a simple conversation can't clear up."

"Seriously. I feel sorry for him because he was born too late. Or too early."

"Meaning?"

"Meaning the kind of prejudice he would like to feel free to declare is, you know, not super-popular out in public. A lot of that public votes. He's had to keep it bottled it up, poor guy, and so he has to choose other targets for all that negative energy he has, else he would go crazy. Safe targets. Like artists. There's not that many of them."

If I could hit him at the right moment, somehow set off one of his hot buttons—that seemed easy enough—and get him right at that moment to transmute his reflexive feelings of powerlessness, white male rage, into an artistic venture, get him to stop beating up on artists and *become* one, would that help my cause?

Wait. Is this what Julio was showing me? Is this the idea I've been gestating?

Was it a long shot? I didn't think so. I mean, isn't this how rap and hip-hop started? Rage into art?

"Show me the article," Sarah said, knowing I would have it on me.

I watched her read it as I had watched Garth earlier in the week. There it was again: that look of extra attention. Was it wonder, surprise, descent through layers, or just doubt? There was so much to the story, in so few lines. Like looking through a finite space into a room of limitless possibilities. More than the excitement of secret sharing took hold of me; she was the first woman I had shown the story to; I was eager to hear her reaction.

She handed it back to me, unimpressed.

"Men look at me like that all the time," she smiled again. "Like they're squinting through a lens. You're all peepers when you can get away with it."

"Whoa," I started to say. But my protest weakened right away—

"No, it's true.," she said. "In fact, the narrower your point of view, the more attractive I look."

I looked at her right breast through a circle of finger and thumb. "You're right," I said.

Then after a pause I said, "I don't think I want him to look at you."

"The Senator."

"Right." I said. "or whoever it is we get."

She laughed. "You want to keep that pleasure all for yourself. Possessive all of a sudden, aren't we?"

"No. I've never asked for that. It's just—look, I'm still working this out," I said. "He wouldn't be able to look at you that way. You'll be with us in the room."

"The room with the hole in the wall."

"Right," I said.

"I'll be helping you."

"Right."

"And there's a naked person in the other room? Other side of the wall?"

"I don't know. I guess so."

"Okay. So, he's like, what, thrashing around in a chair and I'm helping you hold him down?"

"Maybe. I don't know."

"Some ringleader."

"I told you, I'm still figuring this out."

"So who is he looking at?" she asked me.

I didn't know. I fiddled with my glass.

At that moment an idea pushed itself into my mind from where it had been waiting in my "ideas-not-yet-spoken" bin. More than not yet spoken: not even fully thought-out yet. I love that bin, but sometimes its contents catch me off guard. Like I said, words, ideas: where do they come from?

I told her about Kyla and Jermayne. I described them to her in detail, surprising myself as always with the complexity of my reaction to their display. I considered, and then dismissed, that it was my own desire, desperate for real love again, maybe feeling for the first time my calendar age. Maybe I was feeling puzzled, too, even envious, as Sarah and I were so far beyond, or short of, their kind of behavior?

No, this was about beauty. This was also about slavery's terrible legacy assuaged in one tiny spot, although there are whole swaths of our population from left and right who would dismiss me, cancel me, for seeing it that way.

But I teach English, and when images of Jermayne and Kyla's loving rose up in my mind, they fit with my chosen memories of literary love, but almost as if the words the writers had chosen to engrave on my brain had fallen away, leaving only sensory data, as if the memories I was reading were my own, of my own life—stick with me on this, okay, it's true!—the smell of the dairy farm and buttery, where Tess of the D'Urbervilles falls in love with Angel Clare; the moonrise on the beach at the end of D.H. Lawrence's "The Rainbow," when the woman, Ursula, rises to so much female power that it spooks her lover, making him nearly irrelevant; or the looming slag heaps in the night in "How Green Was My Valley" when Bronwen and Huw confess their impossible love to each other.

If I taught Great Love in my honors class, how could I not honor theirs? Even if their love was just chemistry, a quick heat-producing reaction in two young lives, it was more than enough to make them look back and remember its power till their two separate lives ended. I was sure of that.

I have memories like that.

"See what I mean?" Sarah said. "They've been titillating you for a whole year. You can't take it any more. Throw literature out the window. Enough of this sublimation!"

"It's not for me. I won't see anything!"

"I know," Sarah said, finishing her iced tea, "I'm just teasing you. What you say is pretty. But Senator Whatsis is not going to see your friends that way. He'll see the black kid with the corn rows, the vulnerable white girl. The pierced nipple. The Liberal agenda. Intermarriage. The Battle Flag shredded. Mongrelization of the master race. All his alarms will go off."

"I know," I said. "I want them to. I'm not expecting anything else. Not at the beginning, anyway. We'll work on him." I figured we'd have maybe five minutes, to teach what typically took me a whole semester: tolerance, love, appreciation for another point of view. What art can do. Challenging, channeling raw emotion into something pure and finished.

"That's one of the things I like about you," she said. "You look around and you see all the negativity and cynicism that everyone sees, and you honestly think you can wall it out, or in, build a big soft wall of acts of love around it. You think you can protect your students that way."

The waiter brought the steak, two plates, two big salads, one big baked Idaho to share.

Wow! Look at that! Reverse synecdoche—an entire state for one potato.

"I never thought of it like a wall," I said; "more like an infusion. They come to me for a daily dose. Make them all immune."

She nodded, while busily dividing the steak, setting us both up for the meal. "I'm going to enjoy this meat," she said, "and then later we can take a walk, soak up the city a bit, and we can talk some more."

She reached out, patted my hand a little too sympathetically— first of many, from her and from others—and speared her first bite with her fork. A big bite.

Chapter Eight

"I never know whether to take you literally or not," Sarah said later.

Her arm was through mine. We were walking around the neighborhood, digesting, looking for a good place to spend another hour or two before going home to bed. The streets were narrow in the old town, and the sidewalks too, with people out enjoying Friday night, most of them unwilling to choose an indoor setting just yet, as the evening was so pleasant. We were in a neighborhood distinguished by random, valiant storefronts, calling folks away from their 500 channels of living-room lockdown, or out of their cars and back from the malls, to spend, please, a small amount of surplus pay downtown on boutique food and clothes they didn't actually need.

"Try me again," I said.

I thought I knew where she was leading, and though I was glad to have her there on my arm for so many reasons, more than anything I needed her counsel, her company along the confused path my thoughts were taking.

"I'm still stuck on you want to go out and kidnap someone."

"I don't know if I'd call it that," I said. 'More like, borrow him for a purpose."

"And your purpose is—?"

I explained it to her again.

"See, that's what I mean," she said. "With you, the line between literal and figurative is hazy. Very hazy."

I said, "I didn't know there was a line. For me, *Hamlet* and *The Inferno* are prime-time news."

"Right. That's you. But have you talked to any of your students yet?" she asked. "I mean, the couple, or the car full of goons you're gonna need?"

"I've talked to one goon so far." I told her about Garth. My description of him made her laugh. But then she was serious again.

"It's just hard to get used to: guy I've been sleeping with for three years turns out to be a criminal."

"Four years."

"Whatever."

"You couldn't find it just a little exciting?" I asked her.

"I don't think so." She looked at me dramatically. "Mister non-violence, Mister-not-a-fighter, Mister teacher-of-love leads his students into a life of violent crime. They're gonna lock you up in some dungeon and throw away the key. You'll never teach Shakespeare in this town again."

I admitted that it looked that way, but I had the feeling that if I only tweaked certain of the details, we could shift the act outside the realm where the law reigned; we could go from literal to figurative. I was hoping that Cheeto had done that already.

Perception would be the key. What I needed here was a good solid metaphor.

"I'd hate to think of it going wrong," she said. "You do something stupid; you run away to hide. We have to meet in secret. You think there's something romantic about being on the lam?"

"No."

"I think you do. You don't know how miserable it can be. How absolutely deadening and lonely."

"I'm sorry."

"I know, but you just don't know anything about it. You only hung out with me in our Chekhov days."

"Chekhov?"

"Yeah. Our country estate, all that October light pouring in the windows. The fascinating visitors on the weekends. The peach orchard, the fall foliage. Sunlight in the apple cider. The home-baked bread. Candle-lit story-telling in the graveyard. Long walks with brilliant conversation down to the river and back."

That got a laugh from me. I'd never heard our community described so pastorally. When I closed my eyes and pictured it, I saw the tilted stinking outhouse with the wind whistling up your backside. The plucked turkey hanging from the porch rafters dripping blood on the floor. The full fly-paper. Trying to unfreeze the well in the wintertime. Peeling frozen manure off the cow's thighs before milking her. Maggots in the cheese. Woolen clothes soaked in perfume of creosote and old sweat. Bodies smelling that way, too. Coming together in sheets gone stiff with cold and lack of laundering.

I mean, it wasn't always like that, but still...

We two had a way of talking, comfortable with ideas, but parrying or dancing away from any truth that tried to corner us. By letting weeks go by, by hardly talking on the phone, by being verbally and physically playful, even ironic, with each other when we were together, we agreed to deny our seriousness. We had never discussed the terms of our agreement and had no intention to.

Later that night, and during her next several visits, I thought we went to a deeper, more touching place. We were brought there by that conversation on the street, by my impractical plan, by her genuine concern. Our focus sharpened, including our focus on each other. That's how I remember it, anyway.

But that was later. Back to our walking:

"All I'm saying," Sarah said, "is be careful. You're inspired. By Julio. It's an amazing story. You've been given this incredible gift, this signal that came to you in the night. A total surprise. You can screw it up. And not just for yourself: you'd find out really quickly how many other lives you're connected to."

"I hear you," I said. "It's just—"

She interrupted me. "Plus, you need to sensitivity-check everything, like *everything,* in your plan. It's like you're intentionally checking every box! I'm talking racism, violence, interstate coercion, microaggression—"

"Wait—"

"You wait! I'm not finished. ...Exploitation, cultural misappropriation, sexualizing teens against their will, trivializing a Black male body, pimping your own students—"

"Whoa. Hold on," I said.

And she did. She held on.

I think in that next silent moment, in spite of her warnings, she was becoming a participant, I could tell; she had to say all that just to sweep the air clear around us. The article had begun to toy with her mind as it had mine, but her mind had already begun to run with the story in its own way. She said nothing to me about that yet. But she'd take a photocopy of it with her when she went home. And wear it out with looking at it, with trying to look through it, even, at the bigger picture.

I had been living with the Julio Parra story for so long that the structure of it didn't strike me as too unusual, or too impossible to replicate. This kind of stuff is routine almost anywhere in Latin America. It's no longer big news when someone gets pulled off the street. Without the art and the nudity, the Parra story would never have earned its few inches of back-page space, in Mexico or in my local paper.

The lives of thousands of Chileans, Argentines, Hondurans, Salvadorans, Mexicans, revolve around the sacred memory of loved ones who were disappeared for political reasons—mostly with never any closure.

The whole idea is distant to us, yet it could happen here.

"*Desaparecido*" is a common word all over Latin America. But now the meaning has changed. In five or six countries I can think of, it's just the daily risk you take when you walk down the street. But not for politics, not even for art. It's the money.

Hostage-taking is a growth industry in Mexico City. In Sao Paolo, Brazil, some wealthy families never use the streets. They take the elevator up to the roof of their high-rise: they hop a helicopter to the foodstore, the office, the kids' ballet lessons. Like rainforest monkeys that never leave the canopy all their lives. Too many apex predators on the ground.

Down below, if you get carjacked or kidnapped, and you manage to survive, the cop who writes up your complaint will wonder what the fuss is all about. "Man," he'll say, "you look all right to me. No visible nicks. Get a new car. Go have your suit pressed. Next time you go out, don't wear your best clothes."

We're not there yet in this country. People would notice. And there were unknowns, like surveillance cameras, hidden bugs...

There were variables, like, how would the Senator take it? Or whoever we chose? Sarah was right; the thing could get us into trouble. We didn't want trouble. I planned to show up for work the next morning.

Okay, our best bet would be for anyone who *needed* to know it was an abduction, to know it, to be told that or to find it out, but not the abductee. Not even him. Especially not him. (And not the witnesses, either, if there were any.) At least for a while: perhaps we could let the victim know after it was over, after the danger to him and to us had passed. Have a good laugh about it.

Sarah and I sat down at a wrought-iron table outside a barely-surviving indie bookstore. Went inside and got some coffee and sat back down. Sarah was facing the street directly, and I was next to her on an angle so that I took her in, and some of the bookcases through the window. I saw a shelf of used hardcover mysteries inviting me into their world of violence, criminal cause and effect, end-of-the-chapter surprises, leaps of deductive insight. Worlds of fictional characters who wouldn't think twice about doing what I was planning, but I was clearly not made of the same stuff.

Not a fighter, what I said. What Sarah said.

My inhibitions were not worth analyzing; they were never going to change. "I keep thinking of Fabian's line in "Twelfth Night," I said.

"What was that?"

"Something about 'keeping on the windy side of the law.'"

Sarah thought about that, then excused herself and went into the bookstore to use the bathroom, I thought. But I was wrong. Through the window I saw her talking to a clerk, a woman about my daughter's age. Both of them talked with their hands and some synchronized head motions of growing mutual understanding. The clerk went out of sight for a moment and returned with a large blue book. Sarah gestured through the glass toward our table outside and the girl nodded. Then Sarah came out and placed the heavy volume down; opened, it took up most of the table.

"*Black's Law Dictionary*," she said. "Fifth edition. With Pronunciations. Expensive to own, for the one and only time in your life you need to know what you're getting into before you do it. She said I could borrow it for a sec. Is she watching?"

I looked past her shoulder and waved to the woman inside.

"Yes. But why is she looking at me so strangely?" I asked.

"Nothing important," Sarah said, about to finger her way through the A's. "How would you describe her expression?"

"Concerned. Head a little tilted to the side."

"I told her I needed to know the penalty for what I was planning to do to you."

"Oh."

She smiled at me sweetly. "What should we look up?"

She started flipping the pages. On page 5, "abduction" didn't really fit.

"No. Too specifically sexual," I said. "Not what I have in mind."

"Not till later, anyway," she said, still smiling.

"Asportation" was somewhat of a detour. The numerous subdivisions of "malice" were enlightening, though I strenuously denied I had any. Anyway, to the extent that malice denoted a "recklessness of the law," I could claim that in consulting *Black's* I was being anything but reckless. Could that cover me in court? Maybe.

My previous two-hour talk with Sarah had laid out the purity of my motive, but we found out on page 727 that "*intentio inservire debit legibus non leges intentioni*"—"the intention [of a party] is subservient to the law." The law, of course, frightened us both, especially in the case of "kidnapping," which seemed so harrowing even in its dry description that it was clearly not what either of us had in mind, even though "interfering with the performance of a governmental function" had its attractions.

There was some truly entertaining hairsplitting under the items, "coercion," "duress," and "extortion." Sexuality, most of it sadomasochistic, licked at the edges of all these, with images of subjugation, the urgency of persuasion, denial of exercise of free will, or, more exactly, "overmastering the volition of the testator" a phrase I committed to memory for use in bed later that night, but could I make it sound more like an invitation?

This led us to "voyeurism," which was worth the journey: The phrase "secret vantage point" hinted at our story, and gave us both an inner Nabokovian thrill, though we publicly claimed the act to be repellant. There's a nakedness to law when you look at it like this. It peels away the fabric of excuses you wrap your actions in; it leaves you stripped to the skin. A good reference, I agreed with Sarah, to read before going ahead with your plans.

Black's—all 1500 pages of it, even the good parts—was scary. It mostly showed me where I didn't want to go. What I wanted was to put the words "kidnap" or "restrain" in quotation marks, but keep them private, creating an event—an artistic event—loaded with enough ambiguity so that at every step in the process what actually happened could be open to more than one interpretation—like the literature I teach by day.

Like a Julio Parra painting.

There would be no smokey-windowed Jeep, no tire screech, no blanket over the head. Wouldn't work here, and anyway I wasn't up to it.

I needed to guide the victim slash volunteer like a rat through a maze to the end I had in mind, with no pressure, no duress—any compulsion could be his own—without his ever knowing that he had been sequestered, and then to release him just when he was about to put all the clues together and revisit his consent!

Now that we had satisfied the legality issue, we could move on to new topics: how could we get creative? How many levels of reality could we work on? How to get the victim to believe that one thing was happening when something completely different would be taking place? Could we deceive him?

Got it. It was beginning to sound like theatre to me. Could we invite an audience; could we deceive them, too?

We could: an audience is always deceived. They want to be.

For at least an hour, as innocent couples threaded by on the narrow sidewalk, with our coffee cooling in the cups and the big book open on the table, with the clerk on the other side of the glass checking up on us constantly, I sat in deep discussion with Sarah—my heroine, counselor, lover, and co-conspirator.

It sounded doable.

Chapter Nine

Late the next morning, Sarah and I walked up to the front of the plate-glass entrance of the Hotel Mercury. Greek Gods and Titans were known to inhabit inside, in frescoes on the walls, paintings on the ceilings, mosaics on the floor, chipped and dented statues in the halls. The architecture was art-deco zodiac Olympian. The name was an Americanization of Mercouri, from the man who'd had the money to build the place back at a time when no one else in the city had a dime. Speaking of dimes, the image of Mercury from the mid-century coin was carved in pink marble over the front door.

Stavro M made money buying and selling and shipping produce to the military in World War One. Everyone else who'd profited from the Great War sank their money in the stock market, but he'd stuffed his into tin cans and fruit crates, and made it through the Crash.

Stavro used his money to start his own private WPA. He hired masons and plumbers and tile-layers and artists, desperate for the work, and they'd built this solid seven story hotel on a corner not too far from downtown. Mercouri was so happy to see the workers toiling with the energy of gratitude, that he let them give free rein to their eclectic whimsy, within the bounds of his mythological premise. The place became a favorite for visitors and paying guests for the next twenty years.

There was a period—late sixties, early seventies?—when the hotel was beyond deserted. Stavro was widowed and drinking; his son went somewhere else for a while, working, escaping, beginning a family. Prospering travelers in love with highways and big cars stayed at the motels on the outskirts of town. The hotel nearly died.

There were a number of proposals put forward to the City Council for developing the valuable property. One wrecking company proposed leveling the place to make it into a vacant lot. A more ambitious consortium wanted to raze the hotel and the buildings next to it, and build a six-story parking garage to shelter drug dealers, deep throats, and obsolete air-polluting mobile hunks of steel and rubber. Still another developer envisioned a brightly-lit mini-mart open all night with room for ten cars on the pavement fronting, and inside, a couple of single mothers working, at minimum wage, their third job of the day.

Just possibly the Council's unwillingness to choose from this wealth of possibilities saved the Mercury, and it stood, a Greek art-deco icon, in a kind of just-near-downtown limbo, while the decades hurtled by.

Now the building gleamed, its façade sand-blasted, its edges sharpened, protected by the National Register of Historic Places certificate framed in the lobby, and people came to stay there either to revel in the decor, or for the expressed political purpose of not giving money to the operators of the cookie-cutter motels out there blinking on the strips.

Mercouri was long dead, but his grandson Alex was a friend

of mine. I'd had him in class, written his college recommenda-
tions, been to his wedding, and encouraged him as he took over
the building. He directed the restoration, and devised new ways
for the hotel to make money. A brew pub in the basement, a little
dance hall in what had been an upstairs ballroom, a few rental
office spaces, a room for the local public radio affiliate...

What Sarah and I liked about the place (we'd even stayed there
a couple of times, for a fantasy): some of the rooms were adjoining:
that locked door next to the dresser made you imagine the temporary life being lived on the other side of the fragile barrier. The
door promised openness; the old brass knob and lock specifically
stated closure.

Once, we had both seen one of those doors opened. Alex had
invited a theatre company to give an intimate performance in an
upstairs room; it was an Agatha Christie type of drawing-room
(in this case, a hotel room) mystery farce. We had been among
the twenty people crowded in chairs in a corner by the bathroom,
as scene followed scene, and one plot twist wrapped the previous
one, spilling from the next room into ours. The action—so tanta-
lizingly close—moved from the bed to the curtained window, with
its suggestion of outside danger, to the door where room service
swished in with a silver tray of possibly-poisoned red wine for
us all, to the polished desk where an actress in bra and bloomers
penned a desperate note.

We remembered that evening well.

Alex saw us from the lobby and came out to greet us. "Hi, Sarah.
Hello, Mr. B."

Once you've been someone's school teacher, you can never get
them to call you by your first name.

He asked us how we were keeping. We told him fine. I let his
desk clerk's look go by without comment. He asked us if we needed
a room. Sarah said not that way, not today. Well okay maybe. But

could we look at a little two-room suite that might be suitable for theatre? A bedroom one-act? Farcical-tragical?

"Room 22," Alex said right away.

He was manning the lobby for an employee who'd called in sick, and couldn't show us around. He slid the room key across the counter, said the room was vacant and unreserved. He fished around in a drawer and handed us a separate key for the inner door.

"Take your time; see you in a while." He turned back to the inner office and the old copper switchboard, which was buzzing.

Sarah took the terrazzo stairs by two's. Sarah always climbed stairs two at a time. She was unlocking the door when I came up beside her. She pushed the door in and stood looking into the room. It looked like one we had stayed in before. I stood close behind her—body touching her, actually—in the doorway miming two heavy suitcases, one in each hand.

"Shall I bring your bags in, ma'am?" I asked her in an obsequious voice, not my own.

"Yes, please, " she said without turning around; "over there—" indicating the low dresser. I left one of the unseen cases on the floor, and with an elaborate inbreath I swung the heavier of the two onto the table top. I sprung two invisible clips, opened the top in an illusory arc, and, bending over, I lowered my whole smiling face to take in the feel and aroma of her lacey garments of my imagination. Let go an audible outbreath.

She slapped me hard where I deserved it. "The play's starting, I see?"

She sat on the bed and I sat in a dark green leatherette chair. We talked, trying to visualize the event we had in mind, willing it into being. We tried to disturb the seen-it-all neutrality of the room. If we filled it just then, with our ideas—the good ones and the bad ones—we could prepare the space for the pared-down drama we hoped to bring there.

"You know," she said, imagining the scene, "you're planning

just the kind of work of art the Endowment can't stand. One with a political agenda."

"True," I said, "but I'm not looking for grant money for it. I'm going to pay for it myself. Not only that, our agenda is: Save the NEA. They've gotta like that."

"I wouldn't be too sure of that," she said. "Sometimes when a politician can't stand a particular organization, he just worms his own golf buddy into the chairmanship, and then they both get a chuckle running it into the ground. Make it wither on the vine. Less blame that way. Happens all the time. I don't know who's in charge right now, but they may not agree with your agenda."

I saw her point, but kept silent. I had decided a while back that I would follow my original inspired impulse wherever it led me, even if I didn't quite understand it all. Actually, because I didn't understand it all!

I could see how I could modify some of the details for deniability's sake, enjoy the process, hope to revel in its possible success, but practice a pre-emptive detachment should the outcome not jibe with my vision.

Take the story, I always told my writing students, one page at a time. Don't invest too heavily in the outcome. Don't even plan the ending.

And speaking of students, I am the same way with them. I will put everything I have into their growing, but if what they become is not what I've pictured, I can live with that. If they happen to come back to visit me, they'll see no disappointment in my eyes.

The noon hour came and went and we still sat there. We had left a wrinkled bed back at my house, towels on the floor, and dishes on the table and in the sink. Now, in this impersonal space that was not our own, and which sat swept and tucked and waiting for whatever customer would come, time seemed to go by very slowly while we talked. We were relaxed and not thinking about the rest of the day. Still musing about the idea. All the aspects of it.

"I wonder whether she was disappointed," Sarah was saying

"Who?" I asked.

"The woman. In the article. Whatever her name was. Think of how much time it must have taken her to plan the thing, like we're doing—"

"You think she planned it?" I asked.

"I do. I think it came from her. Think of how exciting it must have been for her to imagine it. And so incredible to be doing it finally. Making Julio watch her like that."

"Making him, yeah," I said. "It's different from letting."

"Yes," she said. "Totally different. And then, thinking about showing the paintings. In a gallery, or to her husband for the first time, if he wasn't in on the secret. Then, I don't know, they're just these flat two-dimensional pictures that are so removed from the experience. If she shows them to anybody, they can't come close to describing the experience. And if she doesn't show them to anybody, it's even worse."

Was the artistic act more important than the product, the outcome? That was one of Sarah's themes, I think, and one of mine, too.

The people who founded the National Endowment for the Arts, I thought, have got to be feeling sad. If they're still around. Its original impulse was similar to the "Art for the Millions" of Franklin Roosevelt's day. High culture in the backlands, yes, but so much more than that: a nationwide fantasy of workers, artists, students, children, getting together to create local art with money magically wafted from above. No, not magical at all. It was taxpayer's money, willingly paid because everyone agreed it was very little, and very important.

It pulled the participants out of depression. But then later it became a lightning rod, a battleground. Somehow their grant money got used to insult the Virgin Mary, dip Jesus and his cross in urine, and exhibit the most racially provocative of Mapplethorpe's photos.

No one expected this. Damned First Amendment. Making the public square safe for everybody: Klan members, Nazis, Christians, defamers, kiddie porn hacks, artists aflame with self expression—

They may have expected the fringe group of yahoos and crazies who came to picket. They asked for it. But no one expected how powerful the fringe would become. How entrenched in the mainstream. They'd reduced the agency lately to an object of public scorn, an irrelevant office of advocacy with less than a hundred million dollars to spend, kept just alive, probably, so that a dozen conservative Senators could raise fistfuls of dollars for their own campaigns by fulminating about the evil things the NEA had done.

Without a word, Sarah took the second key and opened the door that led into the connecting room. She went in, and I heard her moving around in there. Couldn't see her from where I was sitting. Something about her quick exit made me just stay there in the green chair and not follow her. Sudden vanishings were a part of her fugitive legacy. I was used to them. I always figured she would tell me if she wanted my company. Usually she went off to take a turn around the block, to scratch some muscular or mental itch. Her return customarily brought good news.

"I like this 'part for the whole' idea," she said when she came back.

"So do I." I said; "why do you like it?"

"'Cause it's how I've always looked at things. It's motivational. Like that Margaret Mead quote everyone has stuck up on their fridge."

"About a small group of people changing the whole world?" I asked.

"Right. But now I can imagine being even more focussed than that."

"What do you mean?"

"I mean I think I see what you want to do. You pick just the right person. One person. He—or she—becomes your catalyst."

"That's what I was hoping," I said.

"Like a seed crystal," she said.

I said yes. I knew her reference. Kurt Vonnegut talked about seed crystals in *Cat's Cradle*. How a tiny drop of transformed water could turn the whole ocean into ice. I've always loved that image. The seductiveness and power of an original idea: when I notice some new wave sweeping the world, say of taste or design or mass behavior, my mind goes immediately to: where did this begin; who was the first person who started doing things this way? And then the whole world stopped what it was doing, noticed, took one breath, and immediately followed suit. Like, what young man on what street first wore baggy pants down past his butt crack? Who—

"Are you listening?" she said.

"I'm sorry," I answered. "I missed the last thing you said."

"I said I think you have the wrong person in mind."

"How's that?"

"The Senator, whatever his name is, is the mouth. You've got to get at the brain."

I looked at her quietly waiting for her explanation. She was standing in the doorway between the two rooms. Legs apart and arms out to touch the verticals, like Da Vinci's drawing of the perfect human form. Like the first time I saw her in those rows of corn.

"It's simple. From what I've heard, the staffers have all the real power in the Senate. We don't know their names but they do the research, the writing, and they network up and down the halls, in the gyms, at the happy hours. They don't actually pull the strings, but nothing gets done without them. You have to get to the right one of them. There's your seed crystal. Change one of them and you could change the whole bunch in a matter of days."

She closed the door behind her, left it unlocked, and came over to where I was still sitting. Strong shiny jade-green chair, just like what the props person would have picked for this scene. She arranged herself across my lap in the chair.

I tried to remember any other time she had ever sat in my lap. I could not. We had never been physically close—well, once or twice—during the year we dovetailed on the commune. I think we kept, or at least showed, a distance between us. She never tried to separate my wife and me. As a group we all expressed our intimacy by working together—hard collective tasks like hand-digging a new well for the barn—and by frequent dancing, by swimming naked in the beaver pond, by sweating together in the hybrid (Swedish-Iroquois) sauna we had built. As a group also we avoided gestures that smacked of any kind of hierarchy, possession, or old-fashioned love.

So no lap-sitting, then, or during the years since she first wrote and offered to come down for a visit. Now, this was another offer.

"So what else were you doing in there?" I asked her. Surprised and delighted by her gesture, my hand crept along her side. Fingers curving around to the front. Enjoying her weight. My eyes were now close to her mouth and I watched her words as they formed on her lips and made it out to the air.

"Scoping it out," she said.

"Hmmm."

"I figured out how I can help you."

"Cool," I said. It never sounds quite right when I say it. I keep hoping it will but it's a race against time. "How?"

"I can help identify the guy you want to get. And I can help you get him here."

"See," I said. "That room has more ideas in it than this one."

"You never know."

"What else did you find in there?"

"There's a big mirror."

"Nice."

"I'll show you."

She dismounted and pulled me with her.

Some time later, when we went back downstairs, we found Alex reading the morning paper in the quiet of the little lobby. So much time travel: morning paper, lobby, Art Deco hotel—the sun poured in and awoke the perfect Aegean blue of the floor. Gilt terrazzo speckles played with the light like on a moving sea surface. You could imagine diving in deep enough to find a long lost statue buried in the sea-bottom sand.

"What'd you think of the rooms?" he asked, when I flipped him the keys. He gave us that desk clerk's look again, but we just smiled.

"They'll do. We'll reserve both of them." I named the night.

"You got 'em," he said. "A theatre event, right?"

"Right. Not a very long one. But I'll pay for the whole night."

"You have to. Hotel rules. Dad used to rent by the hour, but I had to put a stop to it. Our name was turning up in too many divorce cases."

Trying to sound like a pro, I made an arrangement to come back and do a tech rehearsal. Bring along the set carpenter, the lighting guy, the house manager. The best boy. Come back alone, in other words.

"Since when do you do theatre?" Alex asked.

"I don't. This is my first time."

"And it's just one performance?"

"A one-night stand."

Plenty of those in this hotel, I thought. There's something about this place.

"Can you reserve a seat for me?" he asked, while we were saying our good-byes.

"You bet," I said; "but don't advertise it. It's by invitation only."

"Wooo. Not For Everybody?" he quoted, theatrically.

"For Madmen Only," I answered.

"*Steppenwolf*," he said. "I loved that."

"Yeah."

"You made us read the best books," Alex said.

Chapter Ten

Before Sarah went back to Vermont, we held a meeting.

I brought my car, and Garth hung around after school, and we picked up Jermayne after track practice. Jermayne was a runner, a hurdler. We went to the restaurant where Kyla worked. My students knew Sarah and were comfortable with her.

Sometimes I bring people in from outside to speak to the class. So last year one theme was, we read some books that were written in a unique voice, with a unique point of view about the historic times they came from. *Huck Finn, The Color Purple, Grapes of Wrath.* I picked some books from the anti-Vietnam war back-to-the-land movement, still fresh in my personal memory anyway. Sarah came to class to help lead that discussion.

My students had showed an interest in those Vietnam years. I thought they would have good questions about the book, or some of the history and agricultural traditions the communards had brought back to life. Wrong again. They just wanted to know things like "An outhouse? Really? Why?" And "What was it like not to have TV?" "People didn't have phones?" "Didn't everyone smell awful?"

I wanted to talk about history, and the good people who wrote about it. How sharing became communal living, how that became co-housing, how co-housing became themed communities, how smelly cabbage in the basement turned into specialty kimchi, how barely drinkable raw milk became designer cheeses that won every international award—

But I was saying that they knew Sarah, and felt free to speak in her presence. She inspired trust.

We sat around a table at the restaurant where Kyla worked after school. No customers yet. She worked as a prep cook, and there was a lot of preparation to do. She interrupted her work and joined us at a plank table.

The restaurant was a second-floor walk-up above a music store. (Music meaning vinyl, replica turntables, posters, and secondhand CD's.) The decor featured real potted plants, folkloric fabrics, and beads from around the world. The cuisine was vegan, not my first choice for dinner. I couldn't get over the impression that here was a new fundamentalist religion being born whose dietary restrictions were more gaga than kosher or halal.

The restaurant's entrees were an earnest and terminally dry combination of seeds, pulses, exotic Andean root crops, fibrous greens, portabella mushrooms, and fake-milk cheese. Chickpeas were abundant. I don't think they cook them. People who live on this, I thought, must shit aromatic little pellets like deer or porcupines. At the same time, I pledged, if what it took to eradicate world hunger was for all of us to eat like this, and stop wasting the earth's land and fresh water and available oxygen to feed supersized loud-mouthed white Christian beef-eating gluttons, I'd be willing to do it.

Although, until the command came to do that, I was not going to make the first move.

We had some haste. In as few sentences as possible, without the background detours you're all too familiar with, I tried to explain the idea I had in mind. Kidnap a Senator. Okay, not really a Senator. Okay, not really kidnap. A theatrical event. In a hotel room. In two hotel rooms, actually.

Capitalize on the man's voyeurism. His hitting on young women.

His racism. Show him a knee-high hole in the wall. Catch him at a moment of weakness. De-repress him a little; make him into a writer. Save the National Endowment for the Arts. Maybe spend an hour doing this? An hour and a half?

My truncated explanation must have fallen a few segues short of comprehensibility. As Kyla absorbed her and Jermayne's part in the play, she chose the words of her reaction with care.

"You're crazy, Mr. B," she said. "A sick man."

Okay, I can't promise those were the exact words she used. But it's what she was thinking.

I felt my idea slipping away. "You don't have to *do* anything. I'm not gonna look through the hole. Sarah won't look. Of course Garth won't, will you?"

"Not me," Garth said. "I don't bend at the knee."

I glared at him. Either he was showing an irreverent streak, or, I decided, he was revealing another aspect of the self behind the camo and shades: a sense of humor that would help out in a battle situation.

Still I had to come up with the right thing to say to focus us.

"You have to think of it as if you were in charge," I told Kyla. Sarah nodded, as if she had already worked that out.

"You're the proactive ones here," Sarah said. "Nothing is going to happen to you." Her own hyper-protective avatar kicking in.

"The door will be locked," I said. "No harm will be done. Plus there's no guarantee he'll even look. All we're doing is offering the man a possibility, offering any of us a possibility, which may or may not happen."

Come to think of it, when art comes to pull you in while you're walking down the street, that's what is happening: a possibility beckons. Only ever a possibility.

"Or, think of it like an art class," Garth suggested.

"An art class?" Kyla asked.

"Yeah. Not like high school art. In college, they're all over the place. You get to look at naked women and draw them." Garth was pleased with his analogy, and continued: "It's one of the perks of bein' at college. Guys get to act cool and studious, like a real pro, squintin' down their piece of charcoal like you've seen one, you've seen them all. Modeling, too. I hear it's one of the best-paid work-study jobs."

"Yeah, Man, I know that, but couples?" Jermayne asked.

"How about Rodin's "The Kiss?" I said. "Go check it out. He had two models for that. Two models who clearly cared for each other. I mean, you can't fake that."

As I thought of it, picturing that sculpture, I realized that I should teach that sculpture. It was only a chunk of marble, but it said more about passion and love's commitment, and exhaustion, than many books I could think of.

"So what do we do?" Kyla asked. She was looking at Jermayne, holding his hand. She who, among all the teen-age exhibitionists who'd studied with me over the years, ranked right at the top.

I'll admit it: that was a reveal. I know; I get it: Kyla had the right to dress and behave as she wished. No one else's business but hers. Do not blame or shame her. Not me. Not you. Period. Jermayne, too. They're both eighteen, agents of their own whatever—they can vote; they can soldier; why not this?

I fought to come up with an answer. I tried hard not to let them see I was treading water here. Improvising.

I have a recurring dream—I'd call it a nightmare except for the fact that I have been there so often that I am used to it, almost comfortable with what happens. I am in a group of militants meeting together for some noble cause. We're discussing some exciting plan of action. We're going ahead, together. We're going to have an impact, together. Someone gives the signal and we rush forward as one: through the door, or down a street, or out on an actual limb.

I feel the incredible rush of participation, of excited solidarity

—and then I look around again and notice that everyone else has suddenly vanished. But I am in full momentum, and there is no stopping or turning back. Up ahead the enemy appears in great number, and as they stand confidently to receive our attack, they see only me. My breathing comes in quick gasps of abandonment. That's when I wake up.

I was fighting against that same sort of feeling here. Certainly the inspiration for the action was mine, mine only. Reading the news about Julio. Making my wild extrapolations. Broaching the subject with Garth, with Sarah. Seeing their bemused smiles. Trying to read their expressions along the way: were they understanding me as well as I thought they did? Were they humoring me? Going along for an improbable ride? Did they sense any danger? Was I reckless, endangering my friends? Would their participation, agreed on now, evaporate, and would the event turn into my familiar dream, and leave me struggling to explain myself, to exonerate myself, to breathe, to hide, to awaken alone?

I had been quiet for a while; Kyla's unanswered question hung in the air.

"Whatever you want," I said. "Like in my class."

I was definitely not going to suggest, either on the record or off, that they become soft-porn performers, though some observers coming into my afternoon class would have said that was what they already were. Morals are constantly evolving, anyway. You either stay stuck on your position regarding what is appropriate and acceptable, or you change and grow yourself, make yourself tolerant and comfortable in the brave new world.

But you have to be honest about it, because teen-agers can see right through an adult's act, and you must not be a voyeur or a predator or even a participant, desperately looking for a way to turn back your own clock.

If you occupy a position of responsibility and trust, politician, therapist, teacher—a position I actively and happily seek—you must use it to draw a line in the sand against exploitation: loveless sex, child pornography, internet stalking, predator priests, cradle robbing, drug abuse, date rape, men who refuse to think about where babies come from, corporations and their advertisers who make us all feel inadequate, ugly, fat, and lonely.

You use every moment of your English class to teach *love*; you make them know what a wonder and a gift it is. Then you stand back and let young people have their fun. You stay away. Keep out. You don't take any advantage of it for yourself. None. That's the only way to be till the Taliban take over here. Or the Christian daddy on his white horse. The one I see galloping around the corner right now.

Kyla seemed unconvinced.

"I mean it," I said, and I looked her right in the eye. "You two have that hotel room for the night. To hang out in. Do your homework. You do not have to *do* anything else. You just have to be. And then, after a while, the rest of us'll be gone."

Garth had this expression, like, give me and my girl-friend that room, Mr. B; we'll show you a thing or two. Well, not you, but whoever's watching. Right. But he was a seventeen year old boy, quick on the draw and probably quick to fire. Not what I'd like to watch. If I were watching. Which I won't be. I just said that.

"Plus the guy's not gonna be looking for long," Sarah said. "Couple of minutes, maybe, tops."

"How do you know?" Kyla asked.

"I've got a feeling."

"How will we know when he's watching?"

"You'll figure it out," I said. I'd been all through that with picturing Julio and the woman.

Jermayne had stayed as long as he could. He had to go to work at the supermarket. I'll tell you, every time I go to a supermarket and see all those high school students at the check-outs and bagging stations, it makes me want to cry. Wearing those badges with their names. "Rhonda. Customer Service Associate." Why don't those badges say things like "Ryan. No Time to Do My Homework: I'm Supporting My Family and We All Live in Post-Consumer-Capitalist No-Health-Care Food-Stamp Hell."

Jermayne gave Kyla a practiced hug, waved to the rest of us on his way out. "I don't quite understand it, Mr. B. You got me with 'free hotel room.' You left me behind with the volunteer writing lesson stuff. But if it's okay with Kyla, it's cool with me."

We watched him leave. Kyla, Sarah, and Garth then turned as one to me, with the mutual hope that I would now hammer in the golden spike of my long explanation, joining tracks of thought that were being laid down for the first time, which no one ever expected to converge, let alone lead to an identifiable destination. But I was destined to disappoint them. How could I tell them that I was hacking my way through an unmapped place?

The Julio Parra article—which I had decided that only Garth, Sarah, and I would ever know about—was vague where I needed the most direction. It came with no instruction manual for the leader of the copycat op. Yes, the story had chosen me. Yes, it was ambiguous. Yes, the leap between the Mexican anecdote and my purpose was huge, if not ridiculous. Something only I could have conceived of.

I tried to form the words to explain how any kind of call, be it to write, to paint, to become a prophet, to set out on a vision quest: any kind of call that arrives to capture an open mind involves a big surprise and a whole lot of unknown material and unexplored terrain.

Something suddenly concentrates on you. Something picks you out with a look that says "Follow."

Then you take a long step in a direction you never planned to go.

Sarah contributed nothing more. She seemed content to radiate an irritating, though charming, detachment-from-the-outcome as I fought to find the right words. She would jump aboard when she knew where this train was going. Garth drummed his fingers on the table top. He had the foot soldier's ability to wait at rest while the officers plotted the next move. No help from either of them.

Garth stood up. "Gotta date. See you tomorrow, Sir."

He left with a quick wave, no salute this time.

I turned to Kyla. She was dressed in her usual way. The perfect white skin; long Scandinavian blonde hair, some up, some down. Something purple with a French name, silky, showing beneath a plunging widemouth jersey top. From the neck north she looked like Heidi the Alpine cowgirl granddaughter, but below her shoulders was the land of entrapment, a deep perfumey cleavage pushed and held artificially aloft.

When you talked to her, you met her eyes and deliberately kept yourself there, although, whenever Jermayne was not around, she would stretch as if her attachment to him had left her with kinks she now needed to pop out, or as if, having dressed for attention, she was waving perimeter, peripheral parts to attract your eyes away from her display—like a mother robin disrupting your interest in her nest.

I was happy that Sarah was there to witness, if not chaperone, the dance. Happy, too, that we were all sitting around a table on chairs that restrained some movement. If you met Kyla while out walking, her moving and stretching often escalated into bridges, sensational walkovers, handstands nearly. All while holding up her end of an intelligent conversation.

"I think you have the wrong idea about Jermayne and me," Kyla said. "But it's our fault, totally."

"You're not in love?" I asked her.

"Of course we're in love," she said. "But we hardly have any time together. His dad works two jobs, or three. His big brother, Bill, lives—I don't know where. So Jermayne has to get up real early and help his two sisters off to school. He irons their clothes. Then he helps his Mom get out of the house and go to work. He makes it to school about a minute before it starts. Right after school he has track, or cross-country in the fall. He's got to work afternoons and weekends. He's really tired at night. I don't like to go to his house because his friends on the street get down on him for being with me. I can't bring him home because my parents, I don't know. They know I see him, and they like him and all, they accept him, but they just don't want us to be like, serious about each other."

Sarah and I were both quiet and attentive; we felt blessed just to have someone her age talking to us simply and honestly, in confidence.

"What I mean is," she continued, "you see us at one of the few times that we can really be together. We hang out so tight in your class because we can. It's like our, what do you always call it...?"

"Protected space?"

"Yeah. Actually it's the only one we have."

Every so often, I let myself pat myself, virtually, on the back. At the end of the day, my teaching day that is, I want two things. Make that three. One, I want the students to feel that reading and writing are exciting, essential things to do. Two, I want them to know where I stand vis a vis the world, because political thought is my passion, and my passion is what made me choose to be a teacher. They can agree or disagree with me but I insist that they start having informed opinions.

The third thing is I want them to feel that for the eighty minutes we are together, our classroom is the actual center of the universe; there's a great big invisible "X" on the floor in the center that marks the spot—I want them to feel like they wouldn't want to be anywhere else, and that the space we have created is protected. Insulated, by "a big soft wall," I think Sarah called it.

You look around the room and see twenty young people who

could just as well be putting each other down. But starting from day one, I lead them in a different direction. In my room Kyla and Jermayne can intertwine if they want. Go ahead. Boys can hold hands, if they want. Anyone can. People can say what's on their minds. Respect for the living, and the dead. The dead are free to speak and be heard. (In the form of writing.) Those dead don't thank me, and I don't work for praise, but I welcome confirmation from the living students that I am on the right track.

"Makes me think of the community kitchen," Sarah said.

Kyla absorbed that for a moment. "The place you both used to live?"

"Yes. There were ten of us. We all kind of fell together. The best thing we had going for us was at the dinner table, when it was dark outside, we came in from wherever, or home from work, especially in the winter-time—"

"—the whisper of the woodstove," I added.

"The woodstove," she agreed. "There was no noise. We were so deep in the woods. There was nothing we couldn't talk about. It was protected. We felt that that space was almost sacred. It was telling us to open our eyes and ears to each other. Not judge. Be kind."

We went back in our memory to what that had felt like, looked like. Kyla pictured it, too. There is a real risk today that millions of people won't know how it feels to be in a protected space, if for no other reason than that as soon as they're in one, they willingly turn on the switch for the electronic presence in their hand. Afraid they may miss something. Even with the sound turned off, the incessant images and texts pull all attention away from the self. No wonder no one thinks, or reads, anymore.

Ideas and visions come to people in protected spaces. Here we are on the far side of a new millennium, and suddenly we're staring at years of geometrically expanding budget deficits, bound to cripple our material world, take away our vital programs, our old expectations and entitlements, but it is not these deficits that frighten me the most. What scares me more is the dream deficit. The more we let them colonize our imaginations, let their creeping commercial homogeneity occupy a greater and greater space in our brains, the more we run the risk of clogging our dream conduits, the imagination synapses in our brains. We multitask, we overwork, and, too tired to write or paint or create we settle and watch those screens which are increasingly more gorgeous, more unsettling, more suggestive of fear, power, wealth, sex.

We let them in and they come all the way in. We give them a corner of a room in our house and then they want to be in every room. We offer them our hand, as the saying goes, and they reach for our elbow. We fall asleep and dreams, our own dreams, can't come to us now, or shall we say, we can no longer go where our dreams are; we find the way blocked. There is a subjunctive world in there that we can no longer visit; our powers of reasoning, of logic, still function in a decadent way, but we fall short of the irrational leaps we need to take to keep visions coming.

Dream deficit. Spirit deficit. Ebbing power vision. Loneliness.

Cell phones are the chemotherapy that shrinks our imagination to a shriveled, vestigial foreign thing we—the we we *were*—can't live with inside us. Then the surgeon comes and finishes the job. You think I'm making this up? Ask an Iranian who wakes up guilty, shaking, in the night, because she's just dreamt an illegal dream in her own bed.

How did I get on to that?

Ah, I was talking about protected spaces.

Hold on to them if you can.

I tuned into Kyla, who was saying, "When we're together, Jermayne and I, what we mostly want is that space around us. We look into each other's eyes and we only see see each other. It's peaceful. Jermayne works so hard. And because he's Black, he's got to work so much harder than me just to get anywhere, to be anything. That's a given. Most of the time all he wants to do is lie right here"—she patted her chest—"and read. The books you assign us."

"Sounds like you *could* use a room at the inn." Sarah said. Deliberate wintry image, on that warm May afternoon, of that archetypal rejected couple someone once based a religion on—

"We could," Kyla said. "I guess I don't mind that other thing. I mean, I really don't care. We're used to people watching us pretty much all the time. For lots of reasons."

"Mostly 'cause you're both so beautiful," Sarah said.

"Thanks. I wish that was the reason."

I let some breath out. I'd been holding it, in a way, I guessed. I thanked Kyla for her willingness to go along. On this walk in the dark.

"Jermayne won't be a problem," Kyla said. "You heard him say whatever was okay with me—"

I must have smiled when she said that, and she must have picked up part of my thought. Her eyes flashed. She almost scolded, but she didn't have to.

Although, in my defense, my thought hadn't been totally inappropriate. In my experience, as a hall monitor, for example, adolescent boys willingly attach themselves to any young woman who will have them. I have seen them, the boys, walk down the halls in a state of perpetual, anxious physical conflictedness: whether they ought to stand up tall to push out their inadequate chest and survey the territory masterfully just prior to roaring, or crawl on their hands and knees, a ring through their nose, leashed along by the pheromone trail planted in the air, innocently, by the female who just walked by.

Too binary for you? Sorry. It's what I've seen.

"You think you can both get away for the night?" I asked. I needed to know that but, again, I had some hesitation about suggesting a ruse or excuse. I was all too in-loco-parentis.

"It won't be hard," Kyla said. "We'll both think of something."

She went back to her job as the thin, hollow-eyed dinner customers began to come in, exhausted from their climb up the single
flight of stairs. I'm exaggerating, of course.

We said good-bye. As Sarah and I went back down to the street
I held her hand—a part for the whole—and revelled in the sudden
synchronicity: an imminent spinning together of pure acts of love,
art, subversion, all as random as a roulette wheel.

Chapter Eleven

One benefit that comes to me from working with high-school
students is that for the most part they don't seem to hold a grudge,
or stick to a position after they've stated it, heard yours, and dis-
covered areas of mutuality. If you give them a chance, they will
often find a reason to go along with what they earlier objected to.

One of the students in that class said to me once, "you got a
good group here, Mr. B; none of us goes to bed angry." I hoped
that just maybe my class helped them get there: we were good
listeners, and part of its being a protected space was that it was
safe to air out even your negative feelings. Then they were mostly
out of you.

After Kyla let me know everything she thought was wrong—or
sick or crazy—with my plan, including its nearly-cubist lack of
reliable detail, she came on board with all her teen-age energy.
Displaying long-hidden leadership skills, next day—one of those
mysterious teacher-in-service half-days of school—she took Sarah
home to get dressed-up. The two women were about the same size.

What they would do, Kyla announced, was go, just the two
of them, to Washington. They would take the Senator's office by

storm, a sudden unpredicted squall of bright clothes, tempest of perfume, danger signals of skin. They'd get everyone's attention, would have the Chief of Staff or Speechwriter or Political Advisor, whoever he was, ready to do their bidding before they even explained their visit. Sarah, in fact, knew whom they would aim for, having spent a while that morning on the internet. She'd phoned ahead, I think, but I don't know what she said.

They took Kyla's car, some kind of recent VW like Sarah and I would never have let ourselves afford. Kyla at the wheel, both of them already laughing, laying out rules for a feminine language they would delight in all the way to Washington. Language I would have loved to overhear, but would not have understood. Sarah in the shotgun seat wearing an outfit like I'd never seen her in before and would never again, I feared.

I closed the street-side door and waved them off on their road movie. They looked like a mother-daughter street team, a sister act almost, but of the most impeccable quality. Had there been a goddess temple on the corner, I would have gone right in and confessed, begged forgiveness and asked for a whipping, for baiting our trap that way. But it was their idea. Can I use that as an excuse?

I just watched their car head up the street, content with their promise to tell me everything when they returned. They were grown-ups, I told myself: one of them anyway, and they could handle themselves. It was Sarah's idea from the Hotel Mercury, and now both of them were taking over my ill-conceived plan. And Sarah Capoeira would have the man on the Senate office floor in half a second if he tried anything. With her or with Kyla.

They walked into Senator Stern's rooms a couple of hours later. Third Floor, Dirksen Building. They liked it all: the metal detectors, the lingering glance of the guards, the walkie-talkies, the ringing slap of their low high heels on the marble, the echo, the heavy elevator. The states' names laid out in a high row down the hall like highway roadsigns that didn't match a known geography.

Bows, handshakes, smiles, with the receptionist. Who kept her job all these years—it was instantly, totally, clear to Sarah—by being a procurer for her Boss, not necessarily of consummated sexual favors—well, maybe those, too—but at least of visual opportunities he wouldn't want to miss, and would keep him happy and grateful to her. Doing her job, she buzzed his inner office and he came out huffing like he heard the special urgency in the buzz, came out and shamelessly looked them up and down. He made no attempt to hide what he knew about himself. Ate them both with his eyes. The teen-ager and the older one. Mature man, comfortable with who he was.

Sarah warmed to him immediately, she who hates subterfuge in any form and would rather see true nature undisguised. Matching, she assumed, the majority of his home state constituents, according to the latest Center for Disease Control statistics, Senator Stern carried an extra seventy pounds in the place where pregnant women grow in girth. Like a fat angelic new life bursting with future health insurance and urgent care possibilities. I had told her what Garth said about the Senator's sexual habits, and her mind filled with cartoon images of what the big man might try and fail to do in bed.

Kyla was explaining their mission. The Senator's arm was wrapped over both her shoulders, his right hand plopped, propped, on the collar bone near her right spaghetti-strap, all four fingers pointing down, and moving, too, toward where the flesh was softer.

"Oh you're gonna want to speak to Edward, sweetheart." He boomed. "We call him Edward Scissorshand 'cause he never met a budget he didn't want to cut. Ain't that right, Edward?" he called to a far corner of the room.

Edward was sitting out of sight behind a free-standing screen, no view into the main room, just a view out to the Mall.

"No, it ain't." he thought but did not say.

The Senator pushed on. "Edward thinks the only thing the gummint should fund is the Air Force and the Marines. He even wants to privatize the the navy. Ain't that what you think, Edward?"

"No, it's not what I think," Edward thought, but, still thinking, he admitted that he no longer knew what he thought. What he thought and what he wrote were two different things, and he was sitting there thinking that this disconnection—building up stress like an earthquake fault—would shake him irrevocably sometime in the very near future.

He was sitting, listening, thinking: I can say something witty here, or: I can go back to doing what I was doing, which, as I recall, was: trying to calculate the precise moment when I lost it, it being my integrity, or: I can make some ambiguous sound, like a grunt or a meaningless chuckle, which, interpreted as assent, might possibly kick the conversation toward a less painful direction.

It was just about then that he got up from his chair, came out from behind the screen, and saw Sarah and Kyla for the first time. Was taken by their unforecast landfall. Had not heard the advisory. Storms carry off what is not nailed down. Nothing was holding Edward down. He happened to be living through an intense phase when, to every stranger who walked into the office, he posed the silent question:

"Have you been sent to get me out of here?"

He recognized his rescuers immediately.

"You take care of these young ladies, Edward, you hear?" the Senator said. "Gotta get back to what I was doing, sad to say." He wheeled surprisingly quickly for a man carrying that weight. Sarah revised her earlier estimate of his capabilities. As he stepped back to his office he slapped the receptionist's desk appreciatively—couldn't reach across as far as her head—like you would pat a watchdog who'd done her job just right.

On the face of it, what the two women were asking Edward to

do was within possibility's realm. A Thursday night. Two weeks hence. A night of theatre, they call it. Why him? Because they have been studying current domestic politics, they know about his senator's leading the fight against the NEA. They don't know whether they agree or not, but want to invite him to some local theatre at which the issue may come up. Will come up, actually; a student has written a play Edward is going to enjoy. There's a neat coffee house down the street, stays open till all hours; he, and they, and some of the cast, could maybe go there later and talk. An education for all.

They wink, twinkle at him. Upgrading the category of storm advisory. How can he refuse? The teen-ager is delicious, he loves her choice of underwear and the colors, too—both items showing strategically—didn't think sixteen-year olds shopped from that catalogue. But what did he know? He was out of the current cultural loop, and the last few before this one, too. He got her age wrong, too.

Meanwhile, the older woman had a Garbo-like mystery he would like to solve. His ego was definitely stoked by their attention; he was aware of this, but he was willing to go along. His imagination raced. He listened to their words and caught their signals on multiple levels. Clothing. Scents. Hormones. Cellular-level messages.

Was there a subtext here, he wondered? Any threat to his safety? But they had mentioned the city, the school, the class, the teacher. All verifiable. Above suspicion, apparently.

The teen-ager—Kyla was her name, he'd got that—broke off and began wandering the office. For a moment he watched her stretching absently, meditatively stroking the marble window sill, taking in the view (She later told me she was deciding, at that moment, to become a Senator, and laying out the professional track that would take her there. College, modeling maybe, short film career, talk show hostess, visible leader of single socially-responsible hot-button issue, passionate decision to ride this current issue to national political power)—

Edward turned his attention back to the other woman.

Sarah, had she called herself? Older than him, he thought, a little, certainly not out of range—and found himself wishing he had worn a less ordinary suit, had let his hair grow, splashed some Bay Rum on his face that morning after shaving, had hit the rowing machine and the stair climber for the past six months; wishing he had checked his horoscope for today, which he absolutely never did, wishing he could just make himself concentrate on the words she was saying and not let his mind wander this way.

If you want to, you can go back now and read this short chapter again. Maybe you weren't paying full attention—you may have chosen instead to concentrate on your own doubt: wait: how does he know all this? What kind of writing teacher is he, disregarding rules we all learned in high school? Meaning how does a first-person narrator who wasn't even *there* know what a man he had never met was thinking?

Are you losing it, Mister B?

No. Obviously, I find out later. Stuff that you learn about later can find its way into the narrative wherever you want to put it. You're the writer.

But okay, how do I find out what I didn't know?

Maybe I'll wear latex gloves and ransack his apartment, find the notes to this first meeting.

Maybe I'll be bound to a heavy chair, and he will scream these things to me before roughing me up—in revenge.

Maybe we will go out fishing a long time later, and while drifting down a river, two men in a boat, he will answer every one of my questions in delicious detail.

Chapter Twelve

Sarah went back north for two weeks and I went back to teaching. Two weeks seemed like enough time for me to organize: my thoughts, the little troupe, and certain details of our production.

I met a couple of times with Cheeto, doing my delicate dance of helping him with his writing, providing suggestions and corrections, while trying not to think how I would express this thought, write this dialogue, if the work were mine.

"If it were mine," I say, but there was little chance of that. Reading, thinking, especially teaching, had taken up my time and energy for so many years; it was a long time since I had written much of anything for myself, more than a poem, a short article, a book review, or one of my letters—rants—to the editor.

I can look back now, either honestly or stretching the truth a little, and say that I put all my energy into getting other people to write, to write well. I remembered the thrill I used to feel when I wrote a novel more than twenty years before: although I was the one clearly striking the keyboard, there was a part of me standing just to the side and cheering like a soccer dad, getting excited about what I saw happening on the page.

I could replicate that feeling as a writing teacher. I cheered the students on with my yesses, my triple exclamation points, my obviously hurried underlinings in red, my dense comments on the last page. Or I'd purposefully be confrontational like a throwback coach, trying to annoy or bully a student into doing his best just to spite his lousy teacher who didn't get the point, didn't understand him. Or her. Or them. Thus, for me, teaching took the place of my own writing.

Sometimes I go back to my tattered copy of *Zen and the Art of Motorcycle Maintenance*. Open it almost anywhere and read a few pages. I love the part where the author, an electro-shocked shadow of his old self, is prowling the university hall where he used to teach, used to hold office hours. It comes back to him: the moment a woman poked her head out of her door and said, "are you still teaching Quality this year?" This question set him off on an obsessive self-examination that led to his madness, almost did him in. Years later he thinks about all this, and especially about Quality, while riding his big Honda across the country.

One afternoon during those two weeks I did my own version of the bike-zen Quality trip.

Here is what I do. When I need to organize my thoughts, or find a new one, I ride my ten-speed on the old canal towpath. My cycle has no motor, no roar, exhaust pipe scald, highway wind howl in my ears. I just ride. Parts of the old canal are left, and there's a wide gravel path that snakes through ten miles of green space. There's a few intersections with traffic, and you have to watch out for walkers and runners and bladers and baby movers and dogs, but if I don't get too lost in thought, I can avoid collisions and stay out of the murky water right down the bank.

I find ideas on that ride. Some have been around for generations; other people had them once, started them, lost them. They hang around like bats, upside down in the trees. Don't go looking for them; you can't see them. They let go and enter your head when you pass beneath. They did that to Walt Whitman ("Song of the Open Road") and they do that to me.

Here are the thoughts that came to me that afternoon.

I recollected my college years, when I had an urge to major in history. I learned to despise most of the history we studied.

"Kings and Wars," I complained to the professors; "can't we talk about something else?"

But there was nothing else to talk about. Only the story told by the victorious, the people who had the money and the power to commission the books to record the dates and facts about the times they stood above. They'd killed off the opposition. And anyway nothing was written by or about the foot soldiers who died of gangrene in the trench; they never interviewed the guy who milled the buckwheat that fed the infantry, or the woman who waited back at the homestead, sewing the quilt.

Hold on a moment: "sewing the quilt!"

I have an old log cabin quilt on my bed. Well, my mattress on the floor. I love how the afternoon winter light brings out the colors in it. I call the woman who made it "Anne." She sewed her story into the quilt. Log cabin: a homely, sincere style, one-by-six inch strips of colored cloth shiny with age. Strips like little logs, they make you think of hearth, heart, home. Like her cabin.

Not a hard pattern for an untutored woman like Anne to master. And she had no help. The nearest neighbor so far away! You see that fading piece of blue linen? That's the good part of the work shirt he left behind. He: her son. The year was what, 1842? The war-crazy Andrew Jackson was the U.S. president. He and his cabinet ministers wanted a piece of Mexico to add to the map.

Anne's son Eben caught the war fever, was mustered out to Texas, fourteen hundred miles away. She knew when he came back his muscles would be so much bigger. He was still a growing boy. So it was not the fear that he would die that made her cut up what was still good cloth from his shirt—his father had worn the same shirt, so that memory was there as well. But she sewed all that memory and prayer into the quilt, in time she could spare from her hard work alone on the farm.

She did not finish the quilt while he was away, but that rosey bit of calico alongside the blue wherever it appears on the outer squares is from the apron she was wearing the day Eben limped home, scared to die in a distant territory, wounded inside and out from the war, with only months left to live. It's all there in the quilt. You can read the emotions in her stitching, a little erratic as she neared the finish. He was buried near his father just a few steps away from her porch.

I own the quilt now. Found it on some antique store shelf. It comforts me. It is both art and memory, a history lesson not taught in the Kings and Wars classes I attended. You have to go up there to the bedroom in the afternoon light, read a few pages of some book, then put the printed words down and read the room. You stop and breathe and take the time to notice. It's getting harder in this historic haze, when the mental environment is so deliberately, so cynically, polluted. Who has the time to pay this kind of attention? But if you do pay attention, the story will come to you.

I am happy to pay a part of the money I make teaching, to buy creative time for artists, artisans, craftspeople. Sometimes they need time to work, just work with no obvious objective. They can't only work for pay or profit.

They have to be encouraged, allowed even, to have moments of such surprising emotion that what they make at that moment with their hands, their minds, their voices, carries a piece of immortality. Unless they've had the privilege of studying at some graduate program and taking on heavy student debt, they maybe have their craft from an old practitioner who is losing her touch a little—none of her knowledge is gone, but the energy downshifts; the eyes lose a bit of clarity, the hand its steady touch. So much to teach, so little time, and here is someone eager to learn! That pattern woven in the wool, that chisel cut, that braided dough: the very art of it must be preserved because if not, ten thousand ghosts will lose their voices all at once!

This art, this craft, this quilt, is a protected space where the dead still speak. This artist, this crafter, slows us down enough to notice.

And if what I am talking of here is an art that nourishes? Three French folk in their seventies in navy blue aprons, wooden shoes, berets: they make an artisan cheese so full of taste it opens all your saliva spigots and rattles your brain; it is a life-filled, nearly phosphorescent, gathering-together of history, tradition, rural life, family, love, milk, spring and summer blossoms and grasses, unique limestone bedrock, invisible microbes in a cavern's air, the breeze off the wings of a butterfly that we never ever see—human traits like patience, care, acceptance, even the buzz words organic, sustainable, terroir—

What if the local government has tried to protect these people and the food and drink they make? What if there is consent among the neighbors, the taxpayers who cooperate toward that end, that that is the right thing to do?

And then the hijacked jumbo jet called globalization plows into the pasture, the old stone barnyard, leaving a pile of rubble in the cave where the fragile work took place. The organizations that make the world safe for free trade, for the unrestricted flow of cheap cheese substitutes—that crash in the field is the new law, the one that nullifies all local agreements.

No, not even your democracy can stop this hijacking. You and I are passengers. We think we're going someplace safely and then we look up from our trance, our doze: who are those men up front there, the ones with the expensive suits in first class? They're going to crash us into that French farmer's field. The local government is trying to protect them but it can't.

Next they'll take aim at that family-owned Chilean vineyard, the one that grows the rare heirloom variety of grape. Or that corn farmer who's no longer allowed to save some of their harvest to replant. Seems they didn't read the fine print on the seed packet, and now the company who patented that seed is suing them, will end up taking their farm. Seven generations gone in a legal twist. Or that organic farmer who finds her fields invaded by GMO corporate pollen. Or that Italian grocery chain that won't sell DNA-tampered grain. We'll crash into them all, burn them, and all the proud people working for them, their window on the world, we'll watch it all collapse. Is this an act of terror? I think it is.

And when something truly uncontrollable happens—some natural disaster no one was ready for—they'll see how they can use that destruction to hurry this other disaster along.

To me it all fits together. I'm pedaling a bicycle by a canal, but I see clearly a long distance. Protecting and preserving what's been given to us, preventing one family's folk wisdom from becoming somebody else's intellectual property—there is no profit in telling this story. Not for me. Not for anyone. Not in the global marketplace.

But let's take some of the money that we all earn, collect it, share it, grant it, to feed and shelter the people telling this story, just so that it can be recorded. It's such a small amount. Pay the artists for their day's work.

That's the only meaningful mission for the NEA.

But why did I think all of that, all of it, just because of an old canal tow path, a twenty-year old road bike, some paragraphs in a newspaper a few weeks ago?

Part. Whole.

Thus in thought, I reached the end of the greenway, and turned my bike around.

Chapter Thirteen

I brought my bike up to the porch and locked it to its corner post. Went inside, started up the stairs, felt my phone vibrate.

"Mr. B. I'm in your neighborhood," Cheeto said; "you want to meet me?"

I heard something in his voice. What he meant to convey was "I think you need to meet me."

"Sure," I said. I'd only been inside for a moment, but when spring starts doing her color and fragrance thing in earnest, I don't want to miss any of it. I mentioned a pocket park a block away, and said I'd be right there.

We met and sat on a bench near where some children were climbing on a made-for-kids outdoor sculpture. I had brought a couple of sodas and a bag of cheesy popcorn.

"I've been kind of waiting for you to get in touch with me," Cheeto said.

I thought we had been in touch. I had followed the progress of his work, from the class discussion, lots of notes, into a dramatic scene, after some prompts from me about the sequester, the motives—into a one-act, maybe two. Along the way what he was writing had evolved into something worthy to be acted in room 22 of the Hotel Mercury.

Feigning spontaneity, faking innocence, I'd floated the idea of premiering it in that intimate venue. A few days before, reading the second draft during class, I said quietly, concealing my manipulation in the transparent trappings of a joke, "the producer's a friend of mine. He asked me to ask you if you could put a hole in the wall in it."

I saw Garth catch that from across the room. He looked up, seemed to catch my eye behind his shades, shook his head slightly, then looked down again.

"A hole in the wall?" Cheeto asked.

"Yeah. A little one." I held out my hand palm down to show him how high it had to be. "The guy's gotta look through it."

"Look through it?"

"Yeah."

"The captured guy?"

"Right."

"You want to tell me what the dude sees?

"I'm not there yet. Okay?"

"Okay. Good idea, Mr. B. You got it. We'll put a hole in." He looked down to his script to see where he could introduce the idea. He looked up to see if I had more to say. I made a flip, though not unfriendly, dismissive gesture with my two hands turned up. Nothing to add. That had been a few days ago.

Now I sat waiting to see why he had called.

"I kind of need to know where you want to go with this. I heard about Kyla's trip, and the Senate guy. So, like, I get the feeling I'm involved in something more than a play. But I don't know what it is. I'd like to help you out, but at the moment I can't."

"Why not?"

"Well, I don't know what you're doing. And, from what Kyla tells me, you don't know either. 'Scuse me for saying."

"I know perfectly well. We're gonna do a staged reading. Or: an improvisation. Your script's gonna be the prompt. Sort of."

He turned and studied me through those thick glasses. At about that time, I lost count of how many people had flashed me that humoring expression in the past two weeks. Were I at all sensitive to condescension, it could have had an impact. Although in all honesty, Cheeto's look included a lot more than just condescension.

"—and you were planning to tell me...?" he asked.

"Tomorrow." I said. "Definitely tomorrow."

I don't normally think of myself as a procrastinator, so my delaying called for some self-examination. I decided that I could now describe myself (to myself) as a man who was willing, even eager, to postpone certain painful things, like the recognition that his plan had serious logical problems. I was in denial. It surprised me that it was a place I recognized.

Cheeto kept staring at me, trying to decide what expression to put on his face.

"Have you met my grandma?" he asked me after a while.

My first thought was "*non sequitur*," but then I realized that there were not going to be any of those in this conversation.

"I don't think so."

"She lives with us. One of my cousins brought her up here. I don't even know how they got here. She still makes tortillas by hand. She goes out for walks by herself, just around the block; I never know if she's gonna make it back. Doesn't speak a word of English. She always comes back with her apron full of leaves, and grass, and flowers. Bird feathers. Little stones. She's a *curandera*. That means a curer, or a good witch. A wise woman."

I waited, but that was as far as Cheeto took that thought.

"So what does she think?" I asked.

"She thinks you should tell me today."

So I did. Showed him the article, too. Which I had in my pocket. The whole story resonated with him. How could it not? He studied it long enough for several close reads.

Now he could finish his play. Now he could smile, which he did. In my direction.

"What?' I said.

"I think I just figured something out, Mr. B."

"Okay—"

"You know how you're always telling us to watch how we communicate?"

"Right..."

"...and to watch out for communication problems we have, you know, like too many 'ums' in a sentence, or speaking too quiet, or too loud, or not making eye contact?

"Yeah," I said. I decided not to help him go where he was going.

"And you keep that list, right? Of all those disorders, like you call them?"

"Yeah. It's a long list. So, I guess you have another one for me? Wait, don't tell me. It's something I do?"

"I mean, I think, you can tell me if I'm wrong, but I think you never want to tell everything. You think you told us enough, you think we have what we need to keep working, but you leave a lot of really important stuff unsaid."

"I do that?"

"Yeah. All the time."

"And I do it because...?

"I don't know," he said. "Maybe it's like you're a card player? And you don't want to show your hand, even if we're like, on the same team. I think, pardon me, you have to work on your trust."

Cheeto looked so boyish just then, with his pudgy unlined face, his hair greased back and up in a kind of flat-top, his baggy soccer shirt. He had made his way to my part of town and called me because he wanted to lead me out of my wilderness place.

Most religions that I know of have a favorite god or goddess who removes obstacles and difficulties from your path. Takes you out of the thicket and deposits you on the path you need. Dusts you off and points out the way. The right way. Sometimes they carry a broom. This spirit is never the most beautiful one, or the most graceful, or simple, or pleasant. In Afro-Cuban santería he's called Elegguua.

In other cultures it can be a kid with a special mark on him, like Ganesh in India, who wound up with an elephant's trunk for a nose. Makes him have an attitude problem.

Usually, they have to be asked, and propitiated, even flattered, if you know you need their help. But to really desperate cases they show up on their own.

So, I almost never give enough information to the people who want to help? Is this what Cheeto was saying? As if, if I withhold some material, hoard it even, I don't have to come to terms with the fact that all I have is really very little.

It's like that moment in *Apollo 13* when the spacemen lay out absolutely everything extra on board the capsule, to show the folks at Mission Control the raw material they have that could maybe save their lives.

I never did that. I never told Cheeto, "there, you have it all."

Instead I said, "here's what I think you will need to help me" and it wasn't enough. Was never going to be enough. Actually, my holding back had hobbled him. He had recognized that before I did. All I had really done was to increase the possibility of failure. For everyone.

Now I needed to accept without reservation Cheeto's outstretched hand, to be led as I would be by a saint, a teacher, a child, a young man with thick glasses, a guide to another world.

Chapter Fourteen

We climbed the stairs. Sarah dropped her duffel just inside the entranceway. She walked slowly down the hall to the kitchen. There was a strong physical energy—more than usual, I felt—between us, moving, as we were, upstairs toward bed, but later, through sleep, toward the next day's action.

Without actually discussing it, we were delaying gratification. The conversation we had begun down in the car, we carried inside as we walked. I had described our rehearsals so far, and had just revealed one aspect of my nervousness: something to do with pretending. With playing a different role from the ones I customarily play: teacher, director, adult—

We sat down at the kitchen table and turned toward each other.

"Pretending's not hard," Sarah said. "I got into it when I was underground. It's not like I had ever done anything horrible. I was just—a fugitive. From justice. Actually, to justice." She smiled at her own word play. "Yeah, to justice. I figured, someone's going to catch me eventually. There's always some Javert out there who's never going to give up. I can't explain why, but I knew there was another story to what had happened to our study group. I knew I was never going to jail. That there would be justice in the end."

"Like there always is." I said.

"No. But I knew there would be in my case. Still, something told me I just shouldn't go up to some cop on the beat and turn myself in. I had to wait till they found me. I should like, let the planets line up till the right time."

"When's the right time?"

"Get everything in place for my acquittal. New president. People watching new TV programs. They'd had those Senate Committees investigating the CIA. 'We're shocked—shocked—to find that covert action has been going on in this country, against our own people!'

"I knew if they found me too soon, the country wouldn't be ready. So I decided it would take a while, and while it took that while, I would have a good time, as much as I could, and be out and about. How'd we get on this subject?"

I had been to the refrigerator and back, serving us two Coronas. I retraced the conversational steps as well.

"Pretending," I remembered.

"Right. Pretending. It's not hard. I had a good time doing it. Most of the time."

She took her first swallow. "Thank you. Here's looking at you. Actually, I did it really well. I'm not, basically, a thrill seeker, but you have to admit that we live for those moments when we feel really alive, you know? When you look back, what you most remember are those times when you felt really alive. What did Virginia Woolff call it? Leaving the ground?"

I thought about that. And about certain moonlit nights on the farm. Dancing, rolling sauna-naked in clean snow, or breathing in the whole county from the top of the orchard hill. Or, more recently, English classes where my hands are waving and I'm leaping, no, vaulting, from idea to idea, and everything is making perfect sense and the whole class gets it, and seems to enjoy it. Even, sometimes, when I'm out riding my bike and everything seems to make sense.

"Is tomorrow going to be like that?" I asked.

We were both sitting now at the kitchen table: old habit from farm days: it's as if there is no other room in the house. Sharing a beer, enjoying the closeness, the privacy, the cliff we were about to go over.

"It could be," she said; "if you're open to enjoying it. You have to enjoy the pretending. Can you do that?"

I shrugged. I hadn't gotten there yet. Hadn't even considered it.

"It would help if you could."

"Tell me how."

"I would look into someone's eyes, we'd be talking, maybe some part of my body would be touching some part of theirs, and I would be thinking, I am going to make this fun! How can you not know who I really am? If you only knew! Isn't it obvious? And everything I was thinking and feeling would be right there in my eyes, my eyes would be glittering; I would almost giggle!"

I believed her. You know the joke, people use it about politicians especially: "I looked into his eyes and there was no 'there' there."

When you looked into Sarah's eyes, you saw so many receding, or approaching, layers of 'there.' Her eyes were a live demonstration of the ontological argument for the existence of God. How it works, anyway. As soon as I saw one layer of Sarah in them, I could instantly imagine, or think I saw, another layer farther back. As soon as I tried to focus on that one, there was yet another, deeper in. We both had fun—not speaking, of course—while the process went on.

She brought me back. "What's that quote you're always using, from Borges? 'Imminence of a revelation?'"

"The one that never occurs," I said.

"Right. The tease. That's the aesthetic phenomenon." Sarah said. "He's so right. That's how I would feel, every time I almost revealed myself. I would think, fuck it, why don't I just take us over the edge here, and then I wouldn't, and it would feel even better. Pretending. It became my art form. My aesthetic phenomenon. I got to be so hooked on it, I started acting in plays."

Sarah was a gifted actress. She had a terrific instinct for the complicated tragic heroines. I'll never forget her as Elizabeth Proctor in the "Crucible," coming right downstage at the end of the play, pretending to watch John on the gallows, hearing the drumroll, and one tear descending from the corner of her left eye; I can still see the fake sunrise catch the wet gleam in the eye and in the slowly-falling tear. Reverend Hale is screaming "Woman, plead with him!"

Her jaw is set so tight; her face is in full view of the entire audience, very little make-up, and she is all those layers at that one moment, Sarah the political criminal with her real birth name almost no one knew, Sarah the underground fugitive, Elizabeth Proctor the character, Sarah remembering the director's blocking, the precise acting techniques going on at that instance, the timing of the cue from the lighting booth; Sarah thinking, I dare you all to recognize me, Sarah enjoying herself immensely—and now I had a better appreciation for the "pretending" of which she spoke: so many things happening all at once that you would need extra adrenalin just to stay organized.

Thinking of the levels on which we intended to operate tomorrow, I hoped I would be up to the task. But more than that I hoped, now that she had explained it to me, that I would be able to enjoy it.

I have my differences with Jorge Luis Borges, the great Argentine writer. I teach a few of his short pieces in my classes, knowing my students will always be fascinated by the onion-like layers of meaning he can pack into a four-page story. But also I think that he was too precious, so self-involved in his labyrinthian word manipulations that he failed to look up and notice that fascism had taken over his beloved country. Then again, he was going blind. And then again, maybe he didn't care.

But I am a collector of quotes that tell me what art is, and his is one of the best. That slipping away and reappearing revelation that wants to play with you, and you allow it, wanting to extend this moment of almost-divination, because you've left the ground and don't want to come down, because a specific, powerful, bundled neuron junction in your brain is being diddled to near-ecstasy with the feeling that you are about to understand Absolutely Everything there is or ever was—

Borges wrote his passage from the point of view of the reader, the audience, the museum-goer contemplating a great painting. But before it passes to the public, the "aesthetic phenomenon" really gives pleasure to the artist. There's that delicious private moment when an image or an action bubbles up from somewhere in that parallel universe where it has been stuck, just shy of forever, until this aperture suddenly appears, and it leaps through it into the artist's consciousness, who seizes the image, holds it for as long as she, he, they, can, and then translates it with a wow, but it never ever holds quite as much pleasure—once it is out there—as it did when it was held *within* for that extended instant, vibrating with potential, that imminence of a revelation which never perfectly occurs.

Any non-artist person can relate to this, of course: you have a vivid dream, and the best moment of it is the instant you wake up and sleep has not quite vanished yet; of course you hunger to return to the beauty you just inhabited one second ago, and of course you can't. Faced with that impossibility, you next try to hold yourself for as long as you can in the threshold place. But when you try to describe this place and what you have seen there, to someone else, it's never as wonderful—

"An actor," said Sarah, "or any live performer, gets to be right near that moment over and over again. There's nothing like it. It's harder for a painter or a writer to sustain. The paint dries. Picture gets framed. The book gets published. Sits on a shelf, words unchanging on the page. You find me a writer who says they wouldn't rather be a rock star, I'd say they're lying through their teeth."

We went up to the third floor. We slowed everything down. Undressing. Individual night-time rituals in the bathroom. Me shaving to soften the expected touch of my face upon her. Her showering. Sound of the shower turning off and on frequently. Sarah was obsessed with water conservation.

Lying side by side. Reading for a moment. Drowsiness intruding. Touching of toes—

It was the last time we would ever do this, though I didn't know it at the time. Maybe I did. Was I deliberately parceling out the moments, savoring the phenomenon in fact, *delaying* the revelation, wishing it would not occur? Or is it just how I like to recall it now from a distance? Maybe, when you go back often to remember all the physical steps of a night you want to hold on to, by the tenth time you go back you put thoughts into the mind of the remembered you, thoughts you never had—another meaning of 20-20 hindsight.

No, I did not think, get ready to print every delicious moment of this, because we won't make love again. I did not know that, though I can pretend I did. We were not *in* love anyway; we both agreed on that. For us, "making" love was an infrequent creation of something that did not quite exist.

They say the Hindu love god, Kama, has no body at all. He lost it somewhere. He lives entirely in the spirit world, invisible, but he misses flesh intensely. His only chance for existing in the physical world is when he inhabits for a few heartbeats the commingled body of two lovers.

I like that story.

Here is how I recall it. Sarah likes to be superior, a nice way to show active gratitude for our friendship. Afterward she will let herself down and cover me, my arms around her back; I'm falling half asleep and willing to take all of her weight. But now right at the top we hold the gaze, and I find myself thinking, here I am, a teacher—as I like to boast—of great love, love that will pay any price to go on being, to be made into flesh. And I am here, doing love's devotion, with someone, I will swear to anyone who might ask, who is only a friend. Just a friend.

Maybe we're both too willing to let it go. I think we agree that this could happen any time. But, I also think, lovemaking is an outlet for our deepest need to communicate. An intentional sharing of all possible information, a chance to hold back nothing!

I can't tell her I love her.

I look into her eyes, and her eyes flash wider for a moment, as if she hears my thoughts. Proof, as I recall her look, that I was thinking those thoughts. And I think, you do this, again and again, because it is a moment of the purest teaching, of revelation offered; you are on the verge of learning the unlearnable—and then the unlearnable is gone.

But I was speaking of last times.

Do you recognize a last time while you are in it? Like the last time you speak to your father. The last time you sit in a classroom as a student, the last time you have a normal day before you learn you have cancer, the last time you held her in that way and now you won't; you can't, ever again.

When it's years too late, you want to be a messenger, wingéd Mercury on a dime. You want to run back into that bedroom, breaking down the door—which anyway was not closed—knocking over, instead, time's barricade, and you want to holler into his ears, into hers, too, both of them, this is the last time! Be there, as never before; don't miss anything, grasp every word, every touch, wake up—

Thinking like this, retooling my memories as if I could: it's palliative for me. I am solely responsible for what happened after. If this was the worm, loss, concealed inside the bud of every victory, I have to accept it. That's Shakespeare for you.

I was saying that making love kept us in practice. It was good for us. "Fountain of youth," Sarah would sometimes sigh, just before sleeping. I would call it an act of the deepest friendship, sustained for years until that very night.

What I miss most: she would, as I said, smile down at me and I would step so surely and so deeply into that opening her eyes gave me, that I would think I was at the edge of an infinite space.

Chapter Fifteen

I am up, and showered and dressed and fed, at least an hour earlier the next morning. Yes, I'm nervous. And it doesn't help that Sarah shows no nervousness at all. She shows me nothing. She pretends to sleep while I get more and more noisy downstairs, hoping she'll decide to join me.

When it's time to leave, I go back up to the bedroom.

She's reading a book by the new morning sunlight. I don't even look at the title. I guess she's reading just to prove to me that she can, and she will, with nothing pressing to do till late afternoon.

"So," I say.

"So."

"Do you need the car?"

"No. I'll just be around here, if that's okay. Take a walk, or a run. Rest. Make myself beautiful."

"You already are."

"Thanks. That was a really nice night."

"It was."

We hold a look for a little while. I want to stretch out next to her and put my head on her, some part of her, for a moment, but that's the kind of tenderness we never do. Although, it wouldn't be a tender act; it would be a request for reassurance, some inoculation against the doubt I know will creep into my day. You know, you wake up excited and confident and then something happens a few hours later—a remark, a glance, a bit of news—and your confidence evaporates quicker than you thought it would.

"I think I'll drive to school. Might have to run an errand. I'll pick you up at 4 or so."

"Okay," she says. "Have a relaxing and productive day."

"Thanks."

I leave the house only wanting to stay behind with Sarah. Make brunch. Make love. Make a whole Sunday of it.

But it's Thursday.

I can't remember much about the morning. The first clear scene that comes to mind has me leaning in that spot and in that way against the front of my teacher's desk. I look out at the afternoon faces, nothing has changed; it's as if I am still in the class on that first day of Julio Parra. No one has moved.

Anticipation takes away the risk of another languid spring afternoon class. I try to act relaxed, but it's hard. Takes acting. Hey, I should practice. I'll need some of those chops later. In the excitement of the run-up, I haven't given much thought to my performance, to some of the givens I actually do need to think about. What should I wear; who's the character I'm playing—I don't want to just go out there, in there, and play myself. Who is this tough guy amateur sequesterer? Is that a word?

But I can't think about all that right now. I've got time after school, back home. Students are waiting; I have a class to teach.

"Someone ask the first question," I say. We need to do something with our class time. Nobody wants to work.

Kyla looks up from her school desk bed. "Mr. B, would you take us through it, please?"

"Sure," I say. "Thanks for asking. Cheeto, come on up and stand here, with me, so you can answer questions, too."

He comes to stand beside me.

"All right," I say. "Show starts at 7:00. You all know where the Mercury is, right?"

Various nods and thumbs up.

"You can join us for dinner first if you want." I name the restaurant. "I've got money if you can't afford it. You'll have to eat cheap, though."

"Okay."

"And it's night-time, so, get a ride if you can. Bring a parent if you can. If you have to pay for transportation, bring me the receipt, okay; I'll reimburse you."

The truth is I'm a teacher. We do okay with salary. I am so obsessively frugal that I actually have money. I even donate a small percentage right back to my English classes, for petty cash, for favors. Everyone knows I keep a stash right in my classroom, and probably most of them know where it is. You just have to trust.

"Cheeto, what have you got?" I ask.

"Okay," Cheeto says. "First, thanks a lot for all your ideas, and for helping me with rewrites and stuff. That's part of it. The other part is that the play is nowhere near done. There's big empty spaces that are like still empty, right?"

"I guess so," I say, and that brings on the evaporating confidence moment I just told you about. I actually feel my stomach drop. I think of the first ten things that could go wrong. I think—

"But we won't worry about that," Cheeto says, "because you'll all be right there and you can like holler ideas to us. We want you to, right?"

"Right," I say. "But, you know, keep your ideas appropriate, and stay connected to the story, okay?"

"Okay."

I look around. "You all coming?"

Jermayne says, "Yeah, no, I can't come. I have to work."

"You knew about this a long time ago."

"I know. I'm sorry, man. One of the cashiers is sick I think. They need me."

Kyla looks genuinely disappointed. "I guess I'll come alone," she says, but without much gusto. That's when I realize that she's doing a pre-emptive deception, one of those magician's misdirections I talked about way back when. There will be just enough expectation of her not being there, that no one will suspect how *there* she will actually be. She and her lover.

Garth looks at me with that bemused expression he hardly ever seems to lose these days. He knows so much more than anyone else in the room, including four or five things that could cause me to plunge deeply out of the generally decent esteem I'm held in here, if he were into revealing stuff he's supposed to keep close...

"Hey Mr. B," Ravinia asks, "can I bring my dad? I think he'd like it."

Ravinia! Have I mentioned them before? I know, I haven't. Like I said, everyone in the class has a story. If you looked through the opening that Ravinia provides, it's a whole other story, captivating in its own way. Raised by a single dad. Dad has some money. Definitely BIPOC. Definitely gender-fluid, definitely into clothes. Strange rent-the-runway clothes. Named after a summer music festival in Highland Park, Illinois. Ravinia—

I catch my wandering mind. "Of course," I say, "but, and this is for everyone: there's only gonna be, what, about twenty seats? Twenty-five? And no standing room, because there is no standing room, so give some good thought to who you think might enjoy the evening. Your dad's more than welcome."

"Okay."

"And remember, this isn't a class assignment. Come if you can, if you want to. But I know a lot of you have things to do after school. I'm not twisting any arms. And it won't affect your grade."

Cheeto says, "Hey, can I bring my girlfriend?"

Becca says, from the seat right next to him, "Cheeto, *I'm* your girlfriend. I'm going. All right?"

"Okay."

"You like, got another girlfriend I don't know about?"

"No!"

I just lean back and enjoy the general banter. Kyla and Jermayne are sitting up now, in two chairs that they're actually using as chairs. They're play fighting a little for the benefit of the others. Misdirections have become a dime a dozen in AP English.

I tell all of them, no, you don't need a paper ticket, we'll give you one in the lobby. Hold on to it, cause it's important, and, no, you don't have to pay. There'll be a donation jar but you can walk right by. God has no mercy on teachers who demand money from their students for anything.

"One other thing. This is a cold reading, and some of what we'll do tonight will definitely be improv. You know how that works."

"We know, Mr. B," Kyla says. "And we also know that you don't like improv."

"Did I say that?"

"Yeah, you told us it's never good writing."

"Sheesh, do you hold me to everything I might have said at one time or another in this class?"

"We do."

"Got it. Well, we'll see how that pans out tonight. But my warning is, with improv you never know. The action could turn. It could get, I mean it could *seem* to get, ugly. So if you're in a delicate phase, or if you think the person you're thinking about bringing might, you know, get triggered or something, leave them home, let someone else have that seat. Okay?"

That doesn't have the effect I wanted, I can tell. Space may be a problem.

"And one *more* thing, the play will start promptly at 7:00. No one is allowed in after the start time. So if you think you're gonna be late, stay away. The door will close. That's it."

"Are we going to lock the door?" Garth asks. Sensible question. Yet another detail we hadn't discussed.

"Well, the fire department probably wouldn't like that," I say. "I guess we won't. We'll pretend to. But, you know, going in or out during the play, that's a no."

I let that thought hang in the air. The closeness: we all have reasons to feel discomfort with that lack of social distance. Also, we'll have a stage with actors on it, so near that you could reach out and touch.

And, it's not like no one knows what the play is about. We all do.

We've shared ideas and thoughts with Cheeto. We workshopped some speeches. Gave feedback, Liz Lerman style: "What did you hear? What did you like about what you heard?"

They know I'm going to play some kind of alpha-dog teacher. The kind I'm definitely not. They know the role that Garth is going to play. That's not hard. Same role he plays every day. We've talked on more than one occasion about disappearances, on other occasions about what it feels like to be an artist speaking truth to power, a general theme in that room, starting with the dead people looking down at us from the walls.

Today I let the class kind of roll on with no direction from me.

"Last thing," as they file out. "Sarah and I'll be at Sal's for dinner. If you want to bring your dad, your grandma, your date, make it a meal and a show. If you need a few bucks to help with that, we're good for it."

"Wow, thanks."

"Maybe see you there."

Chapter Sixteen

Another warm spring night. We were downtown.

Sarah and I had gone for an easy bike ride after school. (I keep an extra two wheels around.) I spent some time alone with my script. I gave Garth some dinner money; he went off by himself to a sandwich place around the corner. I thought he looked so scary he might frighten Edward—was that his name?—away.

Jermayne and Kyla sat on a bench outside the restaurant. Jermayne looked especially handsome in a blue blazer and khakis and tennis high-tops. They were leaning in quietly to each other, working on an English assignment, I knew—a normal one. Jermayne kept pulling a well-thumbed folded paper from his inside pocket, taking a quick look, putting it back.

Shakespeare! Learning lines.

Edward arrived on foot. Had put his car in a garage: expense account, an official trip. First he drove around the block once and saw us standing in front of the restaurant. Looking amateur, outside-the-Beltway, harmless, as he supposed. We didn't see him. He parked two blocks away and came on foot.

Sarah saw him approach first. I was talking to her and saw her eyes look away. I followed her gaze up the street. He had dark curly hair in a studied disarray that I thought he must have stopped to arrange in a storefront reflection. He wore a yellow oxford under a dark gray sports jacket; clearly, he had left his necktie in the car. He was twelve hours from his most recent shave and this gave a Nixonian shadow to his face, but that made me feel instant sympathy for him. Nixon always thought, if only someone had given me a shave and a little pancake make-up before that first debate with Kennedy, it could have changed the course of history.

There are some people whom you see for the first time, and

you find yourself liking them in spite of yourself. I felt that way about him as he came closer and more into focus, and he helped that impression grow in me by radiating a disarming awkwardness, displaying to my eye anyway every objection he'd had to overcome in order to just show up.

He noticed the women, moved toward them. I introduced myself, and Jermayne, to him. I saw him hesitate for an instant. Saw him feel like a fifth wheel. Two pairs, one student couple, one of the parent generation, approximately.

Where did he fit in? Sarah saw this too and before another second went by she signalled him with her body that, at least as far as she was concerned, the structure of this five-part grouping was fluid. Either it was an actor's practiced instinct to save a scene that was about to break apart, or some entirely different, though natural, motivation which I admit I was surprised to notice.

Not to dwell on that, I thanked him for coming and said "Let's go eat; my treat." He said no, he had his expense budget; I said let's save the taxpayers a few dollars. He was all for that.

The same place where Sarah and I ate before. Not the vegan one. We were about to move us all into unmapped territory, so I wanted familiarity all around me now. I waved to a group of students and parents already eating and loudly talking around two tables bunched together. Their special evening had already begun. The hostess knew me, as did the waiter. All calculated to make Edward relax and feel unthreatened.

We sat. I turned away from Edward and talked with Jermayne about his plans for next year. His family had very little money, but he did beautifully in school. With my help, and that of a few other teachers, he hoped to get a nearly-total scholarship to the state university. It was only in the past year that he had softened all his edges, gone to dreadlocks, fell in love with Kyla, let go of the fear that his only avenue to higher learning would be through sports or four years of the army first, then college if he weren't blown to bits in some war we didn't yet know about.

I had gone to his house—Jermayne's brother invited me; have I told you about him? Bill? I never had him in class, but you couldn't miss the big guy in school. He was smart, and strong: lineman in football, heavyweight in wrestling. Later, he was a self-taught, self-appointed social worker out on the streets. Bill wanted college for his younger brother.

I talked to his mother, overcome her suspicion, told her we could get the young man to college without forcing him to be a soldier first. How many hundreds of thousands of young Black men had joined the army for purely economic reasons? A class thing: watching their white peers move easily on to higher ed. With no military draft in sight it was ridiculous to think that the men in power would willingly change any part of the economic equation that brought them all these fine young multi-colored men and women every year to fill their uniforms. Of course that could change if the anti-immigrant fervor got uglier...

In this case I could at least work to deny them one bit of cannon fodder. I looked at Jermayne, saw scholar, poet, teacher, youth leader. I didn't see soldier. He was as different from Garth as he could be.

We all ordered; we ate, exchanged pleasantries. It was on purpose that I conversed with Jermayne, and he with me. We were casually letting Kyla and Sarah do table talk with the man in the blue jacket—no, now he had taken it off. Desperate attempt to look casual, I supposed. I looked at him, Senator Stern's go-to-guy, from the corner of my eye. There is a shadow of a decent man in there, I thought, and I remembered my mother's counsel. I could like him.

We all have a sixth sense, although what it consists of varies from person to person. Some people see auras, some get glimpses of the future or the past. Part of mine is: occasionally when I look into someone's eyes, I can see, almost hear, their cry for help: "get me out of here!" I would be at a loss to describe the anatomical coordinate that gives me this information. I can see it clearly, though. Saw it that night in the restaurant. The streets are full of prisoners, out walking.

Speaking of prisoners, I began to tune in to what Sarah was talking about. She and Kyla had decided not to go easy on the man. They saw themselves as softeners. If he was going to be the bull in the arena, they would be the picadors drawing small but bothersome bits of blood.

"How many people are locked up in prison in the United States?" Sarah was asking. "More than any other country in the world. Is it two million now?"

"Something like that," Edward said.

"It's actually more now. We don't even have to talk about why. I know we're not going to agree about that. We're a big, free country, and in order for most of us to be safe, we need to put the misfits away, right?"

"More than misfits, I dare say," Edward answered.

"Agreed," said Sarah. "We've got more murderers, for instance, than all the other western countries put together."

"Right," he said, "and we've got a good record at putting them away. It'd be an even better record if the laws didn't favor the criminal."

"Not gonna go there," Sarah said. "But let's do some numbers. Let's say there are five thousand young men, many of them people of color, on Death Row or right next to it. Did you happen to know that like, lots of them are there because they killed the guy who was beating up their mom?"

"Is that true?" asked Kyla, unbelieving.

"It's a lot; it's a big percentage," said Sarah. "I've studied this. I fund-raise for three different prison reform organizations. Now are you going to tell me that all these people are natural born killers? Or there's nothing we can do to intercede between the abuser and the kid's mom, so the kid doesn't have to kill? Doesn't have to find the man's loaded gun and snuff him with it?"

"I hear what you're saying," Edward told her.

Meaning he didn't have a ready reply. Meaning he was falling for her super hard and he would say what it took to keep the conversation going.

"What about this?" Sarah asked: "Two million people behind bars. It costs the state or the federal government thirty thousand dollars a year per criminal to keep 'em locked up. What's that add up to? Sixty billion dollars a year! Think of all we could buy with that money."

"I know. I've thought about it," Edward said. And I believed he had. How had he ended up working for that blowhard?

She went on. "And not even to mention all the people who are locked up for non-violent crimes, or things they didn't do, or they're just poor and waiting for trial, or they can't make bail, or they missed their ride to a probation hearing, and wham, they're right back in—"

I knew where Sarah was going. We had had this conversation. She was looking at people before they did what the State said they had done.

"Now just suppose the creative arts are really effective intervenors in a young person's life. Just suppose one song or one piece of live theatre can be a lifeboat for some young person who's about to get into serious trouble. And this is not speculation. We know it works. Some kid who is ready to explode gets a chance to channel all that energy into howling, raging, hip-hop, or, into a mural project, or, even better, a theatre group where he has to be a team player, where they love him to death for all the things that are wrong about him, that could easily get him gang-banging, killing, shooting up. Isn't this worth supporting? When the annual NEA budget is one half of one percent of the prison budget? What's the matter with spending that money?"

"It's not the money," Edward said.

"Not the money?"

"No. It rarely is."

I agreed with him there. For me it wasn't about the money. The NEA hardly gets any money anymore. It's another part for the whole. It's the canary in the coal mine. It's the place I watch to see if the rest of us are going to survive. If we see it go belly-up on the bottom of its cage, we know we only have a limited amount of time left before we go, too. We have to hurry up and get back out to where we can breathe.

This administration is erasing everything we used to assume that a government would do, by the people for the people, since the New Deal and the Great Society. They want to roll us back to the 19th century, to the robber barons—

"It's not the money. It's the principle," Edward was saying. "Government has no business supporting the arts or artists. Period. End of conversation."

"You believe that?" Sarah asked. And he said yes but I don't think anybody sitting at that table—and we were all listening now—believed his belief.

"Who's gonna support them, then?" I asked.

"The free market." he said.

The free market, I thought, that recently brought us thongs for seven year old girls, available in Playboy-bunny or cherry motif?

"The free market." he repeated, and gestured to support his answer, but what should have been an authoritative finger jab in space suddenly leaked all its energy in mid-flight and became a tentative hand to his own curly hair.

Okay, here's something else my sixth sense told me. The man had been a thumb-sucking hair twirler as a toddler, and the old habit hung on latent to re-surface in adulthood when he was stressed. I saw a stressed look take over his eyes. I saw the child's hand reach up to twirl.

Maybe at the same time he realized, in words not yet quite formed, that Sarah was about to become a formidable part of his life. Or on another level that it was not pure coincidence that had brought them together. I stood up from the table, thankful for the qualities she had, qualities you look for in a sidekick. She was a researcher, and she had come up with a lot of goods on her own about Edward. She was organized and thorough, with a graphic designer's eye. Turned that eye upon herself and upon every situation she was in. She knew her audience and her message.

I folded some money into Sarah's hand to pay for dinner, and left the four of them there. I greeted students and parents at the other table, and as I headed out, I heard Sarah airing out another peeve: you call it a free market, she was saying, when a single radical-right broadcaster can buy up two thousand radio stations from coast to coast, push non-stop white supremacist Christian hate talk onto every boondock radio.

Where is the connection to people, to roots? To local history, to school boards, to what they're talking about down at the senior center, the grocery store, the grandstands in the little league field. Where is the public access? You go into one of those radio bunkers, and all you find is a satellite dish, some blinking lights, and an AI robot on the phone selling ads. Some free market.

I'm with old Bob Marley on this one:

"Babylon system: suckin' the blood of the sufferers!"

Chapter Seventeen

You just can't, I was thinking as I walked over to Hotel Mercury, let the free market be the only arbiter of what survives, what dies, in the world of art. Eventually late-stage capitalism will wake you up one day, I swear, and you'll find that every thread to your past has been cut.

Time for a last-minute check. Like what the stage manager and the head usher do before they open the house. There were a few people already gathered in the bright hotel lobby, losing themselves in the oversized sofas. A plaster Apollo looked down on them from an adjacent plinth. I greeted them quickly and headed up the long terrazzo stairway. Looks like mosaic from far away; up close you can see it was poured, ground, and polished years ago.

The dominant colors on the stairs were wine red and seaweed green: thank you, Homer, for the epic hues. At the top step Mercury, wings on his helmet and heels, pointed the way, with his missing arm, to where the second-floor hall turned its first corner. There were triangular cut-glass wall sconces pointing down the corridor, which ended not too far away (small hotel) in a window and a plaster reproduction of an Elgin Marble frieze.

Our room 22 hugged the near corner on the left, and a little farther down, the next door, which was closed, read 23. Our space still looked good to me; Garth had pushed the one double bed—not a king or queen—right up against the window. He lay on the bed reading Cheeto's script, his black boots gleaming and hanging carefully over the bed's edge.

The window was covered with a pale blue curtain, Radio City Music Hall deco-style print. Garth had set up—squeezed in, rather—twenty-two folding chairs, between the bed and the bathroom. Some of the audience could camp right on the floor. We needed to keep the bed mostly clear, in case any action spilled over there.

A low mahogany dresser with a TV hugged the wall about five feet from the foot of the bed. We pushed the TV to the far left, closer to the window. That gave room for one of us to sit on the dresser if we had to. Moved the wastebasket out to the hall. At the non-window end of the dresser, closer to the room's main entrance, was the door into the other room, where Sarah had stood and talked to me. That door would be our center backdrop, and it could serve as a top-center entrance to the stage, if we wanted it to be.

We didn't want it to be.

The door was locked.

It was standard-issue paneled interior door, multiple-paneled, and each panel was held by intersecting thicker boards, rails and stiles, with four or five levels of relief edges to catch the light. Right in front of that door-that-adjoined was our performing space. Maybe seven feet wide, five deep. Tiny: but for my money, the smaller the performing area the more electric the performance. Within a severely limited space, actors go critical with each other—in the nuclear sense.

There was some yellow spike tape on the carpet in front of that door. When Garth reached out and grabbed the big green chair, he could swing it through the air and land it on the spike tape. He showed me how he'd been practicing: to scare the front row of sitters with the swinging chair, to land its front legs on the spike tapes just so. Then whoever was going to be in the chair— we knew who that would be—would sit at eye level to the hole I had drilled in the door. He would lean in that direction, but he could twist and face the audience, too. The spotlight would be on him from above. We'd plugged in an orange extension cord and a strip, hung a couple of clamp lamps pointing down. When the room lights were out—except for one small lamp at the head of the bed—we had a theatre. To the actor in the chair it would feel like an interrogation.

Garth stationed himself by the bathroom door. Usher in full military dress uniform. Like a palace guard for a second-tier despot. I wondered again, where did he do his shopping?

I stood in the hall just outside Room 22. Signaled to Cheeto at the top of the stairs.

"House is open!" Cheeto called down to Alex and the rest downstairs. Then he went down to get his mother.

Beside me was a chrome plant-stand. I'd stowed the potted plastic ivy on the floor, and put a Damon-Runyon style hat upside down on the stand. For tickets. People paid a few dollars donation downstairs, if they had it. Help rent the hall, we told them. But everyone got a ticket.

And everyone was excited! Just like in some metropolitan theater lobby: that first sharp footfall on the terrazzo. The stairway to the loge. Everyone stepping up and out of their routine: the old elevator on the left, unused, uncalled-for.

We'd printed twenty-four tickets. Numbered. Hold on to your stub. There was to be a drawing partway through the evening. A lottery in the Borges sense, I would say, since the prize would be non-monetary and probably unwelcome. We already knew who would win.

Cheeto came up first, his mother on one arm, Becca on the other. Everyone had decided to dress elegantly for their special evening. But their idea of elegance veered sharply from current national norms. Not a big-time mall shopper among them, I was proud to observe: they dressed themselves from thrift store racks, from Grandpa's closet, Grandma's trunk, from the bins in the high school theatre costume loft.

Cheeto had a double-breasted grey suit which I recognized from the "Guys and Dolls" of the previous winter. His mamá, who was plump and nowhere near five feet tall, even in her high heels, had on a tight green shiny skirt and a low-cut flowered Guatemalan peasant blouse. Her high heels clicked and wobbled dangerously on the terrazzo steps.

She'd taken to wearing the peasant blouses once she'd made it to the United States. Peasant clothes had been outlawed unofficially in Salvador for sixty years. Wearing them now was an act of defiance. Becca had on a bold black-and-white Jackie Kennedy vintage flaired shirt-dress with a matching pillbox hat and evening bag. Tyrell had a pink pinstripe zoot suit, navy blue shirt with white tie, spats and a pork pie hat. Bolo was wearing a snow-white fleece sweatsuit ensemble with retro black-and-white high top sneakers.

Ravinia and her dad? I forget his name. They had on matching Armani-knock-off coppery-beige rent-a-suits, with also matching silky bronze ascots, red-carpet style.

The seats filled.

There was no sign of Jermayne and Kyla.

I saw Sarah and Edward stop at the foot of the stairs. She took his elbow and whispered something into his ear. I saw him look at her, stare up for a moment, and then nod. I could not hear them but she was coached, and I could read her body language:

Your ticket number's going to be called. In the raffle. It's an audience participation improv. Also a cold reading of a script. Act like you didn't know. Go along with it. Go along with everything.

They continued to climb. She stopped him again.

Did he understand? Could he take it, however it turned out?

He nodded.

Do you trust me?

He nodded again.

Her hand stayed just above his elbow all the way to the door, where they stopped, a couple out on the town for dinner and a show. We three looked at each other for a moment. Eyes full of meaning, opposite to the thoughts inside. Like at a blackjack table. I tore each of their tickets in turn, told them to keep their half, glanced at each stub's number as I tossed it into the hat.

Alex was the last one in. He'd left an employee to do the front desk. I shut the door. The audience filled all the seats. I gave a brief introduction, and Sarah, Garth and I took our places. So much anticipation in the room. Not an ordinary night. Not an ordinary art form, actually: so new we didn't have a name for it.

Edward looked around; Sarah's face was the only familiar one, but some of the others nodded to him. Just friendly, I supposed, not a real recognition, but a friendly gesture of camaraderie among the specially-invited. Then I realized that Sarah's special instruction would have put him on his guard, and he might think those nods meant—I lost myself in the permutations and gave up.

Sarah looked up at me and smiled, then glanced down at her printed program (one folded 8 1/2 by 11 piece of yellow paper) and cocked her head at me. Obviously reacting to the quote from Antonin Artaud I had written above everything. I'll put it anywhere I can get away with it:

"And if there is still one hellish, truly accursed, thing in our time, it is our artistic dallying with forms, instead of being like victims burnt at the stake, signaling through the flames."

Chapter Eighteen

The two first acts were Shakespeare. Two quick scenes from plays we had been studying: what they had in common? They were two fictional bedrooms. *We* were in a bedroom. The first scene was an edited Hamlet in his mother's royal chamber, berating her, scaring her, killing Polonius, bringing on his father's ghost for the third and final time. The actors were three students from my class, reading or remembering their lines. Then they sat back down, to warm applause in their audience seats. I have always loved Hamlet's opening lines in that scene.

Come, come, and sit you down. You shall not budge!
You go not till I set you up a glass
Where you may see the inmost part of you.

—A good mantra to have in my brain, it occurred to me, as students file into my class on any ordinary afternoon. It passes the Artaud test. And the Julio Parra test, too.

Our second bedroom offering was Juliet loving Romeo for the first and only time. Bidding him good-bye.

JULIET: O, think'st thou we shall ever meet again?
ROMEO: I doubt it not; and all these woes shall serve
For sweet discourses in our time to come.

He leaps down from her balcony and loses himself in the trees. Then her mother comes to announce the impending marriage to Paris, the nurse hard on her heels, and Old Man Capulet right after her, ready to rage. More than half of the possible human dramatic emotions come on display in this scene, and that's why I love it.

But these were, only, scenes. Olios, they call them, sometimes while the main event gets ready. They didn't add up to a full night of theatre. After the audience applauded and stretched a bit, and high fives all around for my students getting back to their seats, I stood again in front of them.

"Okay, me again. Just a few words here. You having a good time?"

More applause, some thumbs up, smiles—

"So now to the main event of the night. Cheeto's play. For me, it kind of came out of nowhere—wait, I take that back: no one, no thing, comes out of nowhere."

I smiled at Cheeto's mother, Elena. I thought of the somewhere that Cheeto had come from. I also smiled at Edward. Certainly he had not come out of nowhere.

"What I mean is, think about this: say you're a teacher, you work with a student—who's always steady, gets the job done, but safely. You can begin to predict how he—or she's—going to take to an assignment. There's no surprises. Then suddenly something that you assign just touches a nerve. They pass in a piece of work that vibrates right in your hands. I can tell some huge connection has been made that will never come undone. Does anyone understand what I'm talking about?"

There were those looks again: tolerant, even indulgent. Sympathetic. Certainly not comprehending.

"Forget it. I tried. It gives me great pleasure to introduce to you: Romero Romero." Applause, friendly, familial, filled the little room.

"Moncheeto, come on up and make more sense than I did."

While Cheeto threaded his way through the few seats, I felt the gratitude that hits me often. For the chance that teaching gives me to get to know truly extraordinary young human beings.

I gave the young man an *abrazo*—a hug. Of all my pupils, the most studious. Glasses like coke-bottle bottoms. Talks English better than any two of us. Always a complete sentence. Unlike me. His parents' dedication to his learning shows. Cheeto reads all the time. His house may be the only Salvadoran domicile in the U.S.A. with no TV, no "Canal Uno" with its flashy Latin Kens and buxom Barbies, high-pitched hollering, screaming game shows, desperate news, Mexican soccer, mind-blasting commercials—his house by comparison is so quiet you can hear subtle ambient noise, the sound of hot oil in the frying pan, the tail-twitch ticking of the black Felix-the-Cat clock hanging on the wall, his little sister's careful penciling on paper at the kitchen table, the rub of his grandma's knees on the rug in the next room, where she's praying.

Cheeto bowed to the clapping and cheers, and then stood contemplating the audience. Before he said a word, I whispered something in his ear. Picture Bogart as Rick in *Casablanca's* Café Americaine, the scene where he tells the young Bulgarian what roulette number to play.

Cheeto nodded, adding a flash of eye contact and a fugitive thumb-up to show me he understood.

"Thank you, Mr. B."

Then to the audience: "You ready to have a good time?"

A small roar of approval. Then Cheeto gave his prepared speech. "Shakespeare's a tough act to follow," he said. "So, by way of excuse, for my play, this is what they call a staged reading. Slightly rehearsed. What we like to call half-baked. It's like, in Mr. B's class, we hand in a first draft and then, no matter if we correct each other's stuff, or Mr. B does, we find out how half-baked our ideas really are. Tonight I get the chance to find out in public. So, sorry in advance for what I could have got better."

He looked down at his notes, one messy half-sheet of paper. "Oh, one other thing. You all know what a fourth wall is?"

Some people nodded; some shook their heads.

"Well, a stage has three sides—left, right, and back—that you can actually see. The fourth side is this empty space" (he pointed forward) "between us and you. That's called the fourth wall. Some actors and playwrights like to break it. You know, step over the line and talk right to the audience. Or go touch them. We might do that. We may even stop and ask you for an idea, or ask how we're doing. Feel free to join in. No fourth wall. I mean, you're all so close, it's like you're in it anyway. Okay?"

Okay it was.

Cheeto's mother beamed at him. She would probably not understand very much, on one level; the size and self-sufficiency of our Central-American refugee community had made learning English less of a priority for her than it might have been. On another level, I thought, knowing the content, she would understand more than most people. If the play came off as I pictured it.

Cheeto and I had decided that he would give some background now. He'd put the audience on the map. So he talked about where his family came from. El Salvador, a land of routine murder of peasants, campesinos, nuns and priests, since 1932. Poverty and hopelessness in the countryside. Right-wing death squads in the 70's and 80's, responding to a popular insurrection. How his mother's brother had been "disappeared."

Were people in the U.S. familiar with that word? Everyone nodded, yes: they were a select, non-mainstream audience. How there was never an official peace, or truth commission to discover who had done what to whom. And how unspeakable gang violence, bred in Los Angeles, spilled into Salvador in the 90's and beyond.

Cheeto was born somewhere under a roadside bush in Arizona after his mother and two sisters had crossed the desert to travel an underground railroad none of us would ever believe still existed, let alone be able to survive in: every safe arrival to the U.S. was no less than a miracle. The railroad had a name: "No Más Muertos!" (No More Deaths).

His mother, over the 2000 miles, prayed every day to the sainted Archbishop of San Salvador. I've mentioned him before. And prayed for the soul of her brother, if he was dead indeed. It's hard for survivors to go on living when they don't have a single scrap of information about what happened to the ones they loved. It's hard to keep picturing how they may have died.

"It's heavy, I know," Cheeto said. "This scene is not about all that; that's just the background? It all came out of a class discussion we had. A lot of us were talking and the word "disappear" kept coming up and sticking in my head. You ever have a word nagging in your mind and it doesn't go away until you sit and pay attention to what it's trying to tell you?"

There were some murmurs of understanding. Garth and I were kneeling over by the bed, keeping out of the way for now, and, listening to the muted audience reaction, I realized I might have to do a little coaching, or even over-acting, to get them to be more responsive. They were too well-mannered, too self-conscious in that tiny space. The more demonstrative they were, the more comfortable the actors would feel, and the more momentum and naturalness the scene would have. I thought about how and when I could coach them.

Cheeto continued, "It's hard for me to believe that someone can have so much power over someone else. That one group can be holding all the cards, and the other have like none at all. That one group can be so all-powerful that they can just make anyone disappear. So that's what this play is called, "Disappeared." It's starring Garth, and Mr. B., and Mr. B's friend Sarah. Oh, and one of you gets to play a part."

He looked the small crowd over. There was the usual response to news like that. Lifting of eyebrows, lowering of heads, futile attempts to hide. People up front wondering why they hadn't chosen a seat in the other row. Some smartass waving his hand to be picked: just the guy you don't want.

"No, we're gonna make it fair," Cheeto said. "We'll draw a ticket stub. So, find your half-ticket, please."

He waited till everyone was holding their piece of paper.

"Good. Garth, the hat, *por favor.*"

Garth brought over the brown fedora.

"Mr. B., please choose a ticket."

I reached into the hat and shuffled the bits of paper. I picked one up—well, I did my one magic trick again—and showed a ticket quickly to Cheeto and dropped it back into the hat.

"Number 12," said Cheeto.

Edward raised his hand. "That's me."

Chapter Nineteen

Do you remember when I pictured the woman who got this whole thing rolling? Way back when? I said something like "Amazed at the idea that struck her then, she was doubly amazed that she would even take the idea seriously."

That's what I felt exactly. I mean, we weren't in San Cristobal; Edward was no roughed-up, street-jacked Julio Parra, I was certain of that. Not in a sixteenth century convent. Just a hotel room, but that's theatre! The idea that we could represent both the horror and the humor of the story, in full view of the audience, *that* gave me a rush like I may not ever have experienced before, and it came on all at once, totally unexpected.

I also saw Artaud's flames again, but they were not the flames of a saint's martyrdom, they looked at that moment like flames of a massive, unstoppable failure. It amazed me: that I was about to let that happen! And in public, too.

I think you need to know here some of what I already knew about Cheeto's play. "Disappeared." Maybe I'm finally learning how to tell people more about what they ought to know?

That word meant more to him than for most of us. Somehow he had found positive aspects of its horror. The word focussed his gaze into an inspiring metaphoric space. It had done that for me. But Julio Parra's disappearance was only thrilling because the kidnapping had a benign narrative and denouement. I mean, I knew how it ended a moment after I read how it began.

Set free from the suspense of it, I had been free to make it into a special lens for looking at my own existence. I had gathered literary passages to support my point of view. These lines from Ariel Dorfman had leapt at me from the page where they sat in a book on my shelf:

The best thing that can happen to a criminal is to be captured, because in his solitary cell, without the habitual defenses with which he has hidden his past from himself, at times the miracle of a minute window opens inside the prisoner's heart, a window that might lead to self-awareness and redemption.

What if suddenly *all* the artists in the western world were to disappear? They go out for their morning coffee, a little rubbing with real elbows, real people, before retreating into their deliberate daily exile. Hours later, days later, their worried families wonder where they've gone. This is the vision Cheeto had when he suddenly began to write so furiously. Yes, what he wrote first was just thoughts, but with my counsel, he found the scene the audience was about to see.

Cheeto made the connection, without any prodding from me, that "disappearance" could be what artists do when they and all their pure creativity vanish into a cynical commercial place. This is what the market powers want them to do. For every blazing virgin genius who bursts upon our scene, from the forest or farm or apartment or school where they have nurtured their uniqueness, there's an agent of empire lurking to make a deal. It's Little Red Riding Hood, her precious basket, and the Wolf Man all over again. I saw this connection early in Cheeto's work, and I offered him this quote from Arundhati Roy:

"When writers, painters, musicians, film makers suspend their judgment and blindly yoke their art to the service of the nation, (or the corporation) it's time for all of us to sit up and worry."

Time to sit up and worry because the people whose peculiar vision we used to depend on went out somewhere and never came home.

Is it that time yet?

Garth, Sarah, and I had our scripts. Cheeto put a fourth one into Edward's hand, and told him to sit in the onstage chair and look through the first couple of pages. Garth hit a button on his laptop, on the table; some evocative Andean music came on. I flipped the switch on the electric strip and the scary overhead light shone down on Edward's curly head.

He looked up with a start, but Sarah gestured him to relax and read. He did so. I was familiar with the many blank spaces on the typed pages, the ambiguous stage directions, and hoped he'd be willing to improvise. Figured he would; don't ask me why. Desperation feeding on metaphor maybe, or desire giving him its blind assist.

Before diving down into the waiting fiction, I bought Edward some time. I broke the fourth wall as it was just being erected, and I took the chance to tell the audience what we hoped for, expected, from them. That this was hotel room theater, a room service melodrama, a suite nothing. That they were a small crowd; that they would have to deliberately raise the volume, bass, and treble of their response. Laugh without self-consciousness when the impulse hit. Let us hear them breathe: in, when their concern was aroused, out when they felt relieved. Clap for a good stage moment. We needed all that.

I patted Edward on his shoulder. First time I had touched him. "We've got a volunteer here," I said. "He's gonna need to hear from you. Maybe he's never acted before. You give him good feedback, and he might find a new career tonight."

Smiles, some laughter.

"What's your name, friend?" Pretending not to know. My first pretending. But just a typical deflective exchange between a prestidigitator and his shill.

"Edward," he answered.

You already know that, his eyes said, irritated.

"Presenting "Edward," I announced, "and the rest of us, in "Disappeared," a people's play by Romero 'Moncheeto' Romero."

The big breath in. For a moment I thought about all the private dramas that must have taken place in that room. Sixty-plus years of paying guests: scenes from marriages or from affairs, one-night stands, tears, tortured phone calls, take out dinners, sleepless vigils on the one chair looking out at the street, night sweats, bad dreams, couplings, rejections, wine bottles, fevered Bible study: was there anything this room had not seen? Now this.

I nodded to Garth, who turned off the main light, leaving lit the scoop above, and the little bedside lamp over by the window. Sarah looked heart-stoppingly beautiful in the chiseled light; part of me wondered whether it was too late to grab her hand and pull her out of there; go follow another vision to some other destination, let the remaining actors deal with the present moment—she produced a pillow case and put it over Edward's head. He almost jumped out of the chair. She squeezed his shoulders to communicate with him.

"I can't read my lines," I heard him whisper to her.

"You don't have any yet," she whispered right back, bending over him.

"Relax, Man," I said, also in a whisper. "This is fiction. You're in a play. No worries."

Then there was a pause. I found myself wishing we'd rehearsed with him. Wishing there had been moments when we all listened while the director told us our next move.

In Nathaniel Hawthorne's great book of short stories, *Mosses From an Old Manse,* there's one tale that stands out from the rest—"*Rappaccini's Daughter*"—and one sentence that has stayed with me since the first time I ever saw it:

> *How often is it the case that, when impossibilities have come to pass and dreams have condensed their misty substance into tangible realities, we find ourselves calm, and even coldly self-possessed, amid circumstances which it would have been a delirium of joy or agony to anticipate!*

So I have felt on a small number of occasions, and on that night especially. The Julio Parra article, the discussions in my classroom, the desire and planning, all came down to this moment. I should have been excited.

Where was my delirium, my joy?

Searching inside myself, I felt nothing yet. Only coldness in my veins. Maybe, I thought, within me but close to the surface are a few stuck things—baggage, obstructions—that I need to move out of the way before I can be completely here.

Isn't that how the article always struck me? How we need to be roughed up and pulled in and forced to focus as we haven't for a long time? All right then, focusing that way now, the first thing I came upon was a general apology I needed to give: to the thousands of people who died real deaths in real disappearances, an act that we would parody here. I sent that out: a sincere "I'm sorry" to anyone anywhere who might think I meant to trivialize the suffering that would go on to define their entire life.

While I was giving out apologies, how about one to my wife, who I said went off without a fight from me; to my daughter who needed to see and hear from me more; to Sarah, whose limits to intimacy I had agreed on too easily. Anyone I'd made some assumption about, that caused me to not see who they really were. Any student I had hidden important information from, as Cheeto said. Anyone I had withheld true feeling from, while I clung to a solitude so superficially amenable to me that even my nightmares about it had become comfortably familiar.

Could all that change now? I had been so focussed on the Julio-Edward character in the drama, and, wanting desperately to change a single man and therefore change a government policy, I never gave a thought to how this experience could transform me, too.

Cheeto had known: when he phoned me that day, he was already transforming. He wanted to share that with me, to guide me along with him. He was confronting a shadow that always lived in his mother's house. He felt it there always: his grandmother grieving and conjuring in the next room. Becca, his girlfriend, coming over to help out where she could, to pick up important knowledge from the older women. His mother cleaning houses, his father working two jobs, two shifts (working so hard he couldn't even come to this hotel room debut): the quiet in the house a constant commemoration of the missing one: his disappeared uncle whom Cheeto never knew, his mother's only brother, artistic idealistic studious like Cheeto, like Julio.

All these forces making him grow up in pieces, and now he wanted to be whole.

Now, writing this theatre piece around a *desaparecido* metaphor, an interrogation in a tiny room, he was coming out, releasing pent-up stuff he needed to understand, a healing of sicknesses he carried in him unaware. Healing that only art can do. Maybe now he will grow up to be a writer, I thought, a fine, bilingual chronicler, writing the great immigrant novel, his family's story—

It will be so popular in this country that finally our population will get it! Yes! About the evil we've inspired: in Salvador, Panama, Nicaragua, Brazil, Chile, Peru, Argentina. The School of the Americas! All because of this kid's writing, and this assignment in my classroom could turn out to be one of the ones that really got him going—what he had been training for all his life in the quiet house.

There was his mother beside him in the audience, arm over his shoulder; so proud of his writing. Understands about half of it, translating each word clumsily as it goes past; no way she would have gotten that last joke, I caught myself thinking.

"I caught myself thinking."

You bet I do. I'm an actor in a scene, for god's sake. Any one looking at me would see my mind wandering. Going up, the actors call it. The body is there on the stage performing the half-memorized motions, but the mind has fled up to the rafters, or miles away, leaving a blank look in the eye.

Where have I been?

I synch up again. Concentrate, I tell myself. Breathe. Be in the present. You wanted this. You're the director too. And the producer. You want to see some changes in yourself? Then be here. See it through to the end. Edward looks up at me, going dry. The wrap is off his head. The scene has been moving along. It must be my line.

I looked down at my script, miraculously landing on the right place.

"You okay?" I asked him. Not sympathetic, just wanting bare information.

"I guess so," he said. He rubbed his neck as if he had just had the uncomfortable car ride of our imagination. Going along with the acting: I liked that. He turned to look toward the audience, but seeing no one there he recognized, his look stayed blank. I bent down and turned his jaw delicately till his eyes contacted mine. Out of the corner of my eye I saw Cheeto shake his fist and smile. I was glad I had told him the whole story.

I wanted to reassure, frighten, inspire, and educate Edward—his stage character and himself—all at the same time. I was thinking of my old friend Julio in the moment of his capture, bag over his head, heart racing, smelling the inside of the car, the heat of the people, the jab of the pistol into his flesh, ignorant of the destination and of the stakes. Thinking of him when they pulled the bag off his head. Then they said those reassuring words. It was time for me to say them to him.

"You mind telling me what this is all about?" he asked, from the script.

"This is a whim," I read. "We're not planning to keep you here long. We think you can help us."

"Who's the us?" he asked. Following the stage direction, he looked around at all three of us. He had an automatic, clearly different, reaction to the eye contact each of us made with him. The man is a natural, I thought.

Sarah spoke. "Let's just say we're a few people concerned about disappearing artists."

"Not that we think you're directly responsible," I said. "I mean, you don't jump 'em and throw them into a car."

"He doesn't have to, Man." said Garth. He knew their related positions—his and Edward's—along the chain of command.

I looked down at the man who wrote the speeches that his boss delivered on the Senate floor. They were both masters at pushing the buttons of the most conservative, benighted millions among us. Though I could almost taste the antipathy I felt for his positions—if they were in fact his honest positions, I considered—I would have to excuse everything to get to the next place.

"We don't have a lot of time," I said. "We're not, you know, interested in your politics; we're interested in your art."

Nice of Cheeto, I thought, to feature the direct quote from the article. Good thing I finally showed it to him.

"What's my art?" he asked.

I flattered him then, tough cop going soft on the captive. "You write," I said. "Don't you write?"

"I guess so. I'm not really a writer, like a real author."

I didn't let him off the hook. "But you do write. You put your words into other people's mouth. Most of the stuff you put there is bullshit. Every word is dripping with "what's it gonna get us?" "How many votes?" "How much money?" or "How is this gonna play?" or "Won't the Christians love this?"

I glanced at Cheeto: I would have written it different, but the point was made. Kids don't know that to make your point you don't have to bludgeon your audience into submission.

Edward almost got up as if to leave. His stint of civic volunteerism was coming to a quick end. Sarah gripped his shoulders and held him down—part of the job description she hit on, that first night I offered her the gig.

That kept him in his chair, partly facing the wall and its door, partly twisted toward the audience. I went on speaking: "The taxpayers in your state are paying for your job. Cushy job. Don't you ever wonder where the writer went? Admit it!"

"Of course I do, but—"

Garth interrupted him. Every time Garth spoke it was the voice of heavy manners. Code Red: nobody moves.

"There's no "but" here, Man. Teacher knows what he's talkin' about." (Pause. Turn to audience. Discover. Break Fourth Wall.) "That's why I'm back with him for a second year."

That was a laugh line, and Garth delivered it just right. Good appreciation from the audience. Many of them fellow-students. Both Cheeto and Garth looking around and smiling. Cheeto understood, from my Shakespeare teaching, that you often need a laugh line in a difficult, even unsuitable place. That's when you need the laughter the most. Even if the line breaks character. And breaks that wall.

But okay then. That must be the deal. I *am* playing myself. Maybe with a little added edge. Didn't realize that before. That can be difficult, in front of the home crowd. And if you don't have a lesson plan, it's even harder.

"So I write speeches," Edward said. "You want me to start writing something else. I get it. Is that why I'm here?"

"No. You're here because your number got drawn," I said.

"Oh, right," he said; "I forgot."

"Funny how that happened," Garth grinned to the audience; "he's the guy I woulda picked anyway." The young man had a natural talent for stand-up. He'd have to throw all those soldier's clothes out the window, or keep a few to use for laughs. Military comedy has been a successful genre for a long time.

"Could I ask a question?" Edward said, deviating from the script. We all nodded.

"Suppose it wasn't just luck. Suppose I was meant to be picked."

"Like fate? This feel like fate to you?"

"A little. Fate, planning, whatever. There's some reason I'm up here."

"Oh, that," I said; "That's easy. It's because you're a synecdoche."

"Beg pardon?"

"Sin-Eck-Do-Kee. It's a figure of speech." I threw it out to the audience: "Anyone out there tell this guy what a synecdoche is?"

One of my students, I think Tyrell, called out, "a part for the whole, Mr. B."

Someone else said, "like a penis."

High school humor, heard it before. Part. Hole. Good mnemonic.

"It's a nectar key," a third male person said, laughing at his own joke.

There's always one or two in the crowd.

There was a blank spot in the script here. Cheeto had decided not to write it. He had given me a cadenza.

"This is for you, Mr. B," he had told me. "You wing it."

So I told Edward about my vision. Told him, but it was the audience I was telling, too. I said that history can turn on a dime if you get to the right person. He could be that person. Build him up a little. We couldn't bring in every crazed apocalyptic Evangelical politico who set national policy on support for the arts, nor every ideological maggot-covered-rotting-cow's-head-in-a-jar left-wing artist. We got *him*. Edward. Our synecdoche.

He looked at me as if seeing me for the first time. Ignoring the script in his hands.

"You think if I change what I write that everything's going to change?" he asked me.

"It's possible. I deal in possibilities. I'm a teacher." But I was the right person to field that question, since, among the few things I believe in, I believe in quantum change. And Uncertainty.

"Then you are interested in my politics."

The man was sharp.

"I admit it," I said. "Look, all we want to do is save the National Endowment for the Arts. In the words of a Senator I know, 'Is that too much to ask?' It means more to more people than you can even imagine. People I guarantee you you would like if you met them. We want you to come around to our point of view. But we don't want to force you, do we?"

Sarah and Garth both shook their heads. No one was going to force him to do that. We'd all pledged on Black's Legal Dictionary not to use any unlawful pressure.

"I will employ no force, including confinement, without the consent of the person against whom it is directed, etc. etc."

"So that's why you got me here?" he asked us, but looking at Sarah.

"You're here to see a play," Sarah said. "I invited you."

Edward: "This is more than *seeing* a play."

Sarah: "Yes. But it *is* a play. See: there's the audience." She said that nice and loud and got the friendly group wave back.

Mr. B. "Look. You got invited. You came. Then, your number was drawn. You got the part. The rest is up to you."

Garth: "What teacher means is, this is like a class. You're a student. You've gotta do the work. There's stuff you need to see for yourself."

Edward: "Like what?"

Now he was not only surprised and uncomfortable. He was genuinely confused. That's when I started to like him purely for the first time.

"For starters, that you can't leave all art up to the marketplace," I said. "Every other civilized country in the world knows this. It's like health care. You can't have profit be a part of every single deal.

When you sit down to paint or write or compose, you can't be thinking about the money. Sometimes yes, but not all of the time. You have to be open to any idea, from wherever ideas come from, when they choose you, without thinking about future sales. You have to be true to yourself. In some cases, you have to be desperate."

Edward looked at the three of us. I could tell he didn't like the sound of "desperate;" maybe it made him think of crazy sixties radicals, bombing multinationals, shooting armored car guards, taking hostages.

He looked down at his script, fumbling for his place, then finding it. The line seemed to fit.

"I still don't understand what that has to do with me."

"That's good," I said; "that's a good place to be." Archetypal moment for a writer, that blank page in the machine.

I let out some breath I must have been holding. Granted permission by that, he did, too. In the last vulnerable second of his relaxation, Sarah moved quickly in to remind us of why we were here.

"See that light there?" she asked, both reading and pointing to the hole. "Say you were a prisoner. Which you're not. You see that light. You know what light means to a prisoner. What would you do?"

He looked at us; none of us moved. Then he peered for a second through the hole, and jumped up to leave. Sarah had her arms around him from behind. Pushed him back down. Strong woman. He shut his mouth tight. I saw so much in his eyes then. That sixth sense I told you about. But I also saw how he felt, having her arms around him.

Remember how I got here. The newspaper article was all from Julio Parra's point of view. Point of view is important in writing. No reporter went to interview the abductors, the guard, the naked woman, or her husband. Julio talked to the press.

So the story was told from the painter's vantage, and I had been sympathetic with him all along. Feeling his capture, his isolation, his concentration, his desire. In any form of art, you the beholder form a natural bond of sympathy with the person whose point of view is being represented. That's what you see in the frame. It's a big part of the circuit across which the emotions arc.

Seeing Rembrandt's self-portraits, following them through the aging process, the wrinkles, the worry, decay, loss, sorrow; you see all of your life through his eyes. You wonder whether you'll have what it takes to look so closely at your own decline. You won't. He was the Great Master.

I had started this whole process empathizing with the victim. It was Julio's story, after all, and I knew him. More than anything, I had resonated with his situation, extrapolated so much from it—more raw material than I could use in a lifetime—having to do with art in general, with inspiration, passion, teaching, integrity, consciousness, point of view...

And then I caught my own self by surprise by choosing to project myself instead into the abductors' shoes, and doing it before I had thought it all through.

I still hadn't thought it through! I was feeling my way, and now my way was suddenly blocked by empathy for the man sitting almost paralyzed near me. I was looking back at me through his eyes. Momentum is everything. In writing, too. When you lose it, doubt jumps into its place. And you stand there wondering, "how did I get here? Can I go on?"

I breathed in and out deeply then. I was inches away from the man and bonding with him. There was no way I was going to get rid of that sympathy. Besides, Cheeto had written it into the script. I didn't know about Garth, in the camouflage and shades. But he would have a natural affinity for the man, in spite of the Senator he worked for.

Sarah felt that sympathy, too. Her face was flushed; she gets red in the cheeks when her blood starts to pump. Ten years had fallen away from her in the space of a few moments. She had been repressing, for all those recluse years, a street barricade energy that used to nourish her absolutely. With all her power she was rooting the man to our side. For a whole complex of reasons, including the physical feeling: when did her arms around him became a different kind of holding? Despite all the reasons we had to deeply dislike the man, we would each of us just have to accept our empathy in all its variety and use it.

Emotions are perverse; you can use the one you're feeling, to give power to the one you'd like to express, even if it's contrary. Like, if you're a rocket, you can use the gravity of one planet to bounce you to another one farther away, the one you're really trying to get to.

Now Sarah talked to him, breaking his bubble as she liked to do, intruding in his space. "So, did you like what you were looking at?"

"It was all right," he said, reluctantly. Lips clamping shut. Eyes on his script.

She snorted. "I'll bet it was all right. Black on white. You ever see that outside of a pornhouse? Maybe at home on your computer?"

"I have never—" he began.

"Hey, we all know what the Senator's into," Garth said; "Do you like the same stuff? You cruise together? That why he keeps you on? You know too much about him?"

Now the audience leaned forward as one. There's a moment when a scene turns; that moment sped by; everyone was gripped by the new dynamic. Edward was looking down. Feeling, thinking, just reading? I kept forgetting that he was the only one who had not had time to rehearse.

"Look," I said, "to paraphrase a bit. We're interested in your art, not your private life, all right? Let's move on here. Getting too psychological." I didn't have to feign impatience. Feeling for him as I did, I wanted him to get it now. Besides, I wore no watch, but I knew we were running out of class time.

Sarah had straightened up. Now she turned and leaned back

down toward his chair; she gently lifted his face to look into hers, inches away. "You're here because we invited you. We got to you through the Senator. You got picked to be in this play. It's a good play. Now that you're here, I'm getting to know you and I'm trying to figure out what you wrote and what you didn't."

"That's important," I said.

She went on. "Take a speech like the Senator's. What's the intolerance about? Either there's big profit in it, you know, like for a politician or a shock radio station. You people mine intolerance like your friends mine coal."

She was off book now, off the script: "Or, okay, say it's not about money. Maybe somebody's hurting or frustrated. Maybe no love in their life."

"Or no art," I said, quickly, not liking the offer I had just heard implied.

"Or no art," she agreed, but lilted those three words upward, waiting for me to fill in the blank.

I went on: "Some big feeling didn't get expressed along the way and now it's putrefying inside. Jackson Pollack would have been a drunken axe-murderer if he couldn't fling paint around."

"So he was just a harmless wife-beating skirt-chasing paint-flinging drunk instead," she suggested. Good ad lib, good audience response. "But a creative one."

"Right." I said, but then I went on, also ad-lib; "I think there's a third reason. There are millions of envious uptight people in the world. They see everyone with their tattoos, boxer shorts down below their butts, teen-agers wearing push-up bras, purple hair, everyone having a good time. White people singin' hip-hop. Somebody making a sexy film about the Virgin Mary. They wish they could do that, too. But they can't, for whatever reason. Usually some fundamentalist reason. So they punish us. They try to make the rest of us suffer 'cause we're having fun. It's an old story, like

Oliver Cromwell shutting the Globe Theatre down. *Twelfth Night* was just too much fun."

I turned to Edward. "This make any sense to you?"

"Yeah," he said. Maybe he thought we'd let him go if he said that, but I wanted to wait till the last bit of insincerity was gone from his voice. How much time would that take?

"Hey Mr. B," someone called out from the audience; "give him that quote from *King Lear*!"

Everyone turned to the voice, with surprise. It was Bolo. He had liked Shakespeare ever since I told him the Bard of Avon was the hip-hop king of the sixteen-hundreds. Bolo was a tall skinny Black kid with a shiny lilac-colored do-rag down to his eyebrows. Never ever spoke in class. Smiled, always seemed to be listening. Being in the first row and involved in a theatre experience can do that, though: it'll make the mute man speak.

"What quote is that, Bolo?" I asked, breaking the wall right back at him.

"The one about the Beatles and the ho," he said.

"That's 'beadle,' Man." Ravinia corrected him; "It's like a deputy priest. Or sheriff."

"Whatever," Bolo said.

"Like the morals police," she added.

"I know," Bolo said.

"Right," I said; "Good idea. King Lear was crazy, but he got that one right."

"Go for it, Mr. B," Bolo said.

So I did, or, I was about to, and then Bolo said, "Wait," and gave me a beat with his two clasped fists, "b, ts, ts, pf; b, ts, ts, k," or something like that, making a rapper of Lear:

Thou rascal beadle,
hold,
hold thy bloody hand!
Why dost thou lash,

lash that whore?
Strip thine own back.
Strip it!
Thou hotly lusts
To use her in that kind
For which thou whip'st her....

Bolo put his hands back down. "I love that quote," he explained to everyone. "Tell them what it means, Mr. B."

"Why don't you tell them, Bolo. You brought it up."

I hated to keep breaking character, but I don't like to miss teachable moments, either. And I was happy to let the hotel room drama spin its wheels a little bit longer. Till we all figured out where we were going!

"Right, the guy is saying—"

"What guy, Bolo?"

"The king! King Lear. He's saying 'Shut up, you stupid deacon or whatever; stop whipping that woman! Whip your own self with that thing. You know you wish you could do all that sick stuff with her.'"

"You got that right, Bolo," I said. "Thanks."

Edward stayed silent. He didn't read his next line. Which gave me an idea. I asked "Edward, did you ever feel like everyone's making too much noise?

"I don't understand."

"I mean like you can't hear your real self think anymore?"

Sarah picked up on that quickly. "Or like if it gets quiet for a minute, everyone's gonna notice you're a fraud?"

That one resonated with me. One of my deepest fears, always. The old imposter thing.

Now he looked at her, at me, as though he would go along, though reluctantly, where we were taking him. "Yeah."

"You ever feel any envy for anyone?" I asked. "Like that beadle did?"

"Yeah."

"You want to tell us who?"

"No."

I looked at him a little perplexed. "Okay. We're gonna give you a chance. But you have to be honest. Your life depends on it." I put that out as a matter of fact, in no way a threat. Just another thing we could all agree on. Anyway, I read that one. We were back in the script now. But I broke the wall again, saying to the audience, "His life depends on it." I was trying to be emphatic, but all I accomplished, I think, was more ambiguity.

But the audience seemed to understand. They let me know that. Don't ask me how. Well, half of them were my students and that was one of their most recent lessons.

I wasn't threatening the man. My character wasn't either. That's not what I meant. At some early point even Julio knew his life was not in danger. And, don't we all want someone who sees the big picture to stop us on the street one day and tell us what we absolutely need to do to save our lives? Whatever I'm busy with at that moment, I won't mind the interruption.

I took a legal pad from where it sat on the dresser, and a pen from my pocket. "Write," I told him.

"About what?" he asked.

"What you saw. Through there." Pointing with my pen. "Take another look if you don't remember."

Granted I had no idea what he had seen, but I was pretty sure that Kyla and Jermayne were in there. That they'd picked up the key at the front desk and let themselves in. And now were doing their homework, just hanging out, but if it was anything like how Kyla and Jermayne hung out in my classroom, there was a chance that we'd get some good writing out of him: either he would react and reveal the racist engine that ran him, and the Senator too, or maybe he would be truer to his better self and see the beauty beyond the form, as I always tried to do. There'd be an image, an inspiration, and click—

"You're out of your mind," he said, his voice taking on gravel. He looked around for support but saw only solidarity—our hope for him—in the other faces on the stage. He looked toward the audience and saw total involvement there. They liked what they were seeing. Friendly, too: they were there to support him.

He looked back down at his script. Making sure the words he'd just said were written there. They were.

The pause went on too long. I looked at the script and I felt for the first time what a trained actor must feel when a character takes him over. When the lines you're supposed to say transfer their potential energy right to you. I took a deep breath.

"Come on, you sonofabitch." I half-snarled at him. "Write me two or three good paragraphs. Then we're out of here. You just gotta get past what someone else has put in your brain."

"How do I do that?" he asked. It wasn't a whimper, but it came damn close.

"How do I know?" I read in a hoarse whisper. "How does anybody write? What the fuck are we here for?" There were several gasps from the audience: my students who didn't know I used that word. I'd have to deny that tomorrow. Or I could just show them where Cheeto had typed it in. And this:

"I can teach till I'm blue in the face but at some point you have to take the initiative!"

I glanced at Garth, who had been pacing nervously. His cue—

He bent down, wheeled the Senator's chief go-to writer guy ninety degrees around, flung him like a duffel bag on a dock, and flattened his face against that place in the wall, right eye to the hole. Edward snorted involuntarily and swung his right arm ineffectually toward Garth's midsection. I pushed my pen against the soft spot just under his shoulder blade, too hard, forcing another quick breath out from him.

I told you I'm not good at stuff like this. Don't hire me to drive the kidnap car!

I hurt him.

And right away I saw, I felt, the audience waver—

That was my fault: it was in the script but I took it too far.

Chapter Twenty

I looked down at the text, pretending I had lost my place, nothing more. I—

"Excuse me. Could I interrupt for a minute?" a deep, pleasant voice asked from the back row.

More audience participation. It was Jermayne's older brother, Bill. The one who no longer lived at home. The street-walking social worker. Ran martial arts classes and drug-counseling in a storefront nearby. He was also a weight-lifter, a serious personal trainer. Jermayne had told me that before moving back home he'd been a Hollywood stunt double and a floor man in human pyramids. He must have been invited—maybe Jermayne figured we'd need someone like him in the room?

"I'm sorry," Bill said, "but I can't sit and watch a play if I think someone's about to get hurt. You all don't want to hurt the guy, do you?" He was looking at Garth. He stood up. He had a shiny, hazel-colored face, a large gold ring in his left ear, a shaved head, an easy smile, disarmingly gentle. He was bigger and stronger than Garth, and a whole lot more relaxed.

"No, Sir," Garth said automatically. We were supposed to be doing theatre, after all.

"Yeah, well, you can make this look a lot more real," Bill said.

"Without doing any harm? Actors get hurt when they forget to choreograph their fight moves and get carried away by the moment. Cheeto my man, when you put out work like this you have to hire a fight director."

Cheeto said, "for a staged reading?" That got a laugh.

"From the looks of it," Bill said. "It's gettin' too real."

He addressed the rest of the audience: "Sorry. Do we have a minute here? Teacher said feel free to join in."

Then he looked at me. "Nobody's double-parked, right?"

I looked down at Edward. "You in a hurry to get out of here?"

"Now that you mention it—" he ad-libbed, but all he got for that was a laugh from the crowd. His best laugh of the evening. He smiled back.

Bill came on to our stage. "I'll show you a trick," he said. To the Senator's assistant. "What's your name again?"

"Edward."

"How ya doin', Edward. My name is Bill."

"Pleased to meet you," Edward said. I've never heard that said more sincerely. They shook hands. I wish I had a photo of that handshake. The colors, the relative size of the hands. The offer of help. One of the hands not wanting to let go. Ever.

"All right, Edward. I know you're just a volunteer, but I can see you're into it. You're all into it. Got me convinced." To the audience: "How 'bout you?"

There were yesses and lots of claps and one stentorian teen-age yowl of approval, and then a spontaneous round of applause.

Bill faced Garth. "You got a career, Man. You got that soldier part down." Garth smiled. All his friends in the audience laughed, including me. Nice moment of relaxation. An out-breath. Then all six-foot-four, two hundred sixty steely pounds of Bill punched Garth as hard as he could in the stomach. We all gasped. Garth flinched, but that was all. Then he peered down to check whether his navel was still there.

"Looked real, huh?" said Bill. "Lesson number one: pull your punches."

He looked at me. "Got that?"

"Got it," I said.

"Good. That was for you."

I took that in. If I had any thought that I had got away with something, I hadn't.

Then he turned to Edward. "Okay, Edward. You're next. I'm gonna grab your hair." He loomed over him, still hunched over in the chair. "I'm gonna hold it, real loosely, but to the audience it'll look like I have two clenched handfuls of hair. Feel that? I'm not hurting you, am I?"

"No," Edward said.

"I'm just resting my hands on Edward's head. Not giving you too much weight, am I?"

"No."

"Good. Now you bring your two hands up over mine and grab them hard. I won't change the grip I have on your hair." Edward did that. He reached up and took one of Bill's hands in one of his, and circled Bill's wrist with the other hand.

"How's that feel?" Bill asked.

"Okay."

"You can grip me even harder," Bill said.

"Okay."

"That's better," said Bill. "Now you have the control. Now what you do is move my hands, with yours, any way you want to. Up, down; back and forth. Your head will follow your hands' lead. Go on, really move me. And make some sounds. The audience will think I'm shaking you around and you're trying to stop me. But actually I'm not doing anything. Just going along for the ride."

Edward did what Bill had told him to. It looked real. Sounded real.

"You're the motor," Bill said. "You decide where to go. So

nothing we do together surprises you. And the danger of you getting a twisted neck or accidentally banging your head on the wall is almost non-existent. What do you think?"

"It's much better," said Edward; "I was beginning to think I was going to get hurt."

"So was I," said Bill, "and so was the audience. Were you thinking that?" he asked them. The audience said yes.

"Now that's all right. We want you to worry a little. It helps the drama along. But we have to be safe. Okay?"

We all agreed. Before he returned to his seat, Bill brought Garth over and had him try the illusion, Garth's hands on Edward's head. Edward doing the moves.

"Does it still look real?" Bill asked the audience. It did.

"Sorry for the interruption," he said. "You can go back to what you were doing."

"Thank you," said Edward.

"Hey, any time," said Bill.

The audience clapped for him as he left the stage.

"No," he said; "don't clap for me. Give it up for these guys; they're doing a helluva job. You too, Miss."

I was just happy Bill didn't know who and what was on the other side of the door. Teachers don't just go and rent hotel rooms for their student couples. Must be some law against that. He'd have to intervene there, too.

I glanced at my script, found my place. We all went back to where we had been, held a mutual freeze for a second, then: action. I leaned close to Edward's ear. "What the fuck are we here for?" I read again, in the stage whisper. Upset, also proud, to have to repeat that word in front of my students.

Garth elbowed me out of the way. He grabbed Edward by the head with one hand, the shoulder with the other. Edward's hands flew to grab both of Garth's. He, Edward, pitched forward like that duffel on the dock, pitched *himself* forward, and his face

came to rest against that place in the wall, right eye to the hole.
Pulling my punch, I pushed my hand that held the pen lightly on
the soft spot just under his right shoulder blade, and heard him
let a quick—scripted—breath out from between his tightened
lips.

All pretend. Edward was totally in the scene, I thought—he was
Julio Parra over the hump and about to engage in his craft. And
he was in charge.

"You're gonna get out of here real soon if you want to." I told
him in his ear. "All you have to do is, write the story. What you
see. What you feel about what you see. You look. You see. You feel.
You write. It's simple."

He still hesitated. Maybe not wanting to have that view again.
In the next moment Sarah came and elbowed me out of the way.
She had been standing to the side through all this, ceding the performing space briefly to the men. Not a place she could ever stay
in willingly for too long. She pressed against Edward from behind
and dug all ten of her fingers hard into his shoulders. That's the
way it looked, anyway. It looked real.

"Just go ahead and write," she said. "Do it." Her face was low
down toward the top of his head and she seemed to pull him violently back against her breasts, though I knew she had taken in
Bill's lesson, but then which of the two of them had initiated that
move? Then their bodies bent forward as one, she pressing him
twisted into the wall. Her hair a partial curtain over him. Garth
loomed above both of them, hand on his holster. I took two strides
toward the door we had all come in and stood there like nobody's
leaving this room. The old newspaper article had unfolded itself
from my pocket like a time-lapse flower and the scene I'd pictured
finally, finally, breathed itself almost perfectly into life. I guess I
had my Hawthorne moment then.

"None of this goes out of this room?" I heard Edward ad lib as
if from very far away.

"Not any of it," Sarah whispered; "you have my word."

Garth looked with menace at the audience. "You won't say nothin', will ya?"

A collective "no" came back to him. Audience functioning as a single organism now.

"We're all doing each other a big favor here," I said. "Way I see it, you make out the best. You leave the ranks of the zealots. You don't like them anyway. We give your writing career a little jump-start. And that's just for starters. This is your night."

This last just leaped out of me unconsidered and unscripted, but I said it looking straight at Sarah, who shot me a look of irritation, accusation, understanding, anticipation, regret, farewell. Of a sort.

"How do I know I can trust you?" he asked.

"Scout's honor, Sir," Garth said. He flicked a hand toward his right brow, probably thinking, shit, when will I ever get to salute someone, anyone, in an official capacity?

Then Sarah relaxed her grip a little and, leaning to the left, bore her eyes into his. He turned back to the hole in the wall. He stayed there.

The audience leaned forward as one, so present in the metaphor, so there for the performance, as if all they had ever wanted to do for all their lives was to look through that little hole; together they had become the leaning, twisted body and he was their surrogate eye; they seemed to respond to every level of discomfort Edward was feeling: his confusion his anxiety his contortion his doubt for the future. When he was finished looking, he turned back toward our room and gave a look that asked for help.

I put the legal pad on his lap and lay the pen on top of it. My choice: I figured it would be the friendly touch of the familiar for him. All over his city, in the clear light of day, lobbyists and lawyers billed 500 dollars an hour for writing on yellow tablets. He looked to all of our faces. None of us said a word. I didn't know what he would do.

When he started to write, we all kind of looked away, but skew to each other, as if this was a private act—contrition? mastur-bation?—we had no desire to watch. Now no one wanted to be there. A hush in the hotel room: you could hear the noise of the pen on the paper. I like that moment in a theatre when a loud and flurried scene turns quiet all of a sudden. You realize the dialogue has been rushing by, filling the space; you realize how much you were needing silence. And then it came at just the right time.

After a while, probably shorter than it felt, he just stopped. He held the pen still. Writer's cramp? Now he didn't know what to do with the paper. Looked at Garth, who shrugged. And looked at me.

I took the pad from his hand. "You game for this?" I asked him.

"I guess so."

"So hang out for a minute while I correct this paper. That's what I do best."

I sat on the near edge of the bed and read it. Got out my red pen and went at it with a vengeance. Instant disappointment. The man was dodging, I thought, not up to the task, or holding it all in. No more than a dozen lines. Like a lazy student trying to get away with doing as little as possible. Questionable content, way off message. I don't even remember it.

I rolled my eyes at Sarah, shook my head. Some guy you picked. A rope-a-dope. Visible slump of her shoulders with a pursed-lip outbreath. Audience seeing that, mirrored the gesture. They got it, instantly. They didn't need to read what he wrote.

Not what I wanted; I could do better than this. Why even bother? Teachers feel this sometime, when students disappoint. We talk about it in the faculty room. It doesn't happen to me much but it happens. You lay out the assignment, put your soul into it; they blow it off. Maybe they're just having a bad day. They came home late the night before and half-drunk Dad beat up on them.

I'd wanted a power vision: what Edward saw, what he felt, Jermayne and Kyla—I wanted the bodies, the surprising challenge like the nude woman gave Julio! I wanted him tricked, abused, but then excited: it's the young woman he met several weeks ago, that body he wanted to see more of, even all of; the young man with her is black, the synecdoche—part for the whole—the right wing is against affirmative action of any sort—confronting his own prejudice—

I wanted it all. I wanted to see a dam burst on the paper. Why did the man think I asked him to write what he felt? I'd seen Sarah squeeze him hard, saw him nearly wince when her nails dug into his shoulders. He must have felt that. No faking there. Hands of pain and reassurance. Didn't he feel her body against his back, her breasts, her mound of whatever it's called, pressing into him? Did he hear her breath in his ear? Her breath turning the corner of his cheek and making it to his nose. Breath like a promise. I know that fucking breath! Couldn't he write about that? Where was all this? I saw none of it. I could have written it so much better myself!

Now I was stuck, not knowing how to continue. I stabbed the red pen across the paper.

Feeling my dejection, Sarah caught it, too.

Turned off, I guessed, to everything—to Edward, to the play, the scene, my idea, *me,* our always partial life together—she swept past us, actors, audience, anything in or near her way, and out of the room. Slammed the door. One of her sudden exits I was so accustomed to. But wished she hadn't picked this particular moment. The audience didn't like her leaving. Cheeto shook his head: not in the script.

My nightmare was coming true. Deserted by my comrades right when it became too late to turn back. Who would be next?

I was also exasperated. It's okay to get exasperated—done that with some of my best students; it energizes a teachable moment if you do it right. I tore off the top sheet of paper, gave it back to

Edward; I felt the scene go ugly. He balled it up tight and stuck it in his pocket. He didn't look at my corrections. Crunched his shoulders up around his ears like a truant kid about to get whipped. Eyes really wild now, finger-combing his hair, but not for grooming.

He's losing it, I think; the man wants out of the scene. Sarah was his only ally, his grounding. Her exit was not in the script. I whisper hoarsely in his ear, stay with it; she'll be back (although I didn't know that for sure); we're coming to the end.

Write, correct, and rewrite: that's what it's all about. Revising. You're going to get it right. I got nothing back from his eyes.

I turned to the audience. "Tell you what, we're gonna take a real quick intermission here. Don't go anywhere, just stand up and stretch. Bathroom's right there if you need it. Cheeto, I guess this play has two acts."

The guests were grateful for the pause.

Chapter Twenty-One

Seeing the audience rise and stretch, Edward moved to do the same. Both of us, Garth and I, still in character, instantly stopped him. Tough in the hand but gentle like Bill taught us, friendly with our voices.

"Stay in the freeze, man; don't break it!" Garth warned him. As if to say, don't spoil the magic we've got going here; something amazing is happening. He retrieved Edward's dropped script and pushed it back into his hands.

"Yeah, You're doing great!" I said. I only half meant it.

He smiled weakly. "Can I have a drink?"

"No!" Garth hollered, startling the audience, who stood or sat, guard down, half-paying attention. But he handed him a water bottle. I couldn't see the wink for the sunglasses, but I knew it was there. I decided I would not want Garth to be my captor should they ever disappear me. Too mercurial. Give me a torturer I can trust.

Some of the audience sat back down, startled. Edward felt bad for a moment, I could tell, then let it go. Part of the show. He's a trouper, I thought. I'll give him that. He made no move to depart, though clearly most of his commitment had departed with Sarah. We'd have to make the second act much shorter. I beckoned to Cheeto to come up for a conference.

"Cheeto, meet Edward. Edward, Cheeto."

Cheeto gave him his biggest smile and they shook hands. Cheeto thanked him for participating.

"I don't think I had a choice," he said.

There was a real edge of bitterness in the voice. I welcomed it. It was better than nothing. Easy to explain, too, to me anyway: he was feeling Sarah's absence, contemplating its permanence and not liking how that felt. I felt it, too. I could have told him that she always came back, but I refrained. Anyway I wasn't sure.

"You taking notes?" I asked Cheeto. "Lot of gaps to fill in."

"Yeah," he said; "thanks."

He turned to Edward. "You're awesome, man. Now just help me get the ending right."

He gave Edward a spontaneous *abrazo*, and Edward let out the biggest sigh I ever saw emerge from a man. Like he would fall over if Cheeto weren't nearly propping him up.

"I'll try," he said. He could have walked out, but maybe he thought that remaining would give him his best shot at seeing Sarah again.

I waved Cheeto back to his seat. He gave his mamá a big hug

and Garth blinked the clamp light once or twice. It looked like everyone was ready.

Edward sat back in the chair and turned toward the wall, I mean the interior door. I went and opened the main door, checked up and down the hall for a sign of Sarah. None.

Back in my spot, I took in a breath to say my next thing, but there was Bill right next to me, hand on my right shoulder. I don't know how the big guy sneaked up that way. And he took up almost the whole playing area. And why were people always putting their hands on my shoulder?

"Just checking in," he said. "Edward, you okay?"

Edward looked up. "Yeah, I guess."

Bill turned to me. "Any fights in the second half?"

"Not really," I said. "None planned, anyway."

"Okay," said Bill. "But listen, the next time you do this play you need to choreograph. You have fights, you need to write the beats down. Number them. And every time you perform it you rehearse every fight by the numbers, first in slo-mo, and then speed it up. That way no one ever gets hurt."

"Did you get that, Edward?" I asked him.

If you can nod your head yes and shake it no in one move, that's what Edward did. "Next time" was not a welcome thought for him.

"Thanks, Bill," I said as he returned to his seat, and "*Disappeared,* by Romero Romero. Act Two, folks. This is where it's really a work in progress."

Edward turned more toward the audience. "I'd like to go now," he ad-libbed.

I ad-libbed right back. "We'd like you to. We just want to see this through first."

"So, are you forcing me to stay?"

"Nobody's forcing anybody. It's a play. We got a few more pages of script, a bit of improv, and there's an audience waiting for the pay-off. People like good theater. That's what they're getting."

Garth moved closer to him, almost touching. We were all almost touching. "You got any place better to be?"

"Maybe."

"You gonna walk around the halls, looking for the babe? Hotels don't like that."

"I don't know, Garth," I said, louder than I needed to; "maybe the man just wants to sign out and go home."

I put the question to the audience. "Think we should let him?"

The question pulled the audience, who were still idling, back in.

"No" they all hollered. Except for maybe a few who felt bad for him. Especially Cheeto's mom, who understood the question on a whole other level. Too shy to speak out, but her eyes pleaded with me to let the man leave. Please. Now. While he still can.

Edward had become her brother now, a man unable, on the face of it, to give his captors what they wanted. For which omission they wouldn't let him go. They would kill him. She felt this so strongly, she turned to Cheeto and started talking excitedly in Spanish.

But Cheeto had this intense expression that script writers and directors get; I've seen it—shut out of the action on the stage, but so involved, they rock back and forth in their seats, knowing the important line about to be said, the good moment that's being set up, the laugh or the audience inbreath that's coming, knowing how it's all supposed to end, but still lost in wonderment, doubt, fear. And trying to hurry the action along; no matter how fast it moves. You know it so well, you want it to move faster, faster than the audience's collective mind. You can't sit still; you drum the script on your thigh, you're thinking come on, actors, we know where we're going: get there! Get there before *they* do!

And meanwhile his mamá, Elena, kept talking, mile a minute deep Salvadoran Spanish. I heard ten kinds of pleading in her voice. I didn't get a word of it.

Moreover, this was a staged reading, not a full production; more writing would have to be done. That was surely in Cheeto's mind, too. Everything was spinning for him, no forward progress: Cheeto kept rocking; his mother's voice rose. Suddenly he got up like he was going to holler, take over from me, be a director, or write more lines on the spot, to break the fourth wall yet again— his mamá kept up with the Spanish, didn't stop for a second, and now Becca half stood up like she wanted to shake the playwright by the shoulder nearest her.

Was I paranoid? Or tripping? They threw looks at me, too, and not the sweet condescending ones like I'd gotten used to, but harsher, like okay Mr. B, this was your bloody idea, we're all here because of you, it's time to tell us, just tell us, what happens next! The whole story! What are you still leaving out?

I looked back at Cheeto, gesturing with my now useless script. And in the next moment—as if it was written that way—Garth, and I, and Cheeto, and the invited guests, everyone I could see, all stared with one mind at the only person in the hotel room, the old stone colonial convent cell, whatever, who had the power to move us to the next moment. If an audience can ever be said to have one mind, one concentrated focus, they did, and they sent all their power to the man in the chair—

And just then something must have gone click in Edward, like, this is how he would get out of here, straight ahead, in a hurry. He turned from staring at us, everyone all at once, even the empty place next to him where his only friend had been, and placed his eye against the hole.

I mean, he didn't just place it. He moved slow and expertly, so there would be no doubt what he was doing. No need for a fake push. He did it all by himself. It was like he was inviting everyone to come along and make the move with him. Then he flung both arms wide and pressed them against the door. The forward motion and the flinging of the arms sent the chair tipping over backwards on its own—awesome sound effect—and he stood, half-crouched, half-hung there like we were all looking at a crucifixion from behind.

The light from the scoop above splashed down his back, picking out shadowed wrinkles in his clothes—there was something at once hypnotic, gorgeous, suspended, about the way he leaned there. Like a dancer by Matisse, or like a cave painting, I thought—

Julio Parra had come to life for me; I wished Sarah could see it. For long moments nothing stirred, but the audience never grew restless. If, in their intent contemplation, they hungered for a movement, he did not disappoint them. At such moments, even the most minimal movements satisfy. There it was: a slight tapping of his right hand fingers on the wall, and then, the sporadic rise and fall of shoulder blades signifying the great work his lungs were doing.

There's a theatre technique I've heard about called "wait-for-it." Was coined, I think, by Debureau, the great French pantomime. You hold a moment for the longest possible time, and if the climactic move is coming, you wait till you can absolutely feel the audience's hunger for completion, and then, when no one can stand it anymore, you make that quick and finishing move.

I just stood there watching him through all that long wait.

Garth, concerned for the man, reached down with great delicacy and put the chair back where it had been. On the spike tapes. Just in time. Edward made the move; he sat back down in the place where the chair should have been, and it was! He grabbed the legal pad from the dresser right next to him, and started writing. The audience clapped wildly. Garth, ever in character, hushed them with a look and a threatening gesture to his holster.

Cheeto sat down. He threw out his two arms and embraced the women at his sides, mother and girlfriend. Edward was writing quickly: inspired, I could see, maybe risking all at last. I paced and breathed, couldn't think what else to do, then I made as if to check the door–the real one, the one we all had entered—and was almost struck on my face by its forceful opening.

Sarah hurried in. She passed by me—no look, no stop—on her way to her place in the scene.

Edward was hunched over his legal pad, hand moving fast like his thoughts. The audience whispered when she came in.

"Shhh," Garth ordered again.

They quieted instantly. Sarah took up her old position. Hands on Edward's shoulders. He shifted a little, distracted, and Garth moved to hold him down but didn't have to. He kept writing. I paced again, as in a cage, around our tiny section of floor. I stopped and leaned back against the imaginary wall that defined the cell, turned my back to the audience and waited till my eyes eventually met Sarah's, back from wherever she'd been.

We held each other then in our glance for as long as we could, but both instinctively trying not to distract, to keep acting, to catch the focus of the audience and guide it where it ought to be, to draw the moment out, give the man time to write, and, at the same time, trying to read each other's thoughts behind the opaque expressions. An unexpected distance rose between us. Old dynamics change when you are thrown together in a little room. Embarrassed, maybe, to see what we saw in each other's look, we took a big step towards each other and embraced. It can be helpful to do that when looking into eyes is too disturbing. Puts you past the glance.

Edward finishes writing. He stands up. He puts the legal pad in my hand. Gives me back the pen. Whatever was on the paper, whatever was in the script, the assignment is over. So is the show. It's over.

The four of us, me, Garth, Sarah, and Edward, in that order, stand in a row and bow. As if we've planned it! To huge applause. People call our names, call "Cheeto!" and clap him on the back. He comes through the chairs and joins us in the bow. The entire audience stands. Becca produces a bunch of flowers for him, wrapped in see-through plastic. Sarah's arm is over Edward's shoulder, in a gesture of thanks, of solidarity, of something more. We're all smiling. Everyone still applauding.

No one has any idea what just happened.

"Did you get all that, Cheeto?" I ask. He nods yes, waving pages of notes he's scrawled.

Garth takes out his phone and does some magic with his fingers. Suddenly "*Sandstorm*"—old techno beat—blasts from the speakers, guaranteed, I guess he is thinking, to keep the audience clapping, and dancing in rhythm—which they now do—and their volume, and the bluetooth volume, maxes out in the small hotel room.

Alex sends me his most intense desk-clerk look ever, like, Mr. B, get some control here, what will the other guests think, and I'm thinking, week night in a non-season, are there *really* any other guests here, Alex, but if so, didn't you make sure to put them on another floor? I know you did. So I do nothing.

Cheeto waves his flowers over his head, in rhythm. No one wants the beat to stop. Till eventually Garth fades it, slow, down, and out.

I want to say, so it's perfectly clear, that what Cheeto wrote, and what the actors filled in, including those other two on the other side of that door, was *art*, no less and no more. The audience clapped because it was good, and because it was painful, and because it was over, and because everyone had some new revelation to take home with them and think about. But no one saw the same thing. You could have squeezed a hundred people into that room and quizzed them after, and every single one of them would have had a different story to tell about what they just saw, a different idea of who and what Edward saw through the aperture and—most important of all—a different and unique feeling in their heart, to cue up and remember for years to come.

The applause ends. The small crowd starts to file out. But the room is so small, no one can get out without being close to us, to the actors. We're like a receiving line after a wedding. Everyone stops to say something. Handshakes. Embraces. Thanks.

Alex Mercouri shakes his head and shakes my hand and exits. I tell him I'll come by tomorrow to talk. At check-out time.

To fix the door, too. Owner of the establishment deserves a little explanation. Bill is next, and I thank him for the right help at the right moment. Without him, I don't think we could have made it to where we did.

He waves it off. "Wow, what an actor," he says to Edward. He offers his big strong hand to Edward to shake, to grip again. And Edward smiles and says thank you. Looking resplendent in his dishevelment.

Bolo holds out a program and a pen. "Can I please have your autograph, Sir?" he asks Edward.

That's a word I've never ever heard him use. "Sir."

Edward signs. He is still breathing hard.

Cheeto's mom and Becca, the last remaining audience members, depart slowly. Becca and Cheeto are almost supporting his mother. She has been crying. Has been too much for her, re-living her brother's capture and certain torture. His disappearance. As I said, she doesn't do English well but will have understood the story on another level—I promise myself I will invite her out, talk to her sometime soon, about all that she experienced, sitting through this play. There will be some harm I'll have to apologize for. I make a gesture of hand and face to Cheeto that roughly means to say, good work, see you tomorrow.

It's going to take us weeks to critique this and get it just right.

The ending needs a little work.

Edward looks at me directly in the eye for the first time that night. Expectant student waiting for the teacher's response. He thinks maybe I will get out my red pencil, do my correcting right there while we wait: slash, underline, stars, "NO!!" "Illogical!" "Unclear!"

Instead I just glance at the first couple of sentences. "I think you've got it now," I tell him; "I'll look at it later."

He nods.

"You know," I say, "if you're serious about this, writing from the heart, getting critiqued and all, I know a really good group that would love to have you join. Maybe time for me to join it, too."

He says yes, he would like that, and thank you.

"They're tough though," I say; "no bullshit. Lots of revision."

He looks grateful for the vision of that. Then, improvising, I turn toward the door. "You two can stay here," I say looking mostly at Sarah; "it's paid for."

Neither of them looks at the other. Or at me. Got that one right, I think.

I go to the door that has the hole, and I press a little glob of carpenter's putty into it. Will do for tonight. For the last five minutes I've been kneading it warm and supple in my left hand, in my pocket, Captain Queeg-like cure for nervousness.

Must have worked because now I don't feel nervous at all.

The wood putty fills the hollow place and I flatten my palm against it. The window to that universe has closed. Privacy on both sides. I felt that would be helpful. Messy but important. Sand it smooth tomorrow.

How about putty for the hole in my heart?

Sarah touches my arm as I walk by her, seeking something from me. Understanding? Agreement? To last till the next time we meet. I give her what I can, I do. Silently, with looks. But all I'm thinking is, don't stop, must keep moving.

"Come on, Soldier," I say to Garth; "I'll spin you home." Edward says nothing in the area of good-bye. His attention has shifted to this room. He has traded one necessity for another.

I wave Edward's paper at him. "I'll correct this and get it back to you."

"Okay."

"Keep in touch."

Garth and I, we don't look back when we walk out and shut the door.

I think I learned that move from him.

Chapter Twenty-Two

We drive around a bit. Stop for some food at a diner, one of those places they serve breakfast any hour of the day or night. Just a cup of coffee and an English muffin for me. Eggs, pancakes, hash browns and bacon for the big guy.

"On me," I say.

"Thanks, Mr. B."

Small talk, we're both mostly quiet, inside ourselves. Readjusting to real time, and real space too, and taking time to do that. Having just seen a good drama will do that to you. You need time to come back from how deep you went.

Back in the car, I drive through the peaceful night in the city. It's a dark night, and Garth has put his shades away. Suddenly, breaking the silence, he says, "Hey. Can you drop me off at my girlfriend's house?"

"It's after midnight, Garth. Is she expecting you?"

"I don't think so, Sir, but she's always up late studying. She's pre-med."

He directs me to her neighborhood. It's not on my way but what's the hurry? There's her big Chevy I've heard about, parked on the street. Garth's initiation place. Maroon low rider, more than twenty years old. Where did she come up with that ride? It's parked in front of prime three-story wooden student housing. He points out her light blazing on the third floor, the window half-open, shade up. I haven't met her, but he has told me about her in his writing—more, actually, than I wanted to know: the dazzling face, the curly hair, the body, the eagerness to teach him everything.

Through the window I see a big red-and-black Che Guevara poster on the wall. The famous Angel Korda photo of the Heroic Guerrilla in his prime. Looks like it's right over the head of the bed. I glance at the young man sitting next to me on the front seat. Speaking of his appearance and his politics, he could have fit right into the infantry who hunted Che down in the Bolivian mountains and shot him full of all those holes, then tore off a piece of a shirt or a finger to take home to the kids.

"What do you do when you're up there, boy?" I ask; "turn Che's face to the wall?"

"No, Sir." It is a gentle no, as if he is gifting me with a revelation of more tolerance—more solidarity, even—than I ever imagined he had. Then he sits there for a moment as if not wanting this part of the night to end just yet.

"We did it, Mr. B." His face has the broadest smile I've ever seen on it.

"Yeah," I say; "we did it."

"Wow."

"Whatever it was that we did," I say.

"Right."

Then, with a mock pulling of rank, I add, "Just don't write about it. Any of this shows up in one of your stories, I'll flunk you. And break your thumbs."

"Yes, Sir," he says. "It's all yours."

There it was. How did he know?

I'm going to break my word to Edward—did I promise him

anything? I don't remember—and go home and write reams about it. You can't trust a writer.

Then Garth leans toward me in the dark car and touches me on the right shoulder. My touchable place. In the quick circular dab I feel a message of brotherhood, as if, in spite of the teacher-student relationship and the pseudo-military ranking, we're equals now, having passed through something that the two of us will always understand better than anyone, and it may always be nearly impossible to talk about, but we will do that, for years.

There is also sympathy in the gesture. I can feel it. He understands the sacrifice I've made. Three couples are getting together in this endless night, and I am going home alone.

Wait. What? Three, you ask? Yes, three. To know that number, you have to remember what, who, was on the other side of the door.

Garth sees all that and understands. Most of us are all blindly bumping into each other in the dark and he has the modern soldier's night vision, the command of the situation. That's okay, I think, patting the pages in my shirt pocket, I've got homework to correct, and I also have thoughts brimming for the first time in a long while in the writer's part of my brain.

Art will be there to console me.

He swings out of the car, closes the door quietly, and leans back in the passenger window, still not eager to break the spell. "Interesting night," he says.

"So far," I reply, indicating I share his expectation of what's to come. "But get rid of that word 'interesting.' Has no place in good writing."

"Sorry, Sir."

"One thing I learned tonight is, it's true what they say: you get to know somebody, almost anybody, you find something about them you can like."

"Yes, Sir. Even the guy you'd shoot under other circumstances."

"That's right," I say. "You get to know him instead, really know him, chances are you'll put your gun away."

Garth smiles again: "Should I put that on my list of Stuff They Don't Want Us to Know?"

"You bet. How long's that list getting?" I ask him.

"Pretty long," he says; "I've been with you almost two years."

"Have a good night, Garth. See you in school tomorrow," I tell him. We're both reminded of the routine world we'll re-enter in a few hours.

"I'll be there, Sir." he says. "Right at the first bell. Half the fun is seeing people's faces when she drops me off in the morning."

"Garth." I say.

"Yes, Sir?"

"Protect yourself. And her."

"Yes, Sir." Boy Scout training. He turns and marches up the short path to her cluttered front porch. Rings the buzzer. Sound of her chair scuffing, up on the third floor.

Later I climb the stairs slowly to my apartment. Outdoor steps, street door, key, fourteen more steps up, inner door, key. I move slowly, reluctant to punctuate the evening as over, period. For months I have been looking at absolutely everything through this tiny point of focus. The gift from Julio. Whatever passed by me, whatever I noticed, had to be there in that particular point of view. That little four-inch article in the paper became what it talked about. Now it's gone.

Pick any paper. Any news. In the features section, you might find several random human-interest stories. Any one could be a focus point into a place where you could get carried away. Now I sound like a prologue to a fifties black-and-white tv show.

"It's night-time in the city. Flickering lights from apartment windows. In every one—"

Sleep is going to have to wait a while. My house, my own kitchen, welcome me with a warmth I don't always appreciate enough. I don't mind being alone in here. My comfort place. I pour myself a beer, taking the time to choose a favorite glass from the freezer. I put some pretzels in a bowl.

I sit at the kitchen table, running my hand over its smooth top.

I've talked about it so many times now; may as well describe it. It's vintage late-fifties chrome-and-yellow-enamel, with four matching chrome and yellow-vinyl chairs. There's a faint faux-marbling in both the enamel and the vinyl. I bought the whole set for sixty dollars at a flea market.

It would look just right in a Pillsbury ad in an old *Life* magazine. 1954. Colors subtle like in a hand-tinted photo. Magazine ads just tentatively acquiring color, evolving toward the total saturation we have now.

Smiling blonde white housewife in a full plaid skirt and yellow apron swirls up from her open oven and is about to place a steaming angel-food cake on a trivet on her brand new chrome kitchen table. You can really see the steam.

Two combed children, a big sister and a little brother, are smiling, standing behind those same matching yellow chairs—only they're brand sparkling new—gripping them with their clean hands. Dad's coming in the door, home from work, smiling, his wide necktie swinging as he reaches up to remove his fedora. The cocker spaniel's bottom is in the air, bobbed tail waving, front legs prostrating toward Dad. There's a big radio on the shelf by the window, and Hank Williams is singing "Hey good lookin', watcha got cookin'?" You'll have to take my word for that. A wind lifts the calico curtain between the door and the stove, and through the window you can see the big maroon Chevy parked out on the street. The soles of Garth's girlfriend's two bare feet are just visible, pressed against the backseat window.

Chapter Twenty-Three

I think about Garth and I smile. Then I think of what must be happening elsewhere in the city. I go there in my imagination discreetly, knowing Sarah will tell me all about it later. Most of it, anyway, if I ask her. When I ask her.

She did tell me, but not right away. Four days later she was waiting for me outside my house when I biked home from school. Had left a message that she would be there. I hadn't seen her since that night. We sat outside on the stoop. It was a pretty afternoon, blossoms in the breeze, inviting us to stay outside. Like Cyrano and Roxanne on the sun-warmed bench in the nunnery garden, it occurred to me, but I fought against the heartrending nostalgia of that scene. I still fight against it.

"You'll have to transfer your affections to someone else," she said.

"I figured that." I said. "Wish me luck."

She linked her arm through mine. "I would say I'm sorry but that doesn't seem to fit."

"We always knew," I said.

"We did. It's still a surprise though."

I was silent for a moment. I was thinking about the word "affection." We would still have that, no need to transfer that. We leaned our heads sideways towards each other and kissed each other a kind of embarrassed good-bye. Good-bye to one part of us, but not to each other. We could go back to being what we used to be for years: confidantes, good friends.

We must have swapped more words of wit to make light of how we both felt—"displacement gestures," Desmond Morris calls them—but I remember none of them. I was working hard to control my emotions, or at least fully understand them. Feeling the responsibility, also, for what had happened.

If, on second thought now, I had wanted to keep her—a silly expression I'd never use—and had in fact lost her, I had no one to blame but myself. Aside from all that, I was waiting for her story:

The door closes behind Garth and me.

Both of them, Sarah and Edward stand and contemplate the closed hotel room, the empty theater, the sealed crack in the inner door. Everyone who filled the room before has departed: the audience, the other actors. The chairs are stacked against the wall. The room is separated from everywhere else. Their eyes eventually find each other. They're like two would-be suicides who, surprised to find each other on the same ledge, contemplate leaping together.

"What just happened?" he asks her.

She continues looking at him. Would like to say, the play's over, but thinks that would be too trite. Or too like scripted, anyway. Not knowing what to say yet, she holds on to her silence.

"I just made a bargain, didn't I?" he asks, almost irritated; "some kind of deal?"

She gives him a look like a wise woman from the Bible. The one she was named for, or Esther, or Bathsheba. Supplicant man comes to ask the wise woman what he needs to learn in order to survive.

"Yes, you did," she says.

"What kind of deal? Was he the Devil, and you're Helen of Troy?" he asks, his sense of humor returning. "Who does that make me?" While saying this he discovers himself in her arms, not sure how he got there. His body vibrates with recognition, as if he knows the woman under the clothes. He feels himself surrounded, looks past her at nothing. At the suddenly unpeopled room.

She changes the subject. "Are you okay? To stay here?" There is unmistakable concern in her voice.

He nods. He has been in white water till now, and she is suddenly a peaceful eddy against a rock. He feels it may be a temporary shelter; at the same time he realizes he is not a captive; some of what happens next is up to him. He could, if he wanted, pull away lightly from her—who is there to stop him?—and leave the room. Leave the hotel, the city. Find his car. Leave. Go home. He doesn't move.

"We don't hurt each other," she asks.

"No," he says. And then he adds, "Never."

The word is out before he thinks about it.

She hears that one word, "never," like a small, powerful hole drilled into a wall, offering her a new place to look through at herself. Someone who pronounces "never" to her has already conceived the "always" wedded to that thought.

She moves away from him; instantly, he misses her. She pulls down the bedspread, blanket, and top sheet. She goes into the bathroom and leaves the door open. He listens to the sounds. He is rooted where he stands. When she comes out she is naked. She walks slowly to the bed and lies there to wait for him. Half of her body is covered. The rest, her midriff, breasts, arms, settle and open to him. "Come and lie down with me," she says, reaching for him. Her own voice surprises her, pitched lower than usual, coming from a depth she'd forgotten she'd had.

Edward indicates the bathroom and goes there. His turn.

His first time in there. There's an old-fashioned light fixture over the mirror, the kind with a thin push button you have to aim at with your forefinger. He notices his finger is shaking, almost misses the first time. How do I know this? I'll tell you later. A warm amber glow from the knobby glass Deco sphere, with crescents, dispersing, of warm light filling the walls, the ceiling.

He closes the door quietly, and feels, almost, disappointment, to see that the little room has no window to the outside. There is no way out. Anyway, they're on a high second floor. He sees her clothes left neatly folded on the side of the tub. He turns and studies his face in the mirror, looking for something he can anchor to. Feeling dangerously unmoored. But the face looking back at him is unfamiliar. His heart pounds hard for a moment, and then he realizes: it's a trick of the light, the mussing of his hair, the adrenalin, the feeling of quantum change.

Can something really pick you up from your old position and, shaking you once in the air, deposit you re-arranged in an unrecognizable place? He has always scoffed at the idea. He tries to return to where he'd started, who he'd been, earlier in the evening. The witty talk at dinner, the seemingly innocent challenging of his views.

Did they really think I wasn't on to them? he wonders, trying to readjust his memory of the night. In his memory now, conversing with the face in the mirror, he magnifies the few prickling intimations he had at dinner, and later in the audience in the hotel room, before the play started. Now he rewrites the play, imagines that it was actually he who controlled the whole event. He who chuckled inwardly at their naivete, and went along for the ride. He rewrites more, shifts his realization more than an hour earlier in time. Some people have such a reflexive need for control, they will go back to an uncontrolled situation they were just in, edit it, and when it is structured satisfactorily to keep their illusion intact, they'll save and print it, able to relax again.

But then he studies the face in the mirror once more. Still unrecognizable. A genuine face from the past. His past. There is a bashful, unpretentious smile playing on the fleshy lips. The thickening places beneath his eyes—he'd been thinking of paying real money to have them tucked up—look suddenly relaxed, languid, fitting.

He remembers the photograph of himself that his parents still keep displayed, the most prominent of all. Him in his junior year at Santa Cruz. His arms are stretched out wide, saying, can you believe this? He's standing on a low bluff over the Pacific, above the sea lions and the gleaming wet-suit surfers. Lighthouse Field, is that what it was called? His hair is longer than it ever was, before or since. His smile floats like a freighter on the horizon line, where the sun is going down, backlighting all. Linda took the picture. They had both just finished their finals. He was studying philosophy, the History of Consciousness. Loving his mind and the ideas it was filling up with. Loving her, too, he remembers.

He hasn't seen her in years. He knows all about her; she keeps in touch with his parents. Divorced, three children. His mother often brings her up in conversation. "Edward, you know, Linda has been asking about you..."

She stayed in the west when he came back east after graduation, with no particular place to put his ideas and energy. Drifting, writing, city jobs—one magazine editorial position that grabbed him for a while. His father suggested a staff internship; the senator was an old college friend.

The number of the years he has worked in the senator's office flashes like a railroad crossing light across his vision. Thanks, he says to himself, as if I don't know. He took an instant dislike to the senator. Saw immediately that, with rare exceptions, people like the senator won elections and people like himself toiled obscurely in the background. He saw that there would never be intellectual parity between them. The man was a huckster on his way to being a zealot. No bedrock philosophy like the writers he, Edward, had studied in school. The man was a pink-hand-outstretched grinner, P.T. Barnum United States style, like he'd marched out of a fifties musical. The kind of American, devoid of taste, irony, grace, honor, depth, that the rest of the world both loves and despises. On the other hand, the staff in the three-roomed marble office didn't seem to mind; they had their own lives, their interpretive tangents to the Senator's agenda.

Edward fell into the way of life, came to depend on the pay, on the rush of crisis votes, the sense of being in the vicinity of power. (Different kind of power from the one he felt beginning now.) At first, his constant accommodation had troubled him: excusing, denying, the Senator's unquestioning conservatism. Denying the rest of it, too. Looking at himself in the mirror just now, he lets himself feel all the embarrassment he's been storing somewhere. The scumbag. How could I always look the other way, he wonders, always bite my tongue?

Okay, millions of people do it. Freud says every individual has to make myriad accommodations to the forward motion of civilization. Rein in your instincts, go with what the crowd wants.

At the same time he realizes the emptiness of that excuse. Freud was talking about the kind of discontent that can disrupt the security of an entire society. He, Edward, had made an individual choice to shut up and learn to live with political viewpoints that used to disgust him a few years ago. And as the whole national balance kept shifting to the right, he nudged himself in that direction just to be able to show up for work in the morning. Repressing intellect, creativity, joy. And, actually, it meant leaving every old friend, even a lover, behind.

Meanwhile he worked his way up in the staff. Admired for his wit, his put-down humor, he'd become the principal position paper writer, the spokesman at the hasty press conferences. Kept company—fake interest frozen into his eyes—with loonies, tel-evangelists, white supremacists, apocalyptic crazies, right-to-lifers, serial abusers, gun control creeps, English-language-only fanatics. How could he have wasted so many hours weeks years of his life?

When you look back can you identify the instant when you sold out? Gave it all up, accommodated? Is it for ever? Can you get it back, whatever it was? Maybe this night *is* an opportunity, Edward thought. Maybe that's what it's all about. Maybe I'm not in charge, though for a minute I thought maybe I was.

That last thought is almost spiritual for Edward. That neither he, nor anyone who peopled that just-emptied room, is in charge. They might think they are but they're not. Not the teacher. Not the soldier, not the playwright. Not even the woman out there on the bed.

It's all improvisation. Everyone saying "yes" and then going to whatever place that "yes" may bring them.

Looking in the mirror, he no longer sees that willingness to sell his soul. That is what he no longer recognizes. Something happened out there; he thinks; what was it? He wants to, needs to, find language for it before he goes out there.

Something nudges at his brain. A gift to himself from a long-buried, never-examined shard of memory.

Santa Cruz. Department of Philosophy.

Aristotle. "The Poetics."

Was what happened, was this feeling, what that old Greek meant by *catharsis*? Edward knows he has never felt so alive. What happened to the great thinker himself, twenty-five centuries ago, to identify the metamorphosis you undergo, the transformation that can hit you *only at a play*? Well, maybe with other art too, but theatre was what the man was writing about. He pictured Aristotle. He had never tried to *picture* him before; that's not how you study philosophy at a great university—just a distant name on an antique book. Maybe one marble bust. Or a painting at the Met.

Now he saw Aristotle alive and incognito in the early morning Athenian crowd, a sunny amphitheatre, living through his revelation, his long beard wet with tears, with sweat, trembling and brain-harrowed, having just *seen* an epiphany, a god in the flesh, having screamed as one with the rest of the twenty-thousand voices, no, don't do it! when some mere mortal, Oedipus maybe, hurled himself against implacable fate.

Aristotle is shaking, shaken; he stands on cue with the applauding thousands—how did they applaud back then?—he rushes from his seat, pushing through the sun-drenched crowd, thinking, I can't stop and talk with Sophocles right now, must get right home and write about this, about how I feel—

"Are you all right?" Sarah's voice calls from the other side of the door. Interrupting him, thrilling him with her concern, her partnership in this. He knows he is taking too much time. Too much time. A delay in the bathroom. A toilet stall, he calls it. Does it frequently down the hall from the Senator's office, when he is so disgusted with what he has become that, had he any valor at all, he would turn left out the door, hit the elevator, and go downstairs, get away for ever.

Woody Guthrie did that, he remembers from some book. He left the hated captains of industry waiting in the Rainbow Room at 30 Rock, said he needed the men's, but took the elevator instead, guitar slung over his shoulder, no fat contract in his hand, and went back down to the streets of New York to find his people.

Edward's mother had suggested he do that, holding his two shoulders and looking at him with her quiet wisdom, missing the young man, the son she loved in the picture—

"Yes," he says, loud enough for her to hear. He moves from the mirror and tries to urinate. Takes a long time, nervous. She must be listening and waiting out there. Holding himself with one hand, he reaches out with the left and turns on the water. For the sound. Less embarrassing that way. When he finishes he splashes water on his face, runs some around in his mouth. Kills the mirror light. Steps through.

She is lying there with her own thoughts. At that moment, she thinks that perception is everything. It will be all right if they can see together what is happening in a rarified light, perfect stage set hotel room, scene light dimmed, atmosphere coming in from outside like moon through a church window.

If they can both see it as an intentional beginning of something: not see a kitsch-Mediterranean, questionable-neighborhood, forgotten Greek hotel, dust in its corners, humble lack of nap on the terry towels in the bathroom, bedspring squeaky one-night stand.

Perception is everything. She knows how she wants to see it and that helps.

He doubts he has anything to offer her. It is all on the legal pad that the teacher carried out of the room. He sits beside her on the bed and she helps him to undress. Sarah turns out the bedside light (street lamp and hotel sign neon now illumine this room). In this half-light he looks at her and sees a smile, freely given, with nothing in the way, that he knows he will never tire of.

For a long while they do nothing but adjust, to the events of the evening, to the altered atmosphere in the room, to each other's feel and smell.

"What did I just agree to?" he asks her at last. He thinks he understands now, but understanding falls way short of belief.

"Nothing much," she says. "You start writing for real. You become a tireless advocate for government support of the arts."

"Is that all?"

"That's all."

His head is cradled between her breasts, rising and falling as she breathes, as she speaks. She is smelling his hair—black curls with just a few silver flecks—through her own fingers. Both her hands are lightly massaging his head. His right eye lies closed against her, his left looking past the breast to the muted colors in the room. He would like to write what he sees from this vantage now.

All you have to do to write something truly fascinating, he thinks, truly beautiful, is to take the time to notice. Pick an original, a surprising, or simply new-to-you, point of view, and write what you see. You end up describing what other people miss, what *you* would miss if you hurried by. He would never want to hurry by this. A few feet away, folds of a curtain like in a painting, pale blue in the muted light, silver deco decoration in the weave, pale yellow street light stealing in around the curtain; close to his eye the rising, falling breast, aroused nipple, part of her right wrist, silver and lapis lazuli bracelet, fingertips he could almost reach out and touch with his lips and, of course, how he feels about it all—

"Are you part of the deal?" he asks.

Immediately he regrets the question, realizing that another, more ironic, part of his mind just put itself in the way.

"Of course not," she says.

Her feelings are almost hurt, but how could he know, know anything?

"This wasn't planned."

She has, folded in her wallet, in her Guatemalan bag on the table by the door, a copy of the article. It is as worn in its way as the one I carry around. She has unfolded it and read it many times, and has reflected on the story she heard for the first time in the restaurant.

Point of view, as I also realized a couple hours before, is nearly everything. And empathy.

For all these weeks, as the story was becoming part of her, she had put herself not into Julio the artist's point of view as I had, nor with the goons and guards, but in the woman's place. She had thought herself onto the divan on the other side of the wall. She had thought herself inside the woman's body. Younger than hers, certainly less handled by others. But maybe not as athletic as hers. A different body. Different genetic mix, she thought, different food digested over the years, to build the cells, power the nuclei. Inside the woman, she had spent time there, flinging her chin to the side and glimpsing the shiny black hair lift and catch Mexican sunlight beside her face, reaching with her left hand to cup her unfamiliar breast, reaching down with her right... She moved slowly for a moment, then stopped and held the pose, for the benefit of the artist watching her through the opening three strides away.

No, not for his benefit, no, just to allow him to do the job she'd hired him for. Not hired, no, captured.

Sarah had thought herself inside the woman's mind, too, inside her upbringing, inside her marriage. A good twenty years younger, maybe less educated. Maybe not. Latino society, upper class. Educated. How do you cope with the jealousy, the macho possessiveness? Or was this just another assumption infecting her thinking, Sarah's thinking? She really didn't know.

With so little information available, she had tried to measure how proactive the woman was. Was this kidnapping, this crazed commission, her action? How had she come up with the idea? Maybe her husband leaves her cold. Maybe she is a deep hot spring waiting to burst through the Mexican bedrock, and he is too quick, premature, too self-involved to notice what she needs. To even care.

She needs the slow, focussed, captured eye upon her, to bring her up and through. The artist's inability to leave her has set her free.

So, do we accept "model" or was she the actual artist of the event itself—a performance piece, in fact—not a painted decoration at the end of it, not a kind of languid, passive bait in the middle, sweetening the incarceration. An artistic creation in and of itself.

There was no description of the pose in the short article! We assumed she was lying supine, an earthbound, tempting presence luring the brilliant male artist down from his customary contemplation of the Divine, to fix his male gaze on the familiar object. Like so many paintings in so many museums. Wrong assumption. Stand up, Sarah thinks. Stand up!

Was the unnamed woman's beauty a physical burden to her? Was it hers to portion out as it was hers to display? If she could, would she dematerialize, pass like no matter through the wall, reassemble perfectly to pull the artist away from his cramped, rampant attention? He hadn't planned to be there; now he rose to the occasion. Would she take charge? Imperious, would she dismiss the guards, pay them, push them both out of the building, then strip and squeeze the artist empty like one of his tubes of paint?

If she could, Sarah thought, she would. She is about to do that now. Her whole body hums with that aboutness.

She had materialized here before, on this side of the wall, in her imagination. Therefore, to say, now, "this wasn't planned" is a half-truth. It was thought about, like any inevitability, but without sufficient words to form a strategy.

"I didn't expect this," Sarah reassures him, and herself. But "didn't expect" comes up short of what she means to say. As she looks around the room and takes it all in, takes him in, reflects on the planned and unplanned steps that brought her here, she looks within herself for surprise, finds not enough to register or measure.

Then that room and the other one, both populated, separated now by an unbroken wall, a locked door, a sealed hole, come into a kind of balance in the peace of the night.

Chapter Twenty-Four

Sitting at the chrome table in my kitchen, I unfold Edward's manuscript from my pocket, and lay it out before me. I swallow my first sip of beer. I breathe out. I pick up my red pencil, poised to make comments or corrections. I read through the first pedestrian page—some self-introduction, allusions to photography (there's a

nice description of an old upright flip-top Ansco camera he used
to love)—and then I come to this:

I know. I'm stalling here, I know.

What I see and feel. Okay.

*What I saw: I looked away too soon, way too soon, because
I just wanted to keep looking, forever if I could, because I have
to say I never saw anything so beautiful—not the same thing
I saw the first time, seems like a long time ago, when it was
the black kid and the white girl in the bed—I could hardly see
them; they had the sheets up past their chins and they seemed
to be doing their homework. She was holding a big book and
she was speaking. I couldn't hear her. You could see (I think)
under the sheet that she had her leg wrapped over the top of
his. They were so nervous. Really nervous! They kept looking
toward the door, I was sure they could see me, so I got out of
there quickly.*

*But then this time, okay, they weren't there anymore. What
I saw: the woman! I was already attracted to her from the
office, and from dinner and from the scene we were acting in
the hotel room. I couldn't take it when she left. I was sure she
was gone forever. And it was my fault! I felt like I had to do
better to make her come back. But there she was. In the room,
and when I saw her I felt everything break out into life inside
me. It was like a vision and I forgot, for at least a minute, the
guy, the soldier's hands pushing me against the wall. I mean
he didn't push, I was staying there on my own.*

*I actually wanted to rip the legal pad out of the teacher's
hand and start to write. No that's a lie, what I wanted to do
was just to stay and watch some more. She had taken her
clothes off, most of them, and she was swinging her legs. Some
kind of martial art. I couldn't see the expression on her face,
the light was low, maybe she took the table light down and put
it on the floor? But what was so beautiful about her was that*

she was so real, I saw muscles I didn't know women have, is that funny?

Okay. I felt I was watching truth happening. It made me shiver. Like I was having all my philosophy not to mention my recent history thrown out the window. I also felt ashamed to be watching her. Then I felt I didn't have to be, because, I mean, she knew I was there. She knew. I felt aroused, of course, who wouldn't be? I wanted to extrude myself through the hole and go molten and cool myself right to her shape, be molded by her. And then I looked for what my mind usually does at moments like this which is to tie an experience up into a neat box of words and couldn't find anything appropriate there.

What I felt, right before I turned away, was like I was a traveler in the early days of fire? And I was peeking into a cave, and inside there were beautiful cave paintings on the walls, of men and women all muscled, lean, gods and goddesses really, hunting and dancing, everything was firelit, the painter was somewhere just out of sight, smiling at his creation, maybe her creation, and it was a gift to me to be seeing it, to be there. I'll never forget that.

Then I realized, still almost feeling like that cave-man traveler, this must be some ritual and I've got to get out of here, they kill people for seeing things like this.

I put my red pencil down.

I realize that I had no idea where Sarah had gone. And I hadn't even given it much thought. Well, for one thing, I was too busy. Directing, acting, teaching—

I still won't give it the thought it demands. I have work to do. Mental work. There are places that could use correction.

I write nothing on Edward's essay. There's no need now. He has hit it right, I think, has fallen into an archetype, and—

—and then my mind, prodded by his writing, understands something it missed before. That the original article that found me that first night was an archetype, one of the Dozen Basic Plots of Greek Myth, of Western story-telling.

How did I miss that?

How could I have waited till Edward's essay defined it for me? The student teaching the teacher again!

When you are stopped in your tracks by something you see or hear or read, maybe it's an unexpected news bulletin from mythological time. Right away something deep within you communicates with something deep and human—and ancient—within the article, or the painting or the song.

In therapy that uses dance or art or music, that archetypal depth-to-depth communication is what your guide beside you is hoping to witness. It's not as if any of us alive today is unique.

Mythical archetypes are old stories we can use to help us understand ourselves. We're trying to place ourselves in this world, so we put ourselves into one of its old familiar stories. I already knew how powerfully Julio Parra's story spoke to me, but I never thought about a western myth to relate to, to help me understand the story's power. Now here she comes: Diana, the lithe, buff goddess of the moon, of archery, of Amazons.

Those sandals! The buckskin mini! The man spying on her through the bushes is the hunter Actaeon, whom we always meet in the myth or see in the Renaissance painting an instant before he's turned into a deer. And just as the thought hits his brain, "Damn! I've just glimpsed immortality, and now I have to die," his own hound dogs tear him apart.

Diana, Artemis to the Greeks, "queen and huntress," patroness of all female fighters, kick-boxers, aikido practicers—it makes perfect sense that she is Sarah's patroness. She may be that without Sarah ever having thought of her; no, I take that right back: knowing her, she probably has. And kept her as a protective spirit through all her years of exile, as a guardian who embodies qualities she strives for most.

I understand without her yet telling me that Sarah's rushing out the door was not one of her usual departures; it had everything to do with erasing any lingering hint of passivity contained in the woman in the original article. The story had gripped her and she had decided to put herself in the woman's place, but only to shake it free of the description in the article.

No! Not the description! Free of our assumptions. The article never *said* she was lying down. Sarah blew those assumptions away. She took over the body and put it to use. Her personal use. Her active use.

It's very late at night now. I contemplate my hands, tired, turned up, empty, on the kitchen table.

Which is how I find myself in another of the Dozen Basic Plots.

Sitting alone in the sudden, abandoned quiet, the mortal lowers his nose to his forearm, creases his brow as he tries both to name and to remember forever, the ineffable perfume left on his skin. Then he realizes he must have had a goddess in his arms. He realizes it only after she has gone.

Chapter Twenty-Five

"Now I'll back up and tell you what I did," Sarah says, "when I rushed out of the room."

We're sitting on my front stoop in the afternoon sun. It's Monday: four days have gone by. She's dressed for exercise, running, walking—I don't know. Long hair in a ponytail, lipstick, some space-age-material shirt. Looking so beautiful it makes my heart ache, and we are both aware of that, of my heart aching. I have no idea where she has been staying. She has a key;

she came sometime when I was out and got her things, her few things.

She's just told me the bare bones of what happened, and I know when I come to write it—I do plan to write it—I will fill it in from my own imagination. Better yet, I'll find a chance to corner Edward, have him tell me what went through his mind after the crowd had departed, after I closed the door behind Garth and me.

"You don't have to tell me," I say.

"Right," she agrees. "You could make it up."

Not knowing, maybe, that I've already read about some of it.

I do want to hear her side of it, though it may hurt.

"You'd better tell me."

"Just listen then."

She had faked exasperation when she left the room. It was not. Either it was pressure building, or inspiration, a moment of hope. Whatever it was, it was an impulse she had to follow. Just like me when I pocketed the article and didn't share it with the class, she went off on her own tangent but with no purpose yet, just the sense that it was the right thing to do.

Sarah had no plan. You can do things with no articulated vision of where you're heading, just a clear call to do something, anything—if someone had stopped her in the hall and asked, "what are you doing?" she would have had no answer.

Exiting past the audience, she closed the door quickly behind her. To the right was the turn and the top of the stairs back down to the lobby: brightness at the bottom signaled a return to the ordinary world, to real time. To the left was the short hall, five or six closed doors, the low ageing plaster ceiling, the amber light from the sconces, the window at the end of the hall with the fake plant below it, the marble quotation above it—a scene from Ovid, as I remember.

She went left to the next door and knocked almost inaudibly.

"It's me, Sarah; can I come in?" she whispered and miraculously Kyla heard and opened, Jermayne's big loving sweatshirt hanging past her knees. Sarah sent them both away, quickly, quickly, with money for the late-night café down the block. Come back in an hour, she said; take your key, you can have the room back, all night long I promise, go, go! Go!

They dressed hastily and were gone, young people having no problem with transitions, thankfully, and still without a plan, she closed the door after them and undressed. The evening clothes were uncomfortable anyway.

Or, now that she thought of it, this was the only way for her to *become* the woman in the story.

The hotel room was too bright. She wanted a little light, so she pulled the lamp from the table and set it on the floor. Still too bright. She tossed a towel over it.

She turned around slowly and felt the room, passing easily into a state of meditative neutrality. She started with a few casual kicks, stretching her arms horizontally to either side, twisting her torso, tilting, checking her alignment sometimes in the mirror. Same mirror we had played with. It was while looking at herself that way that she saw in the mirror the reflection of the other door with its bright point of light coming through, and in that precise moment, the light disappeared as the hole was covered by a face.

In that first moment of being watched, instead of playing the role of the wealthy Mexican woman, she found herself doing what she did when she felt about to explode. In her underground years when pressure built up, either from the outside when she felt about to be recognized, or from the inside when the stress of pretending was too much, she had had to do something. If she didn't she would break apart, or she would laugh out loud and grab someone, anyone, friend or stranger, and reveal herself.

At those times she needed to do some centering meditation.

Preferably while in motion—hiking up a mountain; or running; or swimming against the current of the river if the weather let her; or, best of all, shutting herself up like this in a private space to do her own mix of capoeira, yoga, tai chi, until she was breathing hard, sweating, until she felt clear.

For this purpose Sarah kept a feminist list in her virtual pocket, "the ten worst things I've ever heard of," she called it, and when she felt stretched, warmed-up and ready, she would kick,—just kick!—take that! Would pretend to do battle for women least able to defend themselves. Would aim for some institutional male face, actual or composite. She'd imagine her foot connecting with some Ayatollah's bearded jaw, or the male part she could love or hate: take that! for letting Iranian men claim "Temporary marriage" for as little as five minutes so they can fuck any woman they want without being stoned to death for adultery: the woman's penalty if caught. Take that! for female genital mutilation, patriarchal clitoricide.

Take that! for every working single mother who has to leave her child at a four pm-to-midnight day care center. An old habit from her undercover days—it both thrills her and makes her sad—all the marches she couldn't run out and lead, the speeches, testimonies before congress—Take that! for having to run a screaming born-again photo-swinging gauntlet on the way to a family-planning clinic. But take that! also, for female babies aborted in societies where families only want sons. This is all she had, all she could do, while her public warrior self went silent.

Once she was back in society things got worse. No one would hire her for any job. She could tell that the technicality that had freed her failed to make her innocent in anyone's eyes. She had a near-breakdown, trying to re-connect all her loose ends, her cut threads. It was too much; she needed to drink, and then she needed not to drink, and all the while her, she called it her "private practice" kept her going.

So, take that! for the nameless woman in the article, who, having hijacked a painter and had a gun held to his head, could think of no better way to employ him, to use that sudden position of empowerment, except to lie supine on some glorified examination table, poised for penetration: passive image of the voluptuous, brainless, violable artist's model stuck in yet another male gaze, apertures available and free—or, wait, no, aim this same kick at *ourselves*, all of us, for picturing that particular nude pose and no other!

Take all that! And thank you for the wake-up call.

Done now with moving and kicking, heart pounding and breathing hard, she noted that the light had returned to the hole. No matter: her experiment had shown her that she did not actually like being watched. Got that out of her system. She sponged off, dressed quickly, and went back to room 22.

How could I not smile at that vision, told me in a way that let me see it clearly? She was happier to describe it than to have someone actually watch. But what you need to know is that by the time she finished her description, we were both laughing. She did those kicks for fun. Her instinct for pleasure and play ran deep. Note for anyone wishing to change the world: a big source of power is the ability not to take yourself too seriously.

Suddenly being serious about someone had not changed that quality in Sarah. We sat and talked on and held hands and as we did, the street filled with cars and buses bringing people home from the routines of their day, and the ground in front of us filled with blossoms like white plumes from the flowering crabs on either side of the path to my front steps.

White plumes.

I mentioned "Cyrano de Bergerac" before. Do you know the scene? I haven't seen it or read it in years, but it stays with you. My memory may not be exact. I think Cyrano was attacked and wounded on his way to visit Roxanne, who is middle-aged now, and eternally beautiful. She is reminiscing about the amorous letters her soldier lover, Christian, sent her. Christian, whom Cyrano had promised her he would protect in the war, until he couldn't. Christian, who had no way with words. Cyrano, who did, who does.

Roxanne takes the yellowed letters out and begins to read them in the autumnal sun. Beside her on the garden bench, the homely, gravely wounded Cyrano holds his hat in his old swordsman's hands. The breeze in the garden stirs the white plume on his hat. The bright October light makes it hard for her to read the words, but that's all right: Cyrano whispers all the lines by heart.

She hears his whisper—voice almost breaking—and turns to him and realizes all at once, as he is dying, that it was always Cyrano who wrote those verses, always he who adored her and put that adoration into words.

I love that scene.

Chapter Twenty-Six

Is there more to tell?

There is more to tell.

I ought to go back several days and describe how it was in class on the very next day: the Friday after the night in the hotel. Before Sarah came and talked to me on the step. I'd only had a few hours of sleep.

Having somnambulated through the morning hours, I ate a sandwich at my desk and waited for my AP students to straggle in. I ate slowly as if still meaning to chew and swallow the events of the night before. Looked out the window at nothing. Drank a diet cola. Wondered how to begin the class.

Thought seriously of taping a "Gone Home" sign to the door. A good day for a slow bike ride or, better, a long nap. I sent an email to my daughter. Someday I would tell her the whole long story. But there was no way to begin just yet. And I was sitting, imagining the comet trail of the sent message in space, when Garth walked in, followed quickly by some others, who would be eager, I guessed, although they wouldn't show it, to process their night of theatre. I abandoned my seat, took a few steps, and leaned back against the front of my desk. Twenty years of leaning just so. I hadn't always had the same room, but had made sure that same desk came with me on my moves. There's a noticeable thinning of varnish on the spot where I rest the backs of my thighs, but it would take another century to wear an indentation in the oak.

"Someone get us going here," I said. "I don't know where to begin."

"Who was the dude, Mr. B? Was he a ringer?"

"You could say that."

Kyla raised her hand and I called on her. "We picked him on purpose," she said; "we enticed him here from Washington." She spun the word "enticed" out slowly, proud of it, and hoping it conjured visuals her friends would enjoy.

"How do you know?" someone said. "You weren't even there."

And then there were jibes at her expense, and Jermayne's, for not showing up. Get them to explain, Mr. B.; lower their grades for the term. The group teasing the dyad for their loving absence from the collective fun. Their *apparent* absence: Garth and I smiled faintly in our conspiracy. Cheeto whose face would have told all: he looked down at his script.

No one else knew how close the two had been to the action; there was only one way they could have been seen. One point of view.

"Yeah, sorry," Kyla said with no more explanation.

"I had to baby-sit," Jermayne lied.

"You'll probably meet Edward soon," I said, moving the subject along.

I told them in a few words who he was and what he did. How he would likely want to meet them and talk with them, after glimpsing them in the hotel room.

"Is he tight with Sarah?" someone asked, and I said, yes, I thought he was.

I lobbed that reply in their direction, but no one hit it back hard at me. I was grateful for that. You have to be careful when you're just getting adjusted to a new situation. Physical changes, mental adjustments, your soul doing its catching up: they all happen at a different rate, so be careful what you say. Your voice can show what you're trying to hide. It's one time when it's okay not to reveal everything you're holding.

Till everything was absorbed, I thought, better explain as little as possible. Also, don't be a teacher and think things through out loud. Not in this case. Kyla's eyes met mine with a quick questioning look, and I must have shown a second's embarrassment—enough to feel heat on my face—before I looked away.

I invited Cheeto up front to take critique. He brought the notes he'd taken at the performance, and now he added all theirs, thanking people for their comments, writing them down. Standing next to him, I appreciated as I always did his surprising self-confidence, his comfort with himself. I marveled at how a very few people come through adversity with an almost saintly willingness to forgive, and an eagerness to emerge from any difficulty with something good to show.

He would always be that way. It was natural for him to dig down and find both artistic and political power in his family's history. When he moved back to his seat the class applauded. Then they clapped for Garth, for his stellar acting. He replied with a wave, but kept his sunglasses on and his long legs stretched out in front of him. Most of the students were seniors, and they tolerated his underclass presence among them. Had to tolerate, in fact, because he was, initially, intimidating.

(Later that day, Garth let me know that he wanted to take my class again next year. All I had to do, he'd figured out, was change the name a little. If it looked different on the registrar's computer, then he wouldn't have to occupy the main office to get his way. I said I thought I could do that. Would like to have him back. Then he turned the conversation to the future, the country's future, his future, and I think his purpose was to let me know two things: that he was reconsidering some parts of his worldview, and that it would certainly be college for him after a minimum military hitch. His pre-med student and I were softening him, and he grinned when I told him I'd be sitting in the back of his classroom one day listening to him teach.)

Before class ended, we planned the end-of-term backyard party I always hold for my AP students. We celebrate that we've gotten through a year together. The yard is small, with a high wooden fence, good only for a small group; the party's not for everyone.

I let the neighbors know a few days in advance. Sometimes we do a little acting, scenes from plays we've read. Every year some Shakespeare. Some of the lines call for shouting, or worse, and I don't want someone calling in the cops.

Chapter Twenty-Seven

Most of the class showed up for the barbecue. There's always a few who can't come: school sport playoffs, jobs, bands rehearsing for graduation week obligations.

Jermayne and Kyla spent most of the evening tight-bonded on the back steps for two reasons: they were pre-emptively nostalgic about their impending separation, and they were running through lines for their Shakespeare scene—another bedroom piece—which they hadn't had a chance to perform in the Hotel Mercury. We all know why.

Their vibe was definitely mature, collected, as if they had always known they might not be for each other for ever, as Sarah and I had known about ourselves. Speaking of Sarah, she was there, too, sitting a step below them and starting a conversation. I knew her plan was to give Edward a chance to pull me to the far corner of the yard for a quick man-to-man.

He did. He eased me as far as possible toward the back fence, which was not very far at all. We sat down on what we could find.

"I guess I need to thank you," he said.

He was trying to pretend to be uncomfortable or at least submissive in this one moment he had to get through. I don't think I meant to claim a status higher than his. I was seriously interested in analyzing how he looked. The man looked like, everywhere in his body that happened to have a thermostat, it had been reset. Everywhere he had a coil or a spring, it had been loosened. His eyes were friendly and unguarded.

I waited, my attitude both quizzical and neutral. My only agenda was not to mention the Julio Parra story. Keep him ignorant of how all this had begun, hoping that Sarah had kept that article folded and put away.

"Sarah's told me a lot." He paused as if carefully choosing his words, but he didn't have to for my sake. "I know the whole story."

("No you don't," I thought. But then I realized: not yet anyway; he will when he reads what I write about it.)

"I didn't do it for you," I told him. That was the truth. I did it for the National Endowment for the Arts. I didn't think I had to say that.

"I'll do what I can," he said. I nodded.

He wasn't going to let me get back to my party that easily. "You must be a great teacher."

"Well, it's what I love to do. It's hard not to do a good job when you love it."

"Yeah, but there's more to it than that. You bring everything to your teaching, all your philosophy. And you're not afraid to take that outside the school and put it all to work."

"Well, I guess I did this time; I'll give you that. But don't forget: I had help: Sarah, and Garth, and Cheeto. That guy Bill. And you. You could have folded but you didn't. That tells me a lot about who you are."

"Still," he said, "I'd like to do something in return."

"I think you're already doing it," I said. We let that sit in the air for a moment. I knew he was beginning to work on Senator Stern and his fellow-travelers to change their thinking on government support for artists. I also knew that he'd invited Sarah to come down and stay with him and start doing what she really wanted to do, which was to be more present in the decarceration fight.

"There is one thing you can do for me," I said.

I asked him to meet me some other time and tell me what went through his mind the night of the play. I said I wanted, I needed, to think about the event in a truly complete way, and I couldn't if I couldn't get inside his head. And I could give him back his corrected paper. Maybe keep a photocopy of it. Would that be all right?

"Yes." he said. "Yes" to it all.

We conversed a few more minutes. We quickly found a political place where we could stand together. We agreed that in the United States right now moderation is nearly non-existent. That the whole country has gone to the ideologues. Had turned mean. The dogmatic sensational artist is as bad as the blowhard cross-wielding senator. A plague on both their polarizing houses. They're like the

Montagues and Capulets. Forgetting the thing that set them off in the first place. Competing for limited space in the diminishing national attention span. Needing each other to survive. We agreed that they could both take a flying fuck at the moon. His turn of phrase. For the purpose of the conversation, I avoided blaming it all on right-wing extremists. Just this one time.

"What's it going to take?" I asked.

"For people to start collaborating again? Start really working together?"

"Yeah."

We couldn't agree on the answer to that. I thought maybe global warming would do it. When the ice caps were all melted and New Orleans was only a memory. Being a skeptic about human-caused climate change, he couldn't see that as an opportunity for mutuality. He was hoping for UFO's, for the landing of extraterrestrials: the "Independence Day" scenario. Unify the whole world against the threat from monster aliens.

So a full-scale invasion from an exoplanet was more likely than the major countries working together to bring our earth's temperature down.

I broke the present impasse. "Let's us do something together," I said. "Do you like fishing? No? Neither do I. See, something else we agree on. I'll see if I can borrow a couple of rods and we'll go rent a boat on the river for a day and do some fishing. Be a captive audience to each other. No bait though."

We shook hands, made a date, and as we walked the few steps back to join my party, Edward told me that he had begun to write. A Washington novel, but hopefully of good literary quality. He couldn't wait to share it with the Tuesday writing group. He had applied to join.

My heart sank. It's probably going to make him a million bucks, I thought. Probably has detailed insider info, great sex, state-of-the-art sequestering, the real kind not the theatrical variant. My idea, leveraged by a person of power! And he's got his foot in some publishing door, I was certain.

I'll bet the guy's a better writer than me, too, but then again I've never had a pistol pointed at my head.

Chapter Twenty-Eight

Kyla and Jermayne met us halfway down the yard. Plates of food in their hands.

"Hey could we go upstairs," Kyla asked. For some privacy? To rehearse.

"That's fine; just leave the bedroom door open please."

I really have to watch what I say.

Plates were piled full of traditional outdoor American cookout. Burgers, buns, grilled veggies, soda, chips. And then a scene from Shakespeare. There's nothing like a Shakespeare scene for topping off a backyard barbecue. Try it some time. This spring we read "Othello," because, watching them all year, I wanted Jermayne and Kyla to get a crack at a scene.

I don't insist that people get off book: (that's theater talk for: learn your lines, put your script away, get ready to move.) But that's when the magic really starts, when the hands and arms are free, and the actor's eyes—windows of the soul—can scan faces in the audience, or check visual cues from the other actors.

Kyla and Jermayne had learned their lines. Which is what I had secretly hoped for but didn't assign. That is in fact what they were doing when Edward's face darkened the hole! Going over their parts, concentrating, giving each other cues.

I wanted their scene to go perfectly, had even met with them several times and helped to block it in a rudimentary way. I had seen "Othello," of course, and pictured it so many times while reading it on the page, but this time I just wanted to kick back in the audience and see my two students channel Shakespeare's characters, bring the old words to life, use the feeling they already had for each other to power the fictitious passion, the destroyed love.

We all gathered toward the end of the narrow yard, crouched or sat on the ground close to the two of them: Kyla feigning sleep on my rusty old chaise lounge, with a pillow she'd borrowed from upstairs. Jermayne quietly approached her from the left, walking so slowly: he can't bear what he's about to do.

I know my Shakespeare, and while it's fun to read and act out the comedies like "Twelfth Night" and "Midsummer," it's tragedies like "Romeo and Juliet" and "Hamlet" that really stick with the students after we part from each other.

"Othello, the Moor of Venice" is different, harder; it's got some truly awful people in it, and it makes you come to terms with three of the worst flaws that human beings are programmed to suffer: jealousy and gullibility, and racism. I hardly ever teach the play. It can make you feel awful.

Ever since I met Jermayne I had been looking forward to this day, and it didn't hurt that he had a ready-made Desdemona. Jermayne's mother was the choral director at a huge downtown church, and he had been singing at her side since he first made sounds. Like I said, he was definitely the sweeter of the two brothers. (Though broad thanks again to Bill, for saving our evening!)

Jermayne had a melting smile, and a singing voice of incredible range. Sometimes I went to their church of a Sunday morning just to hear him sing. His version of "I Stand Still:" that's the track I want pumped into my coffin for at least the first year I'm down there.

Here is what I think and teach about the great Shakespearian tragedies. Bear with me for a moment here. This is not a detour from my story.

Fate is not the relentless instrument of destruction that it was in Greek drama. Here, mere men are at fault. Men destroy themselves, along with the women who love them and who are infinitely smarter than they are.

(Thinking about this now, I realize that the fear of being lumped in this unfortunate male grouping will always make me hesitate to rush in and commit a *true* crime.)

Either men are fatally impetuous, like Macbeth or King Lear or Romeo, or they take so long getting around to the action called-for, like Hamlet, that tragedy spills all around them in the interim.

Iago, the evil, envious, cynical one, looked at Othello and saw a man who could be gulled. For whatever reason—race hatred, personal ambition, envy, concupiscence, Desdemona's rejection, torture in his soul—he wanted to bring the Black man down. Not surprising in a white villain. *Othello* is the perfect story of how you can find out someone's weakness and use it to destroy him.

Jealousy was the weakness Iago found in the Moor. It's the worst human emotion. It's not the focused clarifying aperture of my story. It's a sickening, shadow-ribbed window. Jalousie. Venetian blindness. We're all prone to it like Othello. We have to be on guard. It's too easy to be gulled, to just go along. The world's too full of liars, looking for us and our soft spots.

We have to fight our gullibility with every waking breath. Our complicity, our compliance. We owe it to the God who made us, and to the place where He put us.

My little part of that place turned beautiful just then. The setting sun lit up the yard, as if the techie up in the booth had pushed the master slide and the two actors, one Black, one white, caught all that pink light on the side of their breathtaking faces. Kyla had on a plain white dress that could pass for a nightgown. Jermayne wore the same blue blazer he'd had on at the restaurant. But he stood so straight and tall in it that it took on, as befit Othello, a military bearing: Air Force blue.

OTHELLO: (to the audience) *When I have pluck'd the rose,*
I cannot give it vital growth again,
It must needs wither; I'll smell it on the tree.
    He kisses her.
O, balmy breath, that dost almost persuade
Justice to break her sword! One more, one more;
    He kisses her.
Be thus when thou art dead, and I will kill thee,
And love thee after. One more, and this the last;
    He kisses her.
So sweet was ne'er so fatal. I must weep,
But they are cruel tears; this sorrow's heavenly,
It strikes where it doth love.
    He touches her. She wakes.
DESDEMONA: Who's there? Othello?
OTHELLO: Ay, Desdemona.
DESDEMONA: Will you come to bed, my lord?
OTHELLO: Have you pray'd tonight, Desdemona?
DESDEMONA: Ay, my lord.
OTHELLO: If you bethink yourself of any crime
Unreconciled as yet to heaven and grace,
Solicit for it straight.
DESDEMONA: Alas, my lord, what may you mean by that?
OTHELLO: Well, do it, and be brief; I will walk by.
I would not kill thy unprepared spirit.
No, heaven forfend! I would not kill thy soul.
DESDEMONA: Talk you of killing?
OTHELLO: Ay, I do.
DESDEMONA: Then heaven have mercy on me!
O, banish me, my lord, but kill me not!

She clings to him.
OTHELLO: Down, strumpet!
DESDEMONA: Kill me tomorrow; let me live tonight!
OTHELLO: Nay, if you strive-
DESDEMONA: But half an hour!
OTHELLO: Being done, there is no pause.
DESDEMONA: But while I say one prayer!
OTHELLO: It is too late. He stifles her.

Briefly—just long enough to show us how Othello could have done it—Jermayne held Kyla down. Then in that beautiful twilight, he stood and real tears rolled down his cheeks.

Take a moment to think about all he was crying for. For their own love—a first love for both of them, they'd told me—nurtured through a school year, soon to be tested by absence, by parting and moving on. For the hard work they had done, learning the lines and the moves to bring Shakespeare's two characters to life. (Like the god of love, Shakespeare also needs warm bodies to inhabit and to stay alive.) For the last performance of a scene: actors will often feel real grief when a play they've worked so hard on is over—

And for the work Jermayne himself had to do, will always have to do, just to survive and stand tall as an innocent young Black man in this strange and threatening racist country. For all the forces assembled over the centuries to cause the warrior he had just played to be pictured as shallow, so capable of hot reaction and irrational violence, so easily manipulated by Iago.

Still Othello, Jermayne bent and picked Desdemona up, and she hung lifeless in his arms. With some trick they had devised, some misdirection, her hair which was always clipped up in class cascaded down and touched the earth and caught the sunlight, too. After some time he put her down gently. She became Kyla once again. Who stood, and then they both bowed.

The class sat transfixed. Visibly moved, Sarah caught my eye and held me in her glance. The languid lovers from the back row of my English class had made the whole universe briefly come aflame in my back yard. My students saw a performance of a quality none had expected. It ground into them, made them feel important, elevated, crashed into.

These are high school students, I thought, and I am their teacher. We are all trained, and we're constrained by law, to bottle up pure emotions, to refrain from touching each other in ways that could express our true humanity, since that might be misconstrued. And I self-censor, though maybe less so than others, when I could talk at greater length about love, and history, and race, and envy. I am usually very careful. Though maybe this narrative gives the lie to that claim.

I looked around to make sure others had seen what I had seen. The sun stopped setting for a moment; the party idled, and no one made a move to get it rolling again.

I felt: affirmed. I do these things with my class, outside my classroom, because I can. Most teachers can't, or don't; something personal holds them back. That's when we need help. We need artists to come in and inspire. Like I said, we've had plenty at our school. But we are the outlier.

When every state can get NEA money, with no strings, to spend on outreach, as they call it, that's assurance that some distant outpost of art can be kept free of corporate colonization. Possibly. The corporations have almost all of it now—the sponsorships, the interlocking global social media, the product tie-ins to blockbuster films: games, action figures, empty-calorie breakfast cereals, happy meals, all the politicos they've bought...

If you only let the market decide, they won't be satisfied with sitting anonymous in the bottom line; they'll want the front seat, they will want to be on the stage, on the screen, in the first stanza of the song, on the shirt the actress wears, the tattoo on her left breast when in the intimate scene he lovingly removes her bra, or on the logo that glows through from her perfect silicone implant.

We will see these things. We'll be ashamed by our weakness, how quickly we were gulled, how easily we accommodated. We'll avoid each other's eyes. We'll stop wondering when this all began, how we let it happen; we'll say, it doesn't really affect the art, but we won't mean it—

I can only go so far. I can put up the quotes and posters in my classroom, get the students reading and talking, scribble red ink on their essays, prepare them for the AP tests, bring them to my backyard at the end of the year, show them a Shakespeare scene that stops the world.

I may hint to them where connections are begging to be made, or drop suggestions in my lectures. But I can't make the connections *for* the students. They have to make their own, slightly different and self-referential, else they get no juice from them.

Still, if I could, if I knew how, I would like to shake up four roomsful of students each day and send them, send a student army, right out to grab people on the street, saying listen to this: the ghosts of the dead are howling; our dead are being killed all over again; they're being smothered! Our soldiers, police, protectors, brains pumped empty by reductive education, by sleep deprivation, dream deficit, disinformation, lies—they're all standing numbly by while our museums are looted, history buried, libraries shut down, books banned, teachers arrested, buildings destroyed—I'd have them holler, look everyone; when did you start being so blind?

We're burning at the stake here! We're crying out through the flames—

Flames: I was in full dream mode, gazing at the glowing charcoal, poked to bright life again by students who, while I was dreaming, had taken the grille top off and assayed an opening round of s'mores.

'Twas the smell of flaming marshmallows that broke my reverie. And my student Becca's voice.

"Hey, Mr. B;" she said. "What are you gonna do this summer?"

"I'm writing a book," I said, using the magic of tenses to move the action from the future to the present progressive. "Always wanted to. Stop talking about writing and actually do it."

"Yeah, well, you make us do it enough. It's about time you did some."

"What's it about?" someone asked.

"It's about this high school teacher," I said, already getting ahead of myself.

"You gonna show it to us? We show you ours."

"Maybe," I said. "In September." I thought, then, most of these students will be gone in the fall, but maybe they'll come to see me before heading out.

"Are we in it?"

"You sure are. See, that's why I don't let you wear corporate logos on your clothes: 'cause I don't want those logos mucking up my movie."

"Wow! There's gonna be a movie out of it?"

"You never know."

"So you're just gonna sit here writing all summer?"

"Actually, no," I said, thinking it through for the first time, right there in my backyard, "I've gotta go down to Mexico first; I need to do some research for the book. Look up an old buddy of mine."

"*Caray.* Don't go to Mexico City," Cheeto said; "you'll get kidnapped. That's how half the people there earn a living. They jack your car and sell it. Disappear you. The real thing this time. Not a play, *hombre.* Throw you in a basement, make a ransom call."

"I won't have a car," I said, "and I don't look like ransom material." But I smiled to myself at how that captured image kept on appearing and shifting.

"Well if they do," Bolo said; "we'll get you. We'll find some money, and we'll come down with it to spring you."

But then the thought took them, that they could rescue me

instead of paying. The kids got excited about that: It's cheaper, and we'll all get a trip to Mexico, too. Let's start training right now! Bolo got down and gave me ten quick push-ups.

"Garth'll lead us, right?" he said. "You'd want to rescue Mr. B, wouldn't you?"

A good summer job for the big guy who that night was wearing vintage camo shorts and beige high socks, what looked like what the Brits on the beach in India wore, pounding Gandhi on the head with their two-by-fours.

But Garth said, "How it is, lookin' around, I just don't smell a victory, and I don't go in anywhere unless I can be sure of the outcome. Would never have gone into Vietnam, man, with one hand tied behind my back."

He was so menacing when he said it: many hands hesitated in the air along the chocolate-marshmallow-graham cracker arc to the mouth. Edward and Sarah looked over from where they leaned in towards each other. Othello and Desdemona neglected to look up from their tender display of forgiveness.

Garth smiled a truly winning grin, and took off the sunglasses at last so we could see his smiling eyes. It was getting dark.

Chapter Twenty-Nine

I've never stepped out of the Mexico City airport.

Looking at the greenish purple afternoon sky, I decide not to venture out of the packaged, slightly more breathable indoor air. Till the 4:00 to San Cristobal, I sit and drink a Corona. Tastes better when it's a local brew. I buy a Mexican newspaper and pick my way through it.

La Reforma. That's how all this started, I think, with a news-paper: a blessing on the assistant editor of my local paper, who scrolled through the assortment of features on the AP wire (no longer a wire) late that night, and chose to fill a few empty column inches with an amusing bit of fluff from Mexico.

Then I'm on the plane, an antique Boeing, Compañía Mexicana de Aviación. I call it a jump jet, for the way it bucks around in the air, as if taking off over and over again. The air in that part of Mexico will do that to a plane: flying over Puebla toward the southeast, it's two volcanoes more than an ordinary thermal. There's Popo, smoking, off the wing to the left, and nearby is the one the Aztecs called Ixtaxihuatl, "Sleeping Woman." It's horizontal, with two or three summits and a steaming vent: those Precolumbian namers saw what they saw in the peaks.

After a night in San Cristobal, I head for a week by the Pacific. It's a rough eight-hour bus ride over two coastal ranges, but at the end of it I've rented a one-room cottage on top of a cliff at Puerto Diablo. It's a short climb down to the beach; you can swim if you want to dare the waves and the rip, and the shark who everyone says will keep his distance, *usually.* To the left is the tortilla lady, and down the beach to the right some palm roofs beneath which you can escape the sun, and buy fish or eggs and warm soda or beer. Oh, and the best coffee in the world.

I have a hammock tied to a porch post and a corner of the house. When the wind blows or when I swing too hard, the house shakes. I use this week to tell myself this whole story all over from the beginning. Start writing it, actually. Brought some paper with me. And I use the time to practice Spanish with any patient person who'll sit and talk to me, especially children. That's my vanity: I want a week of current Spanish under my belt before I meet Julio Parra. In the internet café in the nearest town, I find Julio's contact info. It's not too hard. The man is a famous artist after all.

Back in San Cristo I check into a hotel near downtown, the *Posada Pacífica*. Then I go find a table in the main plaza, the Zócalo, where most visitors come for some part of each day. A lot of life takes place beneath the huge trees, or under the earthquake-proof archways on the square. The "*portales*," they're called: portals to the stores and restaurants along all four sides of the square, and portals to history, which is everywhere. Every wall is pocked with three or four centuries of bullet holes.

My history is here too. I look around and remember the park bench I calmed myself on, years ago, right after Julio was dragged away. There's the Cathedral of Our Lady; with its open steeple where I used to watch boy bell-ringers flinging their bodies into the sun, giving all their weight to the thick ropes and the big iron bells.

Around noon I meet Julio just outside the portales, on the corner close to a street that heads north. Maybe it's this very corner that he was heading toward when his trip was interrupted. I see him in a small crowd waiting for the light to change. He has the same uprushing black curly hair from when I knew him: "pelo chino," they call it here, "chinese hair,"—don't ask me why.

And the circular wire-rim glasses: Leon Trotsky only spent a few months in Mexico, making love with Frida Kahlo and hiding from Soviet assassins, before one of them got to him, hatchet in hand. Politically he never gained much of a foothold, but it looks like his influence on fashion will never quit.

Over *café con leche*, Julio shows me the scars he earned in prison as a young man. Mexican prisons are some of the worst in the world. I see him scanning my face to locate the person he met once and forgot about till now.

We get reacquainted over coffee. Friends stop by the table to greet him; I'm introduced: old friend, school teacher from North America; all their names escape me in the rush and the city noise, the diesel engines and the hundreds of birds that make the park their home. Then we leave and head up the hill to where he has his studio and a nearby gallery that shows his work. Maybe we walk near the place where they sequestered him. I don't know.

As the sounds of downtown recede, at last I begin to tell him about seeing the article. He doesn't know that the news traveled through the English-speaking world, but that is only his first surprise. I tell him the whole story. We walk, slower now as I take him through all the steps since I first read the article. We stop when I need a moment of stillness, or when he needs to stop for some better eye contact with me. Then we walk on.

"*Hombre*," he says; "you've got some balls."

I thank him for that, and for inspiring me. I thank him for giving me the idea. I thank him on behalf of all the artists and arts advocates en *el norte* for helping me save the National Endowment for the Arts.

We reach his studio. "You want to see some of the paintings?" he asks. He actually has some. Even at gunpoint, an artist can bargain. You can lead a painter to a hole in the wall, but you can't make him paint. What he had bargained for at that moment in the room was the right to hold on to some sketches and studies.

I had been hoping to see them. I'm not much of a critic. I know what I like. I mean, were I to try, I could write art criticism. It's not that hard. You write what you see; you think and write about the whole universe beyond the frame, following suggestions from within the confined space. Part for the whole. You let your mind travel to a time beyond the present moment. You let your other senses, like hearing, like smell or taste, inform your choice of language. Seems to me it's not too hard.

They are beautiful. They're all he has of what he went through, and I feel so close, so powerfully connected, to what he went through, that the sketches carry me away. I thank the wisdom that leaped uninvited into my head when I first read the article. It had come again in the hotel room when I refused to look through the hole near Edward's head. I want to see the art of it, not the real thing. I had been hoping for this chance.

They are oil pastel, or paint sticks, I suppose. The face of the woman was sketched quickly, and clouded over, rubbed anonymous, as if a wind or a wave of time was passing by her in the instant she was seen. Or as if he had agreed without speaking, to keep her anonymity safe. The impossibility of approaching her is rendered visible in the painting. The woman is not recumbent, as I had imagined her. In some of the sketches she is dancing, twisting, arms flung to her sides, like Sarah.

Even with no wall, and even coming near her, you would never catch her. She's a nymph in the first rush of metamorphosis. A goddess letting go her human form. She could of course, if she wanted, stop, turn on a dime, and catch you in her arms. Her body is clear, reliefed, sculptural, in focus through the tiny aperture, like the figures Vermeer saw through his camera obscura and nailed their emotional truth for the centuries with a delicate dab of paint.

Julio Parra never learned the woman's name.

She is young and supple, Matissed and Modligliani-ed, brightly colored in the palette of all Mexican artists. There is no submission in her pose, no bent-over back, no power pulled from her. The painter focussed in on the apogee of her being—now I have no doubt at all, no doubt that the story is true, and no doubt that she herself directed the operation.

Witnesses saw armed men seize Julio Parra off a street in the southern city of Oaxaca on Feb. 11. He wasn't heard from for four days.

"*Cuatro días?*" I ask him. "Four days?" He knows what I mean by the question. He knows I understand maybe better than anyone, now that he's heard my story.

"Never have I had four more intense days," he tells me; "I almost want them to come back."

Confirming what I'd suspected. "*Comprendo,*" I say; "I understand."

"I never left that room. They made me sleep there. But who

could sleep more than a few hours? They brought in my food, led me to the bathroom."

I look through all the paintings again. We talk a little about concentration, about the moments in one's life when it seems as though one's intuitive powers have never been so clear. How sometimes those moments are just visited upon us. Pure accidents brought about by nothing we are aware that we have done.

"These are just the studies, right?" I ask him.

"Sí, ése," he replies; "she kept all the finished ones. The real paintings."

Now Julio Parra invites me to choose one for myself. For all my trouble. I look into his open face, see generosity, solidarity. I pick a standing, moving one; some rich streaks of cinnamon and gold leave her body at an odd angle, as if to show a breeze her own body stirs in the still room's visible air.

I try to pay him but he just winks. She will always be with me. You know who she reminds me of. I'll pay for a good framing back home. I have a wall in my kitchen where she will look good—not as good, I think, as she must look in the gilt-framed finished painting in her bedroom, the one her husband likes to look at, now that he's over the shock. And now that he treats her body with more care.

We leave the studio. We walk to Julio's house. I stay for dinner, at three o'clock in the afternoon. I meet his wife, his children. He invites me back sometime for a longer stay. Maybe next year, I say. Who knows?

It's my last full day in Mexico. Last trip to the market for chicken soup, the local tortillas. Find the bakery on Independencia that makes the best flan. Last time to sit in the zócalo and people watch, and finally I'm back at the Pacífica, drowsy enough for sleeping.

Chapter Thirty

Next morning, early, I hail a cab from the hotel and go to the little airport outside of town. I like the feeling of walking through one of the two gates and crossing the tarmac in the open air—no jetway—as the summer sun starts to soften the asphalt and a hot wind whips the palm trees. I'm anxious to get back home, to keep writing. I finish my night's sleep, flying near the two volcanoes but not seeing them, and change for the international flight in Mexico City. Julio's painting, rolled up in a cardboard tube, is safe above me in the overhead bin.

Flying toward the hub in Chicago, somewhere over the Sonoran Desert, the big plane shudders as it hits some turbulence and I look out the window at my right. I look down and just happen to see our tiny shadow cross the Rio Grande and then we bank to the right, seeking the Mississippi and the corridor due north.

I reflect that the country below is changing in ways none of us ever expected. I've been away for a few days, and wonder what I'll notice first. That so much uncertainty could hover in the air about the very system of governance we would have next year, or five or ten years out: it frightens me. There's so much discord below, so many ugly fists of hatred, isolationism, pure anger aimed at each other and at the rest of the world.

I wonder if I am up to the task of living through what I fear.

Something surprises me with tears. Shudders me like the turbulence in our flight path. Traveling, meeting Julio: these have been diversions, and now my mind is telling me to deal with what I haven't thought of, to get a grip on what I've lost before I'm back in my element. I can suddenly feel and taste all the intimacy with Sarah, all I had enjoyed but always kept at arm's length, like how in a museum, your stillness and respect, not to mention the guard by the doorway, keep you at a distance from a painting you love.

Maybe one result for me from all this will be that I am ready to go all out for love, if it is not too late. If I can find someone.

Often something happens to me when I go to a museum, and every time, really, when I sit in a cinema. Does this happen to you? Halfway through every film, I suddenly remember that I am going to die. Not right then but someday. The awareness slips in from where it's been resting and waiting.

That same awareness hits me now; I realize that it's been a while, and I wonder—now that I've been shaken up—if it is not too late to sing in a chorus, to fall in love, to go half-time on my teaching job, to set up a loom in my front room and learn to weave a beautiful Zapotec blanket, learn to throw a decent pot, to paint, to create, to write—if it is not too late.

Does art-contemplation happen like this for most people? Is every work you resonate with like a green light into a wide new terrain of excitement, a hope of humankind, yes, as F. Scott Fitzgerald wrote, but also a momentary sighting gifted just to you? An invitation, a welcome, into a generous spirit world where the artist has been, and where you can go too, but where you can never be satisfied, and that fact alone just adds to the delight.

You can't get such a message from a piece of marketing art, because that art is scientifically calibrated to come between you and your thoughts. It's not about you and your unquenchable potential, your hope for renewal. It's a twisting of your desire, a reaching—not into your spirit, but into your wallet.

I said a long while back that I am not too spiritual a person. But I am open to becoming more so. Or at least more mindful. Looking down out of the window, I feel tears running slowly down my cheeks.

I know I didn't do a good job explaining to myself or to anyone why the Julio Parra disappearance story made me think of the National Endowment. I could have done better. The looks of doubt and sympathy I fielded, the touches on my shoulder, that was all my fault. I fell so short of describing clearly how I entered into such a surprising, inexplicable, slanted personal space.

You know how you can start crying about one thing, and as soon as you're into the flow of it, the motivation multiplies; there are so many things your tears could be for. In my case, for the closing of an aperture, the completion of an event that won't repeat, the vanishing synecdoche, and more: the feeling of powerlessness that comes from being an inner emigrant in my own country, and of course, the loss of Sarah.

I had to make that sacrifice. Sometimes you have to give up something deeply important to you in order to grow. You have to die to the routine order, precisely because that order did not give you, or your partners, the satisfaction required. Therefore Sarah let me go. For the first time I allow myself to feel the full regret for letting go of her, and go deeper into it to see the huge space it takes up within me.

I find that regret does take up a big part of me, most of me, but it leaves me a little room for this progression of thought: I remember my meditation from the first night I sat and studied the Julio Parra article, my clear understanding that a similar hijacking had just happened to me and for me. I remember wondering whether I would be up to the labor offered to me. I remember thinking that I had no idea how long the chance would last.

We always have a choice to ignore a sign, to reject a gift. We can see that special opening and turn away from it, and go instead to where the majority is heading. Or, without a plan in hand we can gather ourselves up and take the direction that's been offered. We can put our precious selves into a fight we might have a hard time explaining, one that only our nightmares understand. We may wake up alone, the only one still standing.

Art is our last, best hope.

The plane cruises northward. I look down through the little window at the very center of my country: the Mississippi drainage, the midwest, today a genuine flyover country.

Somewhere down there, somewhere special to the people living there, but almost never visited by folks from either coast, some place like Norman, Oklahoma, or Davenport, Iowa, I can almost see a theatre. Old vaudeville house, for forty years it's been frequented only by sorry old men with their flies open—remember what Garth told me so long ago? Rain comes in the roof, runs down the walls, stains the old WPA murals. Some dumb luck or rural inertia saves the place from the wrecking ball.

Now a local group, Friends of the Savoy, Friends of the Opera House, have got it all fixed up. Local artists donated materials and time to restore the murals. The Chamber of Commerce helped raise money for new seats. NEA grant funds helped a lot. There's community events. A downtown revival around it: cafés, new shops—

Some kids are doing "Much Ado About Nothing." A downtown store donated cloth for the costumes and sets. Good, talented people come together to volunteer after school and on Saturdays. They work with energy, love, respect for each other. A retired accountant good at crunching numbers just won a $10,000 State Arts Council Presentation Grant, partially funded by National Endowment hinterlands-outreach money. It's not much but it could mean survival of the Civic Little Theatre for another year.

Children get bussed in from the local elementary schools to watch the plays. At one of the performances a ten-year old kid who was born here, who's never met his dad, son of a single-mother Haitian immigrant with no health insurance, working as an unseen motel chambermaid by day and at the Dollar Store from four to eight—the kid sees this live play and decides to become an actor. He signs up for after-school classes at the Little Theatre. Gets a full scholarship. His mother is relieved; he'll be safe from the streets for those hours she can't see him.

He loves the voice training, the scene study, the camaraderie. The teachers take a special interest in him, guide him through school, encourage him to go to college. When he grows up, he'll be handsome, articulate, grateful, self-assured. Trustworthy, with a velvet voice you'd want to package. Later on, he will always remember how and where he started; he'll go into politics, be the first Black governor of his state. Maybe run for President.

The marketplace wouldn't have done that. It's all because Senator Stern changed his vote, stopped talking his repressed bullshit and got others to do that, too; all because of a hole in a wall, my old friend Julio Parra, a naked woman with no name, a night editor in a newspaper; and Sarah, Cheeto, Garth, Jermayne, Kyla, Edward, and me.

But the kid won't know this. And I'll never tell.

THE END

Take as long as you want, to sit with "THE END."

You made it to the finish.

Writers want their readers to linger on those last lines for a while. We want you to feel unwilling to close the cover. Not ready for the screen to go dark. Or for the music on the audio book to tell you the story's over. Really over.

But let that feeling go, and come along with me for this unexpected part, okay?

With *me*, Peter Gould.

Do you need to do something first? It's fine if you want to go get a beer or make yourself a cup of tea. But then come back.

All right. Like we do sometimes in theater, like Bob B. did back in Room 22 of the Hotel Mercury, I'm going to break the fourth wall and talk to you directly as the writer.

What you need to know is that the story you just finished is fiction. I guess you knew that already. It says so in the Roman numeral pages. But the news article, that news article, was *real*. The artist is *real*.

I'll still use my made-up name for him.

"Don't put the man into more danger," my wife says. I have to agree with her.

Bob B. never read the article. There is no Bob B! Like the rest of the book, he's made-up. I am the person who read the article.

I'm holding the actual newsprint in my hand right now. *"Seized Artist Says He Had To Paint A Nude."* I took it down from where I push-pinned it to my wall after I cut it out of the *Brattleboro Reformer.*

But the way I told you the story caught his eye? That was not fiction. That is how it captured mine.

I saw it by accident. I read it. I said to myself, "there's a novel there." I kept it and told no one about it till I was ready.

It took me five years to find time in my own life to start the first draft. That's how long "Julio Parra" took up space in me and waited. Till the aperture opened and I could focus on him.

Three years into the project, my wife and I took an anniversary trip to Mexico. We went to the city where Julio lives. I had a second or third draft that I liked. I brought a photocopy with me. I hoped to present it to him. We asked around. I had never met him before, of course. I had never *heard* of him. Only that one time.

Life imitated art imitating life.

I gave a local painter friend of mine a brief review of my experience. By now you get it, I love to tell this story.

He said, "Pedro, I know Julio. I know where he lives. You want to go meet him?"

"Sí, por favor," I said.

We were sitting at the corner of the central plaza, at the same café (it does exist) that Bob B. imagined Julio heading to, when he was kidnapped.

Our friend got Julio on his phone just like that, and the three of us took a taxi to a neighborhood away from downtown. It was fringed with fields that stretch out to half a dozen native villages, centers of vegetable and flower farming, and of crafts that have been there for five hundred years. The villages are famous for their high-quality artisan work. Today their crafts are threatened by cheap knock-offs from the global market place. And you can't always get tourists to spend money on beautiful folk culture any more. They want to spend their money on upscale cocktail bars, a modern Air B&B with a pool, the newest neo-hybrid restaurant with a glowing review in the *Times*.

There are human rights issues in the villages, too. If you look past the colorful crafts, you can see them. We don't hear about them much in the U.S., but they're what sparked the Zapatista revolution in Chiapas. Loss of farmland, destruction of habitat, energy exploitation, inequality, racism, domestic abuse, women's rights, water rights, cultural imperialism, and often the violent disappearance of people who protest too much.

Why am I telling you about this? What does this have to do with—

Wait. You'll see.

Here is Julio! The real one, not the one I'd imagined—

I saw him for the first time ever; you can feel how exciting that moment was for me. He opened his gate and let us into a large yard. We never made it to the house; his studio was close to the gate. We went in there and waited while he found three chairs. He is the elegant, quiet, intelligent, indigenous gentleman I described in the story. Not physically as I wrote him—I got that wrong—but we'll let most of the real description go. Different hair, same glasses. I was right about the glasses.

He greeted my friend, and my wife and me, with dignity, with grace.

In contrast to his contained calm, his paintings are enormous, eccentric, splashing color out towards the edges, as if each painting were a part of a greater whole, but forced to remain inside the frame.

I saw no pictures of the nude I had pictured so clearly. No sketches. Of course I had a secret hope to bring one home. That came out clearly in the story. I was already thinking of where I would put it.

I speak Spanish. I told him about the article.

Julio was surprised that the story had travelled so far. I told him about the associations the story had planted in me. About my rendering of his experience, the characters I'd created, the hotel room, the copycat-crime-as-theater, our National Endowment For the Arts.

I then presented my manuscript to him. I autographed it. He listened with a patient smile to everything I said. I waited for him to excuse himself, get up, and go to where he keeps his archive, his studies, his secrets.

But Julio didn't get up.

He waited until I had finished. He just sat there holding my book in his lap. An unexpected gift from another country. Wondering how to begin, I guess. While I spoke, his fine hands played with the plastic binder, and he ran two paint-stained fingers over the first page, as if he could read it like a blind man. As if he understood English.

When I was finished he was silent for a while. Taking his time, waiting for the right words. Caring about me, this new surprise acquaintance. And then,

"*Es muy complicado, Pedro*" he said. "It's complicated."

I nodded. I knew it was.

But, really, I didn't know. I didn't have a clue.

He had made the story up.

Should I repeat this?

Julio made the story up!

There was no rich woman. No paint, no brushes, no easel, no paper.

No hole in the wall.

I was so surprised, and deeply disappointed. I had been held captive with him, seeing what he saw, dazzled by the image, the synecdoche and all its potential. With so little raw material, I'd spent years improvising an elaborate fiction grounded on and inspired by what had happened to him.

But it had never happened.

I won't quote him. I won't make up dialogue I can't remember. I feel more comfortable doing that in fiction. But this is the gist of what he told us:

The people who saw Julio dragged off the street were telling the truth. He was curb-jacked, pushed into a car. How that looked to the witnesses, I got that right. He disappeared for more than three days, held in a room he would not be able to find, if he ever tried to.

His captors hurt him. He was afraid he would be killed. Had no reason to think he wouldn't be.

"It wasn't for his politics, it was for his art," he had told the reporter, in the article I read. But really it was for both. The same people who had tortured him in the late 1970's had him in their hands again. New younger faces maybe, if they had been visible, new tactics, different senior advisors in the room—but the same brutality, the same abuse of power, the same odd mix of hatred and mercy, the same implied, off-stage chain of command.

But why?

Julio was making his way toward fame and prosperity in the arts. His name was beginning to be known beyond his region. He was influential. But he never lost the connection to his roots, to those villages that circled his studio in the valley. He mixed gratitude and solidarity, going to these villages to teach painting. He was one of them. Zapotec. Indigenous. He brought them free materials; he worked with them to mix the paint and wield the brushes. Some of them already knew how; in fact, they were famous for folk art, but Julio inspired them to move beyond the inherited comfort zone of their naive crafts; he brought his knowledge of the wider world.

And then, neither he nor they wanted to stop there. A collective energy kindled. They wanted to hold pageants! They wanted to show off the work of adults and children, too. They wanted to build huge puppets like they had seen in pictures of that famous

Bread & Puppet troupe in Vermont. (He knew about the state I come from!)

They wanted to use their new power of expression to tell their stories, to denounce the injustices I listed above. They planned a parade—in their plaza, in front of the church, by the police station and past the market, the army barracks. They set to work with purpose, with joy. Julio loaned them all the power of his reputation.

When Julio was only making his paintings and no more, his work sold well. The patron class boasted of owning him. They clinked wine glasses with him at his openings; they posed with him for photos; they carried his work from the gallery to their living rooms.

But now, he was doing Arts Education. That is, in fact, what I do when I'm not writing. I've been doing it for forty years, so I know about what I am about to say:

Arts education is a danger to the State. To be any good, that's what it has to be. Inspiring like liberation theology. Subversive like a literacy class in a rebel zone. Dangerous because the waters we sail into together are uncharted.

Arts Education may be all we have left. When books are banned, when Slavery is whitewashed, Indigenous lands are paved and pipelined and mined for precious metals, when candidates run and win on their success at thwarting education, denying science, rounding up immigrants, altering history, what hope is left?

Artists can get into and out of a school, a community, add to the collective story that still needs to be told, and we can get out quick before someone notices what we've done—

The last thing the powerful wanted was for Zapatista-style uprisings to spring up in every region, led by painters and printmakers and puppeteers, jesters, clowns, musicians, and art teachers—and children.

I don't know what happened with Julio during his disappearance.

He didn't tell me and I didn't ask. It follows the model, from Argentina to Chile to El Salvador to Mexico. If you come back in one piece, at least on the surface, you don't tell much about it. You move on. You stay quiet about the details.

We know they didn't drop you still living from an airplane, or throw your corpse into the Río Mapocho, or pull a living newborn baby from your womb and dump you in a landfill, or bury you in an unknown orchard like the fascists in Spain did to Federico García Lorca in the forties.

Something happened to Julio, and then it was over.

I think of that scene at the end of Orwell's *1984*—that novel that never goes out of print—the scene soon after Winston Smith finally caves in to Big Brother, betrays his lover, agrees to drop his futile opposition and just go along with the regime. You do that, and somewhere down the line you revel in your survival; you can't help it; you experience the thrill of the crowd, your belonging to it, your exultation at the triumph of the very people who dangled you helpless at the edge of death and then allowed you to live. You are so relieved; your happiness is so intense, you have no room for shame.

I'm not saying that Julio Parra went that far. But he made a bargain.

Maybe his captors were gentle and caring while giving him all that pain, whatever kind of pain it was, electricity or water, compression or violation. The deal they offered him was generous: prosperity and notoriety in the art world of his city—the same people who bankrolled the security of the regime would pay as much as he wanted for his paintings—his splashy colors so reminiscent of the great Mexican muralists, but with all those painters' fierce denunciations transformed into the semi-abstract apolitical energy of his allowed canvasses.

"*Es muy complicado, Pedro*," Julio repeated, still holding my novel—*his* novel, my gift to him, such a small compensation for his gift to me.

"The military and the ruling class, they have the power, and they will go on doing what they want to do. As long as they can."

Politically active artists and arts educators have a choice. If compelled to, people like Julio may arrive at their buckling point and give in. They want to see their children again. They'll leave the villagers with their half-built pageant and parade, and take the deal they've been offered.

In the end it's a matter of survival.

The men who held Julio made the choice for him. He was famous enough to be dangerous, maybe not important enough to kill.

They told him, "You keep painting, *hombre*. Be successful. Forget this Arts in Education. We know where you live, your wife; we know you want your children to stay safe."

They told him, "You know, you do that parade, something bad could happen to some of those villagers. You don't want that."

Wherever they had taken him and whatever they did to him, the men cleaned him up. They checked him for damage; they gave him a shot of *aguardiente* and then they bundled him back in the car and drove him back empty-handed to his neighborhood. They took his hood off when they were almost there.

Almost there!

The car stopped near the same curb, engine idling, and then a moment suspended, when nothing happened. No one moved. The choice they'd given him still hung in the air. While it was hanging, its influence traveled in an instant around the world and back, causing multiples of people, real and fictional, to adjust themselves in ways that were too subtle even to register.

A moment like that on a stage or in a movie—that "wait for it" moment—can stretch out till it seems many seconds longer than it is. It has to be long enough for the audience to consider—and understand—what could happen next.

Would Julio leave without a word? Would he thank them for his freedom, or would he turn and say something that would break the bargain? Would his kidnappers change their minds? Not let him go? Would the tires spin out again, the car accelerate, head back to the same place or—no, to some other place, a vacant warehouse parking lot, some desolate arroyo near the mountains?

Would he never make it back; and therefore would that strange news article never be printed? My life would be so different! I would not spend years writing this book. Sarah and Garth and Cheeto, and Kyla and Jermayne, and Bob B, especially Bob B, would stay hidden in that cavern where undeveloped literary characters lie waiting to be awakened, to be born.

Then the moment moved on. Julio said nothing. He wanted to live.

Just before they popped the door, Julio Parra told me, the guy in the back seat leaned close to him, and gripping his shoulders hard, he said:

"*Adios, hombre.* You better make up a real good story about where you've been."

And then they pushed him onto the sidewalk and sped away.

ACKNOWLEDGMENT

I wrote and rewrote and rewrote this novel between 2003 and 2025.
*(therefore some events in the book precede Trump's gutting of the NEA,
and the now-frequent street kidnappings by our own Secret Police)*

Thanks to my earliest reader, Howard Norman.

Thanks to Michael and Deborah Krasner, constant cheerleaders.

Thanks to Pantaleón Ruiz, for connections and counsel.

More than thanks to Mollie Burke, my best friend and my wife.

Thanks to Gabriela, Tim, and Chloë for how this book looks,
to the many real people who donated parts of themselves to these
fictional characters, and thank you to the *Brattleboro (Vermont)
Reformer.*

www.ingramcontent.com/pod-product-compliance
Lightning Source LLC
Chambersburg PA
CBHW032008050726
47590CB00006B/2086